Deep Fried

Mark Doyon

ISBN: 979-8-9850353-4-6
Library of Congress Control Number: 2024933600

Wampus Multimedia Catalog Number: WM-133

Cover art by R.E.D. Design. "Statue of George Wythe" courtesy of FCIT. "Man Standing on Empty Parking Lot" by Gonzalo Carlos Novillo Lapeyra. "Pigeon in Flight in City" by Harri Hofer.

www.markdoyon.com

For Lew, Al & 'Hew

MAY 2014

1 | Arjun

Wedged in a crack in the asphalt, baking in the heat, sat a shiny, fresh penny reflecting sunbeams at the sky. Shoes brushed past it. Tires rolled over it. A soda can soaked it, stagnant like a tiny pond. The silhouette of Lincoln watched the amoebas and the rotifers and the insect larvae, chasing their dreams, making plans for the future, getting busy.

Lincoln tanned in the glare, a crusader in copper. He knew it was over when they put him on a coin, and on a stamp, and when they sculpted blocks of granite in his image. By then they just wanted to look at him. They didn't want to listen.

They had heard it all before.

Candy Carney was starving. She flicked off her desk lamp, pushed in her steno chair, and checked her lipstick in a pink compact. She slipped past the Xerox room and queued at the elevators. Since her coworkers at EverSafe Solutions had started teasing her about having the same thing for lunch every day, she had taken to eating alone on a bench outside.

Last night had been the usual. Five years out of college, and she was still hanging out with her girlfriends at Curly's Grill & Bar, singing Gretchen Wilson songs at karaoke. Everywhere she went, she found Bobby lurking, reeking of Axe Body Spray, claiming he just happened to be in the neighborhood.

She toddled into the parking lot. The food trucks accosted her with alluring aromas and bright colors and whimsical designs. Her favorite truck was painted sky blue with yellow trim and plastered with cutouts of smiling Indian movie stars and clapperboards. She peered in the window.

"Hi, Arjun!"

"It is a beautiful day!" the young man said, beads of sweat dotting his forehead. "Would you like a curry eggroll? Perhaps a Delhi tea?"

"Yes, please!"

"Did you take my advice about your Bobby?"

"He's not 'my Bobby.' He's just a creepy guy who likes me."

"You are tormenting him," Arjun said.

"Oh?"

"I would not let you torment me. I would sidestep you. I would be nifty."

"Hmmm?"

"Like quicksilver." Arjun pulled the eggroll from the fryer, wrapped it in foil, and passed it through the window. "Okay, now let it breathe. Savor its aroma."

"Yes, I know." She smiled.

"And then take it into your system."

She sauntered to the park bench, which was bolted like a bus stop shelter to a concrete slab. Lately she had been waking up in the middle of the night and raiding her refrigerator for the closest thing she could find to a Bollywood Eggroll. In the glow of her kitchen, she gulped frozen entrées in a fever of fantasy.

She lifted the eggroll to her lips. Her mouth watered.

She was late for her two o'clock.

Arjun wiped the stainless steel counters. As an only child, he had grown up playing in his father's shoe store in the Lajpat Nagar neighborhood of Delhi. The little shop had carried fake Nikes from China. Arjun would drag his chair to the window and watch the *mehendiwalas* apply designs to the hands of tourists. He would see the same faces come and go each day, dark-eyed men who murmured with his father and lingered over masala chai.

Don't just sell them what they want, his father had whispered on a rainy day when the shop fell quiet. *Sell them what they need.*

Arjun had played cricket in the streets, oblivious to adult business, sowing dreams of glory. He had fantasized about making the Indian national team, winning the Cricket World Cup, and catching on with a professional club as a charismatic wicket-keeper.

In his mind, he had always been leaving for some faraway place where he would shed the shackles of his birth and clothe himself anew in the threads of possibility. He would meet a beautiful girl and settle down in a shining Western city. He would succeed in business. It was intoxicating.

His phone vibrated in his pocket. "Hello?"

"Hi, sorry, I forgot to ask you before, but can you let me know if you see Bobby this afternoon? I don't feel safe."

"How do I know if I see a Bobby?"

"I'm scared, Arjun. He follows me. He watches me do things, like loading my laundry at the coin-op. Please tell me if you see anything suspicious."

"I know nothing about a Bobby."

"I'm afraid something bad is going to happen. Everywhere I go, he's there. You're the only friend I have in the lot and—"

"Okay, I will stop what I am doing and call you if I see a nondescript man in a car doing anything at all."

"Thanks, Arjun. You're sweet."

He surveyed the lot for prospective customers, but aside from the pigeons encamped and sunning on the east flank, all was quiet. He returned to cleaning the counters.

When Arjun was sixteen, his father had run afoul of the local police by declining to meet the request for *baksheesh*. Fearing for his kneecaps, he closed his accounts at the State Bank of India and rushed his family onto a flight west, settling just outside Tucson, Arizona. Arjun enrolled in the tenth grade, his mother clerked for the public library, and his father managed a Foot Locker at Park Place.

Arjun ran cross-country and made the honor roll. He was hired on sight to wait tables at an Indian eatery in Oro Valley. And when he received his acceptance letter from the University of Virginia in a neat linen envelope with his name in an elegant serif font, his parents wept with pride and put him on a plane to the Old Dominion.

Growing up with a single closet for all his worldly possessions, he had been used to living simply. But after seeing his father's customers in Delhi leer at leather boots and pointed heels, he had noted the complexity of desire. *Meet the needs of others*, his father had said, *and you make your own happiness.*

His phone buzzed.

"Is he there?" Candy said. "Is he lying in wait for me?"

"Lying in what?"

"Please, Arjun. I don't know what he might do."

"There is no one here. There is no one who might be a Bobby or not a Bobby."

"I'm scared."

"Close your eyes. Imagine you are a great, powerful cat. You have no fear. You have no need to call Arjun."

"I have to go," Candy whispered. "Thank you."

He lifted the basket out of the fryer. He swiped the net through the reservoir, removing chunks of burnt batter, shaking loose remnants of eggrolls past, and emptied it into a plastic bucket. He picked up his paperback about Preston Tucker, a 1940s magnate who had to shut down the world's largest auto factory after producing only fifty cars.

If you weren't making moves, Arjun thought, *you were a pawn in somebody else's game.*

After graduating from the University, he had become a sous chef at an Asian fusion restaurant called Jiyū. The owner, Seiko Okuhara, blended her native Japanese cuisine with Chinese, Thai, and Vietnamese. She added cayenne and Parmesan to wonton soup. She put cinnamon in panang curry.

Arjun had studied this visionary like a monk at the foot of a master.

He watched a rusty, old Honda Civic creep into the lot. A young man waddled out the door and opened the trunk. He withdrew a long, narrow instrument from a hard case, mounted it on a tripod, and aimed it at the EverSafe Solutions building.

Arjun thought at first the visitor was a surveyor. But then he noticed the man's pants, sagging below his waist, hugging his abdomen. He tapped the number of his most recent incoming call.

"Hello?" a voice whispered.

"I see a Bobby, maybe your Bobby."

"Bobby? Here?"

"I thought he had a gun, but it is just a telescope."

"What? What is he doing?"

"I presume he is taking his measure of you."

"I told you he was stalking me! Oh my God, he is obsessed with me. He can't stop thinking about me."

"No doubt."

"Can you tell him to leave?"

"No, I cannot."

"Well, can you call the police? He is stalking me!"

"I don't know what he is doing."

"Oh my God, Arjun!"

Arjun hung up. He wandered across the lot, in the young man's peripheral vision, and lingered in the adjacent parking space.

"Excuse me," he said. "Are you hungry?"

"What? No."

"May I ask what you are doing?"

"No."

"Why are you on this lot?"

"She is cheating on me," Bobby said.

"Candy would not cheat in open view of an office window."

"She would!"

"I think she would at least go to a supply closet."

"Agh!" Bobby wailed.

7

Arjun walked back to his truck and called Candy. "I talked to your Bobby. He is bereft, miserable, a shell of a Bobby. But you will be fine."

Candy hung up.

Arjun returned to his paperback, but his concentration was broken by shouts. Across the corporate campus, he spied a woman sprinting across the manicured median, her long hair whipping in the breeze, her purse bouncing off her knees as she hurdled the curb. Her face was contorted in anger, or exuberance, or perhaps a capitulation to carnal need.

"Baby!" Candy wailed.

"Baby!" Bobby screamed.

Candy leaped into Bobby's arms, nearly knocking him to the pavement. He swung her around like a lasso, straightening her out in midair, and pulled her body close to his. He kissed her eyelids, stroked her hair, and locked his hands at the small of her back, whispering words that seemed to calm her.

Arjun wondered if someone deep in the cosmos was watching, eating popcorn and rooting for the plucky, dysfunctional couple. The film was no Oscar contender, but he knew it was the formulaic fare, the grist, that resonated.

2 | Burger Bombs

The Broadnax County Courthouse gleamed in the sun. The lawyers and their clients huddled on the steps, sipping coffee and spinning fanciful adaptations of circumstances and state of mind. Before being arrested, each of the accused had endured a hard day at work. After stopping at the Curly's bar on the way home, each had received bad news in a phone call from a distant cousin. And standing before the magistrate, each had worn remorse on his face like a plaintive tattoo.

Looming over the food-truck lot, the courthouse held forth on Greco-Roman architecture—columns, arches, rolled-up scrolls molded into the grand edifice. Fountains.

Drunks peed in those fountains all the time.

Arjun recognized one of the defendants ambling through the lot, a young man clad in a Washington Redskins T-shirt and beanie. The prospective customer took off his earbuds and approached the window of Bollywood Eggrolls.

"Yo, who these faces on yo' truck?"

"They are stars of Hindi cinema. They are celebrities."

"Why they on yo' truck?"

"They are from Bollywood."

"Put Beyoncé on there. Put Tyler Perry. Who the shorty with the spot?"

"That is Katrina Kaif. She was in *Jab Tak Hai Jaan*. Did you see it?"

"No, I didn't *see it.*"

"Would you like an eggroll?"

"Fasho, no curry."

"The eggrolls are drizzled with curry."

"That's wack."

"Then I cannot help you."

"I gots to eat."

"Go to one of the other trucks," Arjun said.

"What? You thinkin' 'homey wants fried chicken?'"

"What is your name?"

"Antwaan."

"Nice to meet you, Antwaan. I am Arjun. Do not take offense, but it would not kill you to broaden your horizons."

"Eggrolls is wack."

"It might open your eyes."

"Somebody gonna drop some science on you, Gandhi."

"I am not Gandhi. Did you win your case?"

"I told the judge I don't pee in my drawers. So, I peed in the fountain."

"And...?"

"Case dismissed! Keep it gully, *Ar-joon*. I'm late for Mickey D's."

Not everyone, Arjun thought, was a Bollywood Eggrolls person. Some didn't like eggrolls, some didn't like curry, some didn't like curry in their eggrolls. Some would never try a Bollywood Eggroll, no matter whose face was on the side of the truck.

Arjun had spent months in his apartment kitchen, experimenting with recipes. He grilled chicken instead of pork and seasoned it with his mother's curry, along with ginger and garlic. He supplemented cabbage and carrots with romaine and onions. A splash of sriracha completed the creation.

He knew eggroll wraps, like ramen noodles, all came from the same factory kitchens in Tianjin. So, he infused his blankets with a dash of cayenne and a hint of brown sugar. They were more like tortillas than eggroll skins, like soft little burritos waiting to be dropped in oil.

"Help!"

Arjun dropped his book and ran outside. A woman was waving her arms, her face pink with panic. A flock of pigeons had surrounded the Burger Bombs food truck and was invading its pass-through window.

"They're *attacking!*" the woman cried.

Arjun ran to the truck and squawked like a giant bird of prey. The pigeons scattered, fluttering toward the front lawn of the courthouse. He peered into the kitchen and noticed a lone pigeon on the counter, its head submerged in sautéed shitakes, spearing them with its beak. He cupped the bird in his hands, holding its wings next to its body. He carried it out to the lot as the woman looked on.

"He likes the food," Arjun said. "I think he is a foodie."

"They'll eat anything," the woman replied. "Rats with wings."

He set the bird on the pavement. "I am Arjun," he said, extending his hand.

"I know. You'll forgive me if I save the handshake for after you've cleaned up," she said, laughing. She was tan and fit, with hard lines around her mouth and eyes. "I'm Melinda McCoy."

"I like your motif."

"My 'motif?'"

"The painted scene with the cows and the barn and the beautiful hillside."

"Oh, thanks."

"I will have to try a Burger Bomb sometime," Arjun said.

"Well, as of right now, I think you get free Bombs for life. Come wash up and I'll fix you one."

Arjun followed Melinda into her truck, where she assumed the authoritative bearing of a chef. She shook a mixture of chopped onions and garlic out of a bowl and guided it with a spoon into a tray of ground beef. She slipped on a pair of plastic gloves and packed the mixture into a fat oval, something between a cue ball and a flapjack.

"You want just a speck of steak tartare in the middle," she said. "The core should be pink, the next layer tan, and the outside blackened."

"You are showing me your secrets," Arjun said.

"Well, the pigeons know them, so you might as well too."

"But we are competitors."

"I make hamburgers. You make eggrolls. Someone wanting one isn't thinking about the other." She tossed the patty onto the grill, pushing it with her spatula toward the back, away from the licking flames. "I'll tell my customers about my buddy Arjun, and you introduce yours to your pal Melinda."

Arjun appraised this bright, calculating woman, commandeering a hot grill, swooping from one end of the truck to the other. "What did you do before?" he asked.

"Before what?"

"Before Burger Bombs. Before the lot."

"I was a lawyer."

"I am flummoxed."

"I practiced *right over there*," she said, waving at the courthouse. "I got community service for the drunks. I charmed the judges. Before that I was a divorce lawyer."

"Why did you stop?"

"One day I realized I was rooting for my best friend to leave her husband. He flirted with the babysitter, and I told her, 'screw that guy.' I knew the value of her case. It hit me while listening to her bitch about picking up his socks off the floor. So, I walked out of Worthington Fairchild and left a sticky note on my computer screen. And I started hanging out on the courthouse steps, reeling in the lushes."

"How did that go?"

"It went great. There were a lot of them, and they all wanted to hush up their problems. Drive a car after a few beers and you're a pariah, worse than Madoff. So, I just hung out on the steps and

asked them if they had representation. A lot of them didn't."
Melinda turned the patty with her spatula, launching flames into
the air. "They were deer in the headlights. And they became my
clients."

"But you stopped doing that too."

"Yep." Melinda flipped the burger once more and pulled it
from the grill. "See that thin, seared shell? Delicious. It's funny
how in a restaurant they ask how you want it cooked, like it's one
way or another. Ground Angus, especially this stuff—locally
grown—tastes different depending on the degree. I get three tastes
out of one cut." She slid the patty onto a pretzel roll and slathered
it in sautéed onions. She grinned. "No worries. A Bomb isn't just
organic, it's pigeon-free."

"Thank you," Arjun said, cradling the sandwich in its
polystyrene foam box. "It is beautiful. And please do not take
offense, but you do not look as if you eat a lot of Bombs." He took
a bite of the sandwich, dripping grease on the plate.

"I eat them. Just not every day."

Arjun's eyes widened. "*Swaadisht!*"

"Yep!"

"So," he said, wiping his lips, "how did you end up in the lot?"

"Well, I used to see the perps in the hallways, slurping 7-
Eleven coffees and eating those gross packaged doughnuts. They
would pace back and forth, you know, nervously, and then bolt
outside and get sick. I saw like twenty guys puke next to the statue
of George Wythe."

"The Father of American Jurisprudence."

"Yes. And then Broadnax announced it was granting permits
in the lot for six gourmet food trucks, which was wonderful,
considering the 'cuisine' in the area. A couple grabbed spots right
away—Saturday Sundaes was first, I think, and you were second—
and I figured I had a shot. So, I bought a step van off Craigslist,
and *voilà*."

"What about your clients?"

"Well, at first, I was going to court in the mornings and working on my kitchen install in the afternoons. I'm talking from before dawn until after *Jeopardy*. Then I closed my practice and started cooking Bombs full time."

"Wondrous."

"Now… not to meddle, but there is something I wanted to ask you. The name of your truck… what is that about?"

"It is a tribute to the movie stars of my country."

"Do people get that?"

"Get what?"

"The Bollywood part."

"Who does not know Bollywood?"

"Um… *most people?*"

A man approached the window and peered inside. Melinda took him through the script of order-taking: mix-ins, toppings, sides. Arjun looked around the packed kitchen, every inch designed to maximize space, and made a sad sighting on the floor. It was a motionless pigeon, wedged in the throes of a failed escape by the zucchini fryer. He tiptoed over to the bird, lifted it from its resting place, and shoved it in the foam box.

"Thank you, Melinda!" he said, slipping out the side door. "I will be back soon for more organic goodness!"

Friday evening brought a springtime rush to the lot. Men in unknotted ties and women in skirts and pumps were lining their stomachs before happy hour. Mature ladies, stuck together like peanut clusters in a tin, clutched their handbags and soft coolers. Arjun filled a basket with eggrolls and lowered it into the oil.

He wondered if people truly were unaware of Bollywood cinema. When they saw the smiling face of Kareena Kapoor on the hood of his truck, who did they think it was? Indira Gandhi? Evita? He had noted during his decade in America that people didn't much care if he liked improvisational jazz or cheered for a particular sports team. They cared that when he spoke, he sounded like the Dalai Lama impersonating the Queen of England. They cared that he had come to America.

They liked eggrolls too, but their affection came from suburban Chinese restaurants, spots that catered to Americans but qualified as fast-food outlets to Chinese people. Arjun wanted to see their eyes light up when they visited his truck, to watch them share his eggrolls with others as proof of their good taste.

He knew that by tinkering with a classic recipe, he might be ignoring his father's advice. Someday, he knew, he might pay a price for following his dream. He had already declined an offer from Seiko to help her manage Jiyū. He had rebuffed his father's invitation to help him open a shoe store. He had passed on an apprenticeship with a popular food truck downtown. He had avoided compromise, and with it, bosses, partners, and investors.

The rush wound down, and the crowd headed for the watering holes. Maybe he could explain Bollywood to them. As they became regulars, they would see the bigger picture. He sat down, pulled out his notepad, and began to write.

Dear Customer:

This is a Bollywood Eggroll. Its flamboyant character honors the grand stars of Bollywood cinema. Created by Chef Arjun Chatterjee, it is prepared with the finest and freshest ingredients.

It is a feast for all five senses, but especially taste!

Bhojan ka anand lijiye!

He drifted into a daydream of long lines of office workers winding around the statue of George Wythe and up the courthouse steps, into the halls of justice, and past the offices of the judges and bailiffs and court reporters. *You can't hide a good eggroll,* he thought, surveying the glorious queue in his mind, throttling back adrenaline as it coursed through his veins.

He thought of Thomas Jefferson, the founder of his alma mater. He remembered his family's visit to Monticello, when he was welcomed into the realm of the Lawn, the Rotunda, and the

Range. He recalled Martha Jefferson's death at thirty-three, after she had produced six children, only two of whom survived beyond age two. He thought of Jefferson's promise never to remarry, and of his subsequent fathering of six more children by his slave, Sally Hemings.

Martha and Sally were daughters of the same plantation owner, John Wayles.

Arjun appraised the statue of George Wythe, Jefferson's mentor and teacher. He pictured Antwaan relieving himself at the base, emptying his bladder on the marble shoes of the Father of American Jurisprudence.

He heard a sound—a rustling or scraping—at the rear of the kitchen. He checked the fryer, the sink, the range hood. He looked inside the cabinets. He sensed movement out of the corner of his eye, on the counter by the trash can. It was the foam box from his Burger Bomb, edging slowly, rhythmically, toward the sink. He placed his hand on the hinged top. *Thump, thump, thump.* He drew a breath, pried it open, and peered inside.

It was the pigeon, eyes alight.

Arjun carried the box outside, opened it to the asphalt, and watched the bird waddle into the wild.

3 | Hungover

Candy hit the snooze button on the alarm clock. She curled into a fetal position. Her thoughts were a jumble. She and Bobby had gone to Cottontail Park and downed a bottle of Boone's Farm in the back seat of the Civic. He had cried and begged her to promise he was the only one. She had kissed his forehead and rocked him like a baby.

Now she was searching her purse for an ibuprofen. But all she found were an eyeliner pencil, a packet of cheese crackers, and her diaphragm.

She stumbled into the bathroom, threw open the vanity, and discovered only Bobby's toothbrush. She rifled through her dresser and nightstand, tossing aside silk lingerie and plastic toys and edible creams. She dove into the kitchen drawers. Finally, she pulled a chair in front of the refrigerator and climbed up on it. Behind a PVC pipe in the cupboard sat half a pint of Old Crow.

She took a swig, grabbed her car keys, and walked out the door.

She glimpsed her eyes in the rearview mirror. Darting behind her bangs, they looked desperate, sad. Her emotions ran like wild horses while her mind tried to take the reins. Why did she always end up with clowns? Was she a clown? Was she born to mate and nest with other clowns? She wiped her cheek with the back of her hand. She wanted a fresh start. She wanted Bobby out of her life. And yet she felt close to him somehow.

During her junior year of high school, her mother had lost patience with her when she started skipping class and smoking pot in the woods. After screaming nonstop for eighteen months, Mom had gone silent, denying Candy her affection. She placed a plate of scrambled eggs in front of her daughter each morning without a word and disappeared at night to her bedroom while Candy curled up in the recliner, texting friends.

In the end, Candy turned in her final project late and barely graduated, charming her government teacher, Mr. Franklin, with a sob story about the public library closing due to a broken water main. She had noticed him staring at her in her purple blouse and chemise. She had returned his teasing in line at the cafeteria. She had stayed after school to make up a quiz and accepted a ride home after missing the late bus. She had bragged about doing tequila shots on her eighteenth birthday, climbed over the stick shift, and strained to please him like a child performing in a school play.

Now Bobby was trying to please her, and she was pleased, but it was the sort of pleasing that led only to heartbreak. She could see it as clearly as she saw the rows of pill bottles on the Cold & Flu aisle at Walgreen's. If only Bobby could live and let live, he would be able to enjoy these fleeting moments. But he was oblivious, dreaming of a future of rascally little Bobbies and darling little Candies, of Little League games and birthday parties and family vacations to Disney World.

Candy grabbed the bottle of ibuprofen and took it to the checkout. She recognized the clerk, a jittery high school kid with chin acne and a walleyed gaze that never seemed to connect with hers. His nametag read "BILLY."

"How are you doing?" he asked.

"Headache."

"Hangover?"

"Yeah."

"That is so cool. I wish I had a hangover." He scanned her Walgreen's card and ran her Visa. "If you have a hangover, it means you were partying." He handed her the bag. "Partying is awesome."

"Right," Candy laughed.

"Me and my friends," Billy said, "we party pretty much constantly."

Candy smiled and headed for the exit. She thought of poor, pockmarked Billy, vending tampons and candy bars and photo prints, watching the clock until he could punch out and go home and watch reruns of *That '70s Show*. Did he have a future? Or was he destined to descend into a cycle of partying and hookups and excruciating hangovers?

She rued the disappearance of Bollywood Eggrolls on the weekends. It was as if Arjun was taunting her with pleasure just to yank it away. He was a sphinx, inscrutable, wise in ways she was not.

Arjun's apartment kitchen was littered with bags and boxes. He was making the curry, his mother's recipe, and rolling the eggrolls for the coming week. His friends at the University had subsisted on curry and pho and sushi and sought out the most obscure dining spots. He had taught them how to order in a Punjabi restaurant and make palak paneer on a budget. He had imagined them as the future clientele at a refined, downtown bistro called *Arjun's*.

He fried the spices in the pan, cumin and turmeric and cayenne. He flashed back to his mother's kitchen in Delhi, where she summoned the recipes of her mother, the dishes perfected by her grandmother and generations of stewards before her. He added chopped onion, browning it until caramelized. He turned down the flame and added coconut milk and ginger and garlic, stirring it to a thick yellow. Finally, he spooned in yogurt and breathed the aroma until his hands told him to remove the pan from the flame.

He waited for the curry to cool, sealed it in a Tupperware bowl, and stacked it in the refrigerator. Small batches. The curry was his secret ingredient, his big idea. His mind basked in a reverie of long lines, restaurant reviews, and accolades. He envisioned his smiling face splashed across a spread in *The Washington Post.* Caption: "When you're one of a kind, you win by default."

His heart pounded. He would ride the wave of attention. He would open other trucks around the city. He would start a foundation for the culinary arts. He would build his parents a home in northern Virginia with a vegetable garden and a sunroom and a Viking kitchen. He would write a book about being the person one was born to be. He would return to Independence High and speak in the auditorium.

His head spun.

He turned on the TV and ordered his favorite movie, *Tucker: The Man and His Dream.* Anyone could succeed in America. But it was best if you had money. With money you had power, and if you had power, you made more money.

Tucker had designed an amazing car. But it didn't matter in the end how reliable or beautiful it was, or whether it was as good as it could be.

Candy lay face-up on the sofa, a damp towel over her eyes. She thought of Bobby in the back seat, kissing her tears. For all his macho posturing, he was sincere. He had risked rejection. He had removed his armor and shown himself to her.

The pills were taming her palpitations, blunting the chaos in her mind. Five years from the graduation dais at Medford, here she was. Still. Except for her accrual of vacation days, little had marked the passage of time. Two years ago, she had been promoted from Administrative Assistant I to Administrative Assistant II and received a raise of two thousand dollars. Last year she had accepted extra duties without pay. This year she was doing off-the-books work for the executive office, planning the holiday parties and staff retreats. Her job was more demanding than ever, and for that she was getting forty dollars more a week. Her rent alone had gone up more than that.

She breathed slowly, following the drift of her mind. She could still carry a tune. She could still perform. She thought of her father applauding her, the only person standing in the cafeteria until everyone joined him in thunderous cheers. She felt her mother's embrace as she came off the stage, the way Mom wouldn't let go even as they blocked the exits of the other performers. She saw her dreams as destiny. She would go to Julliard. She would perform on Broadway. She would share her gift. And then, gradually, after her father left, after her mother hit the brown liquor and they moved from Briarwood to the trailer behind Best Buy, the dreams faded like Candy's old jeans, threadbare and ill-suited to adult life.

The older boys at school had always looked out for her, bringing her along on joyrides into the flats and trips to the bars of Midland. She was their cute little arm candy, tagging along with a fake ID, kissing them playfully in the back seat of Randy's father's Ford. At night's end, Randy would drop the boys off at the ice-cream parlor and drive Candy down the gravel road to Pioneer Park.

He was a gentleman and never told a soul about her abortion after Christmas in eighth grade.

Arjun freed the padlock on the pass-through and rolled the steel door into the ceiling. It was a crisp day punctuated by birdsong. He fired up the fryer. The lot was filling up with early risers. The Finn brothers at Three Bucketeers were setting up for the day, laughing and singing along with Cee Lo. Arjun smiled and inhaled the sugary aroma wafting across the lot from Doughnut Hounds.

Melinda, clad in a bright red apron that matched her glasses, was packing Angus into Burger Bombs. Arjun waved at her. He liked the camaraderie, the sense they were all in it together. He remembered his father talking up the virtues of the other shops in Lajpat Nagar. *A rising tide floats all boats.* A customer who stopped by for a Saturday Sundae would return for a Bollywood Eggroll. A fan of Doughnut Hounds would sample ribs from The Pig Rig. Working together, the chefs would carve out a niche for each truck.

Candy toddled on her heels across the lot. "Good morning, Arjun!" she chirped, sidling up to the window.

"A nice weekend with your Bobby?"

"He's not my Bobby."

"Eggroll? Tea?"

"He's just a guy who likes me."

"Okay."

"I have been thinking about you all weekend. I can't be happy without one of your delectable eggrolls!"

"If you want to be happy," Arjun said, "you must find your happy place."

"Hmmm."

"You have a map inside to guide you."

"To my 'happy place.'"

"Yes. When you find it, you will sleep happy and you will wake happy. And you will not want."

"Will not want what?"

"Whatever you wanted this weekend."

"Everybody wants things," she said.

"Not always." He pulled the eggroll from the oil, drained it, and wrapped it in foil. "Remember what I told you. Let the eggroll breathe. Savor its aroma. And then take it into your system."

Candy bid adieu with a wave of her pinkie. For a woman who was so high-strung, Arjun thought, she was quick to laugh. She was probably quick to cry too. Maybe she knew joy and sadness were two sides of the same shiny penny.

He felt something flutter by his ear. He turned to find a pigeon on his shoulder. He held out his index finger. He noticed the bird's markings—white lines on its breast—and recognized it as the stunned creature he had entombed in the foam box. The pigeon looked at him.

"Hello again, Pidgey! To what do I owe this pleasure? Do you have a message for me?" The bird cocked its head, cooing in a language both universal and oblique. Arjun furrowed his brow. "What news do you bring, Pidgey?" The bird stretched its wing and dragged it over Arjun's forearm.

All was mystery, he thought.

22

He grabbed a pen and a yellow sticky note from the drawer. On the note he scrawled the first question that came to his mind: *Why am I here?* He folded the scrap around the bird's leg, glue against glue, and pressed it between his thumb and forefinger. "Go, little friend," he said, cupping the pigeon in his hands and setting it free.

Business was as brisk as the weather, a parade of attorneys and perps, all of them hungry, all of them hurried. Bollywood Eggrolls wasn't as mobbed as Burger Bombs, but the rising tide was floating all boats, and Arjun filled a stream of orders. A group approached the window: a lawyer in a tailored suit, a young man in jeans, a young woman, and a little boy holding her hand.

"I know it sounds funny," the lawyer said to the young man, "but it's actually better for you if you urinate *next to* the statue rather than on it. The law is very specific. Urinating in the grass is a natural act, but doing it on a monument is a desecration. Do you understand what I'm saying to you, Javier?"

The young man nodded.

"You are being charged with a desecration. So here is my advice, and I suggest you take it. The officer will testify he saw you urinating on the statue. You say you were relieving yourself in the grass and lost control of your stream. You say you didn't mean to foul the monument. You say—and this is important—you have *urgent bladder syndrome.* Then you say you're sorry."

"That's a syndrome?" the young woman asked.

"Mommy, I have to go to the bathroom," the little boy interjected.

"In a minute, sweetie."

"All right, listen carefully," the lawyer said. "I'm sure you didn't intend any harm. And I'm sure, if you could go back in time, you would dash into a McDonald's like a civilized human being with a shred of self-awareness. You've got a family, you've got a job of sorts, but you could be deported anytime. We know it wasn't your best self who disrespected a *personal hero* of the man who will decide your fate. And a hero of mine too, by the way."

"Mommy!"

"In just a minute, baby."

"No, Mommy—look!" The little boy scraped at the blacktop with his fingernails, digging a small object out of a thin crack. "Look!"

The woman turned to see her son holding a shiny penny up to the sun. His face beamed with pride.

"Mommy, look! Abe Ham Linkin!"

"That's nice, honey."

The little boy jumped up and down, his arms waving like the wings of an airplane. "Abe Ham Linkin! Someday I am going to grow up to be president. And my daddy won't have to be in the jail. And Mommy and Daddy will live with me in the White House. And I will have a puppy too!"

The boy planted his foot, cocked his arm, and launched the coin toward the Burger Bombs truck. Arjun watched it glimmer, etching a motion blur through the sky. It clanged off the roof, bounced over the hood, and skipped like a stone off the chrome bumper.

4 | An American Classic

The silhouette of Lincoln watched the ants in their toils. They built homes, communities. And when the rains washed away the fruits of their labors, they rebuilt what was lost. They dug into the dirt and got busy.

He watched people walking across the lot, moving paper from one office to another, pining for retirement. Freedom gave them the chance to be who they really were.

The failure to exercise it, he thought, was a kind of death.

"Play in somebody else's wheel well, boys," Melinda said, sweeping the anthill into the air with a broom. "I have a permit for this patch of asphalt."

She waved to the singing and dancing Finn brothers and smiled. She had never felt such joy in the offices of Worthington Fairchild, had never known such contentment on the steps of the courthouse. As an employee, she had never plotted her own course. She had only watched the instruments set before her by others.

When her girlfriends had asked why she had given up her lucrative law career, she had stammered, "Because I love food!"

And they had all laughed. Everybody loved food.

Melinda's daughter Aubrey loved food, but her complex relationship with it, and with the recent stormy departure of her father, had rendered her a bulimic and a cutter. At thirteen, she had made the honor roll and the cheer squad. At fourteen, she was seeing a psychiatrist three afternoons a week. She was purging, the doctor said, to cleanse herself of experience. She was mutilating herself to express emotional wounds.

Aubrey dropped by her mother's truck on the way home from school, her backpack hanging from one shoulder, a scowl on her face. Long sleeves protected her from prying eyes. She hid under the brim of a baseball cap.

"Hungry, sweetie?" Melinda called from the window.

"Nope," Aubrey said, setting up a lawn chair behind the truck.

"Did you have lunch?"

"I had a snack."

"What did you have?"

"Like, crackers."

"Crackers are not a meal."

"Just *no*, Mom. Okay?"

Melinda walked down the stairs, to the back of the truck. "You know what the doctor said."

"That I'm messed up?"

"He said to enjoy simple pleasures. Like eating. Like stroking your cat. Like going to the movies."

"Burgers are disgusting."

"Aubs…"

"Mom."

Melinda placed her hands on her hips. "I am going to make you a Bomb, and you are going to eat it."

"Hey, Bhagwan, here we go," Arjun muttered to himself. "Looks like it is going to be the other kind of beautiful day."

A man with a silver hot dog cart, his shoulders hunched and rounded, rolled into the lot. "Angry" Eddie O'Day was an interloper, uninvited and unwelcome, and he made no effort to please. All that mattered to him was his vendor's license from Broadnax County, which allowed him to sell hot dogs and potato chips in locations throughout the downtown area.

Arjun took Eddie's existence as a personal challenge. He greeted the crusty Vietnam vet with a smile, asked about his family, his bursitis, and his "mangy dog." He offered him free eggrolls. Eddie declined with a grimace that seemed to come from some old Western set in a lawless town. He had no use for small talk. He was interested only in customers, whom he lured with the words printed on the canopy of his cart:

Hot Dogs $1.00—Free Ketchup Mustard

He wheeled his cart into the space next to Bollywood Eggrolls.

"Hello, Eddie!" Arjun called from the window. "It is a beautiful day!"

"Too damn hot."

"We can enjoy it together."

"Uh-huh."

"Let me tell you something. Wherever we go, we carry an invisible backpack filled with smiley faces. Some of us do not have many smileys—maybe eight or ten—and some of us have a lot of smileys, as many as a hundred. Today I have a hundred smileys in my pack, Eddie. How many do you have?"

"None, zero. *No smileys.*"

"You must have at least a few."

"Haven't sold a dog all day."

"But your dogs are an American classic."

"And that's why you and your artsy friends are going to be collecting unemployment soon."

Melinda approached Eddie's canopy. "Move it along, mister."

"I'm working."

"This is a food-truck court. You are not a truck; you are a cart."

"I'm not going anywhere."

"You are poaching."

"I'm selling hot dogs."

"You are hawking grub."

"At a fraction of what you charge for your frou-frou. Sorry, lady, but people like this cart. They like the price. They like the free ketchup and mustard. They like the free pepper."

"Free pepper?"

"Lady, I'm busy."

"You have to leave now."

"This is a public lot."

Melinda turned on her heels and looked at Arjun. "Do you believe that damn fool?" she said.

"I do not disbelieve him."

She marched back to her truck.

On Mondays, Eddie wheeled his cart around the campus of EverSafe Solutions, luring the restless from their offices. On Tuesdays, he posted up in the median across from Trader Joe's. On Wednesdays, he hit the vacant lot by the McDonald's, and on Thursdays, he set up on the sidewalk in front of the Sportsplex. On Fridays, with the end in sight and a weekly nut to make, he lighted outside the courthouse, by the food trucks.

He wasn't on the premises to socialize.

"Look over there, it is Melinda's daughter," Arjun said.

"Uh-huh."

"I think she is going through a difficult time."

"Hmmm."

"It is not easy to be a teenager."

"Uh-huh. Spoiled and lazy. Full of herself."

"No... she is a good kid."

"Um."

"She is."

"Kids today. Fat and *not even happy*. Worst of both worlds."

"But she is thin."

"Yeah, well, she needs a hot dog. Two. She needs to get off her tush."

"She goes to school."

"Uh-huh."

"She is not getting what she needs. She is hungry."

"Uh-huh."

Arjun looked at the sky, at the trees, at the birds soaring from the EverSafe Solutions building to the courthouse. He thought of the way he felt when his family arrived in Tucson. The houses, the sidewalks, and the little stores in the strip malls looked different from what he had known. And he was changing too. He was a stranger in a strange land, with little to ground him but his parents and his memories and his dreams of the future.

Had he stayed in Delhi, he would still be studying the finer points of counterfeit athletic shoes. He would be an ant in a hill, working with others in a world enslaved by routine. His parents expected him to meet a nice girl, settle down, and produce humans for a planet already overrun with them. How would that make the world better? People needed to grow, to evolve, but all they ever did was recycle their greed and aggression and glorify themselves in gluttonous consumption and conquest.

Who was making the world better?

"You should not judge Aubrey," Arjun said.

"Who cares?"

A lot of people were misunderstood, Arjun thought. They were wandering through the labyrinth, searching, reaching out for answers, but finding little in the maze to lift their battered souls.

The EverSafe Solutions data pool, a crew of typists dubbed "keyboardists," provided clerical support to the management staff. Candy sat at her desk, digesting the employee evaluations of CEO Brad Paxton. Comments ran the gamut: "A lost puppy," "Ill-equipped to tackle the challenges facing our industry," and, in exquisite penmanship, "As fine an executive as I have encountered in my thirty years of service."

Upon being promoted to Administrative Assistant II, Candy had been awarded a window cube on the west side of the room. The spot was supposedly a status symbol, but more closely resembled an oven that baked its occupant to a glistening gold by late afternoon. The longer one stayed with the company, the more likely one was to be deep-fried like a Twinkie.

Charlene, an EverSafe lifer, prowled the aisles like a housemother, enforcing rules on attire, supplies, and decor. She relied on Candy to perform important tasks. Anything requested by the executive office—transcription of dictation, digitization of business cards—landed in the "priority" tray on Candy's desk.

Candy looked over the evaluations: "He's always been nice to me," "Great if you like a boss like that," and "NOT A CHRISTIAN." These comments would be forwarded without attribution to the executive office, presumably so CEO Brad Paxton could "take the temperature" of his staff, reflect on their criticism, and improve his performance. Candy knew the evaluations would be used to inform the company's internal PR, the relentless spin placed on every scrap of information targeted at its workforce. Would there be layoffs? It all depended on the success of their efforts to sell security systems and yard signs to homeowners by the end of the fiscal year.

There was, everyone knew, a revenue shortfall. And that meant all hands on deck in the sales effort.

"You don't want to have to freshen up your résumé," Charlene said to the pool, her expression grave as she peered over her reading glasses. "Looking for a new job is no fun." It had dawned on them that their jobs weren't fun, that their days were spent in such numbing repetition that carpal tunnel syndrome loomed more as destiny than danger. "I'm sure everything will be fine," Charlene said in a motherly tone. "I know what this staff is made of. I know what it can do. It's up to you guys now."

It never seemed to be up to Charlene, or to Charlene's supervisor, or to CEO Brad Paxton. It never seemed to be up to the board of directors.

"I'm so grateful for you guys," Charlene said after bonding with her direct reports over fears of unemployment lines and the loss of health insurance. "Can you imagine this company without you? It would grind to a halt. It would crumble to the ground! And that is why we need to hit our numbers this month and next. So the company doesn't have to limp along without its most precious resource. *You.*" Faces paled throughout the room. "And that is why," Charlene continued, "starting today, keyboardists will spend evenings marketing the Family Sentry system by telephone to targets in the mid-Atlantic region. Is it a promotion for you? Hold your horses, it's better. You are players in the game now, guys. EverSafe is your company too."

The pool was silent. Candy sat in her steno chair, legs crossed, filing her nails. She envisioned Charlene pinned beneath a skidding monster truck, screaming for help while the mudflaps dragged debris over her face. She imagined the grisly state of Charlene's body, flattened and punctured by gravel and glass, as emergency medical technicians loaded it onto a stretcher. She watched Charlene patrol the aisles and wondered if this woman had ever been young, making her way in the world.

Candy remembered sneaking out late to meet Randy after her mother had passed out while watching QVC. She remembered Randy in his father's Ford, his hand on the small of her back, his breath in her ear. He said he was going to make the A&M football team as a walk-on, that he was "just gonna show up" at practice some July afternoon and start doing sprints on the sidelines. The coaches would notice his speed and ask who he was. He would say he had worked to help support his family in high school and hadn't had time for sports. They would laugh and nod and throw him a jersey. He would join the drills.

Randy was expelled three weeks into his first semester for selling redneck cocaine out of his dorm room. When he returned to Midland, he was caught packing it in baggies in the men's room of Burger King and sent to jail for fifteen months. When Candy drove out to the flats to visit him, he looked at her blankly, coldly. When she pressed her hand to the glass, her eyes searching his, he motioned to the guard and turned away.

Bobby was like a less talented, less enterprising Randy, an exuberant bro with a heart the size of a beer keg. But Candy saw his limitations as plainly as she saw his childlike need for love and approval. He would never be the dreamer Randy was on those hot summer nights. He would never rise above his boyish wants.

Now Candy was bolted into her cube, making phone calls and interrupting families with a prepared script in the middle of dinner. She was intruding into the lives of mothers and their babies, injecting fear of the unknown into their private bliss. Most would hang up without speaking or ask how she had gotten their number. But a few listened to her pitch, hearts skipping, thinking of all they stood to lose if they became crime victims, and asked what it would cost to keep their families safe. Those were the ones who occupied what Charlene called "the sweet spot."

EverSafe had a solution to every security problem. Motion detectors spotted prowlers. Window sensors tattled on intruders. Alarms alerted the police. A text message informed you of a breach as you checked into a motel in Kansas City on business.

Candy raised her hand. "What if the person already has an alarm system?"

"Stoke her fears," Charlene said. "If she already has a system, she needs a better one. Get her in touch with her anxiety."

"How?"

"Hit her with the burglary data. Pound her with the pedophilia stats. How would she feel if somebody busted through her basement window and grabbed her four-year-old?"

Billy reclined in bed and scrolled through the photos on his phone: Candy at the counter, Candy in the aisles, Candy at the bar at Curly's. He had noted her name on her credit card when she came into the pharmacy. Now he knew her home address, her birthday and birthplace, her high school and college alma maters, her employer, and her record of moving violations in Broadnax County. He knew her parents' names. He knew she had played the role of Nellie Forbush in a Medford University production of *South Pacific*.

He stuck the photos to the wall by his bed. He had seen how Candy looked at him. He wondered if she was thinking about him right now, sitting at her desk at EverSafe Solutions, daydreaming about kissing him on some moonlit night on a breezy beach. Would she come back to see him? He was sure she would. Any reason at all—to pick up photo prints or a miniature American flag for her car antenna—would be a great excuse to drop by.

Maybe she would be hungover again. And he could nod knowingly, a shared moment between hard partiers. He could ask her, in a hushed whisper, to buy a twelve-pack of beer they could share. She would wink and tell him to meet her later at the 7-Eleven. Maybe she was like a bored, young teacher who hung out with students in the back seat of her car after school. His heart raced.

A knock at the door brought him back to Earth. It was his mother. "Have you taken out the trash, Billy Boy?"

Melinda grabbed a folding chair and sat down by the truck next to her pouting daughter. "I'm just looking out for you, sweetie. It's what moms do."

"And it is helping a *ton*."

"I know it hurts now. But your father loves you, even if he was born without a capacity for empathy. He loves you even if he's a disgusting animal who mated with his substance-abuse counselor while I worked to pay our bills. He's just part dog, you know, and dogs are wild. I know he loves you."

"I'll keep that in mind."

"It's better that he lives in the wild, you see, where he can prey on someone besides his loved ones. He can send us birthday cards, call us on Christmas. But he can't smash Grandma's bud vase or pass out face-first in his meatloaf. We're just letting him be himself now. It's a kind of love."

Aubrey scowled. "Whatever."

"Did you get enough to eat?"

"Yep."

"Food is love, you know."

"That's what fat people say."

Arjun cocked his ear for signs of the pigeons but picked up only the whir of the trucks and the breeze through the trees. He drew a breath and opened his ledger. Bollywood Eggrolls, home of the most distinctive deep-fried confection in America, was barely getting by. He couldn't afford anything extra, like a folding chair or a pair of Levi's. And that wasn't the plan.

An eggroll, he thought, had an esoteric value, like a painting or a book or a song. If it was going to change the world, it might take a long time.

He spotted the flock of pigeons on the courthouse lawn, pecking at the turf, foraging for an afternoon snack. He scanned the grass for a splash of yellow. In a flash, Pidgey was on the windowsill, his eyes darting from fryer to sink.

"Hello, friend!"

The bird shook its leg, holding out the sticky note like a little flag.

"News?"

Pidgey teetered.

Arjun stroked the bird's wing and felt its heart beating like a tiny snare drum. "You are excited, I see." The note was crumpled and torn and stained. It was attached differently than before, wrapped tightly around the bird's ankle, making it difficult for the little avian courier to stand.

Pidgey emitted a sharp cry.

Arjun removed the scrap. At the top he observed his query: *Why am I here?* Underneath it, in dull pencil, he noted a blunt scrawl. He stared at it for what felt like an eternity, an ominous demarcation of a dark history.

To be my bitch, it read.

5 | Don't Be Afraid

A flash of light filled the sky. The blast rolled across the lot, scattering food and coins and fryer oil. A side-view mirror landed at Arjun's feet and splintered into pieces. People shouted for help. Arjun pulled out his phone and called 911. "I am at the food-truck court on EverSafe Drive," he said. "There has been an explosion. Like a bomb in the street..." He began checking on the others in the lot. Everyone seemed to be moving. He scanned the trucks—Doughnut Hounds, The Pig Rig, Saturday Sundaes. His eyes settled on Three Bucketeers, cranking the Black Eyed Peas through a speaker mounted on the roof. The back of the truck was gone. Arjun spotted Melinda and Aubrey, their faces grimy, their sobs drowned out by the strains of "My Humps."

Paramedics dashed in, pulling stethoscopes and trauma shears from their packs. They checked each person—pulses, lungs, eyes.

Arjun spotted Candy on the edge of the circle.

"Arjun!" she called out. "My desk shook!"

He flashed back to the car bomb in Lajpat Nagar, the way it had reverberated through the retail district. His father had sprinted into the street while Arjun watched from the front window of the shop. The mehendiwalas had fallen in prayer while mobs trampled everything in their path. Arjun had locked the front door and jammed a chair underneath the doorknob. The world he knew, with its reliable rhythms, had vanished.

"Don't be afraid," Arjun said.

"I can't help it," Candy said.

Arjun thought of how the car bomb had blown fingers into the trees. "My father could not do anything," he said.

"Your father?" Candy put her head on his shoulder. "This kind of thing isn't supposed to happen here, is it?"

Arjun remembered his mother saying Lajpat Nagar was not the third world, that somebody hadn't read the travel brochures.

The bomb squad pulled up in a Humvee. Armed men parted the crowd. "We are setting up a perimeter. Move behind the lines."

Melinda wrapped her arms around Aubrey. Debbie of Saturday Sundaes ran toward the statue of George Wythe, trailed by Sharon and Sully of The Pig Rig. Ron of Doughnut Hounds walked through the crowd, handing out free jelly doughnuts.

Candy tugged on Arjun's sleeve. "Do you believe that?"

"Seeing is believing."

"I can't eat. Where are the Bucketeers?"

"They are okay."

"How do you know?"

"They are speaking with the police."

"Why?"

"Because shards of glass from their windows are embedded in the statue of George Wythe."

Antwaan slinked through the lot, hands in pockets, his eyes shifting from the trucks to the courthouse to the EverSafe Solutions building. He wore the expression of a man who preferred not to be noticed, who wished to remain on the periphery. "Lookin' for a G," he grumbled. "Blame ol' Antwaan. Blame your boy for the state of the world."

He had just left the magistrate's office, where he had paid a ninety-dollar fine for taunting pigeons on the courthouse lawn. The judge had intoned that the mistreatment of "native populations" would not be tolerated. He had pushed the spectacles to the end of his nose, peered over them, and told Antwaan he did not want to see him in his courtroom again.

As Antwaan's frustration began to ebb, his curiosity started to flow. He picked out familiar faces in the crowd—the eggroll homey, the hood rat with the sparkly purse, the jake with the bullhorn. As reluctant as he was to be seen in the vicinity, fascination bubbled inside him. He gravitated toward the commotion.

"Yo, Ar-joon!"

"Antwaan! Where is your Big Mac?"

"D's is wack. I am back."

"I am temporarily closed."

"What went down?"

"We are waiting to see."

"Smells like somethin' got lit up."

"You did not hear it?"

"I was assed out. In court."

"What did you do?"

"I was playin' with the pigeons."

Arjun pondered this scrap of data, rolled it over in his mind like a sticky note wrapped around a pigeon's foot. He wondered if the amiable Antwaan was his anonymous pen pal. *To be my bitch.* One could not always discern between friend and foe. Sometimes a person with poor social skills turned out to be a gem of a human being. Other times a maker of good impressions was revealed to be a poisonous snake.

Arjun looked at Angry Eddie, propped on a stool, balancing a pair of reading glasses on his nose and frowning at a newspaper. Even in a crowd, the vendor was a solitary figure. Arjun imagined the upbringing that produced this irascible character. He saw a stern father and a meek mother, chewing their food silently night after night, storing their love and anger for years like bottles of unopened soda. He saw a boy searching their faces for affection and approval. He plotted the arc of a life, from neglected child to antisocial adolescent to crotchety misanthrope.

"Poor Eddie," Arjun said.

"He looks content, doesn't he?" Candy said.

"I suppose he does."

"He likes it this way."

"I do not think he likes it."

"Why?"

"No one likes to be lonely."

Melinda and Aubrey sat in their folding chairs, wrapped in blankets, sipping coffee. Melinda's former colleagues, junior partners at Worthington Fairchild, had been flushed out of the courthouse like ants in a flood. Skilled at spotting the bereaved, they moved in stealth, spreading words of encouragement, canvassing for business. The police marked the scene with yellow tape. The ambulances remained empty, their stewards standing at attention.

"Goddamn kids," Eddie said to Melinda. "They blow up mailboxes. Egg you when you walk out to get the paper. Light bags of shit on fire."

"That's enough now," Melinda said.

"Their parents won't discipline them. Schools won't stand up to them. They tip over toolsheds. Let the air out of car tires. If they lay a hand on my cart, I'll ring them up. I'll take them down."

"Maybe they need to speak with a professional," Aubrey said.

"Or a drill sergeant."

"No—I mean, like, a therapist."

"Fort Benning, baby. Fort Jackson."

"Eddie, stop," Melinda said. "Don't punish others with your anger."

"Oh, it's fine," Aubrey said.

"See?" Eddie said. "She knows what they do. They haunt you, torment you. Maybe they make you cut yourself."

"That is *enough*," Melinda said. "You think a woman won't flatten you?"

Eddie laughed. "Okay, it was the unicorns that did it. It was an accident. With the horns."

The crowd let out a murmur. The brothers from Three Bucketeers—Casey, Chester, and Buddy Finn—were led to a cruiser in handcuffs, their eyes shielded, their heads down. Melinda and Arjun traded glances. Surely the brothers had done nothing wrong. Surely it was all a misunderstanding.

Aubrey sighed. They all could have been blown to bits, she thought. Her father would have gotten a call on his cell phone. He would have arrived at the morgue late at night. *I was in Philly,* he'd say. *On a sales call. Yeah, that one is my ex-wife and the other one is my daughter.* He would be wearing a blank expression, like the one he wore the day he left. He hadn't hugged Aubrey. He had just thrown some things in a duffel bag and driven off to the gym. He had come back the next weekend with a U-Haul and asked her how she was doing in school. He had tousled her hair. But Mom had hidden in her bedroom with the door locked. Aubrey hadn't said anything. She had just sat in her chair at the kitchen table, eating a bowl of Cheerios and staring at the cover of *Cosmopolitan.*

After her father identified the bodies, he would go to the bar and sob on some woman's shoulder. What woman's heart wouldn't swell with sympathy for a man who had lost his family? She would console poor Jim, who was still alive, still enjoying beautiful spring days, still unpacking boxes in his new condo. Poor Dad. He would be the only one left. Just like he wanted it.

Aubrey pulled an Exacto knife out of her purse. She used it in art class. She also cut herself with it. She sliced her forearm in cute little shapes, emojis that rose in a deep pink from the surface of her skin. When she pierced her flesh, anxiety escaped like steam from a teapot. She would make an incision and look at the blood and feel her lungs relax and expand. She would close her eyes and visualize oxygen rushing to her bloodstream. She would remember a time when everything was as it was supposed to be, when her mother and father had made her snacks of macaroni and cheese, when they had thrown parties for her birthdays with the neighborhood kids in a Moon Bounce.

Now she was checking herself for damage, wondering what had gone wrong. Even if her parents were estranged, even if they disagreed on the directions of their lives, they had made a commitment. They had a little girl, a symbol of their love, who needed them. But Aubrey wasn't a kid anymore. She wore makeup. She filled a bra. Maybe Mom and Dad thought their job was done.

"Mom, I'm scared."

"It's okay, baby."

But Aubrey knew it wasn't okay, that her mother wasn't sleeping, that her father wasn't calling, that the locomotive of her life was taking the turns too hard, ignoring the lights at the crossings. It was only a matter of time before it plowed into a school bus, crushing it like an anthill and taking her innocence with it.

She dragged the point of the blade over her forearm. The blood turned red when exposed to air.

"I do not think the Finns are terrorists," Arjun said.

"They don't look like terrorists," Candy said.

"Did you know Osama bin Laden played soccer?"

"What?"

"He ate and slept and went to the market like everyone else."

"But he wasn't like everyone else."

"He was."

"But he was different."

"He needed something different."

"I need lots of things I don't have," Candy said.

"When I was a boy," Arjun said, "a cat came to our back door. He was skinny and trembling and sad. I was afraid he would scratch me. Amma sliced the end off a sea bass and gave it to him. He purred and rubbed against my leg. He came back the next day for some red snapper and saag."

"Nice mom."

"People do not want to feed a stray."

"Why not?"

"They think it is alone for a reason."

Arjun remembered an old schoolmaster who had said people were all basically the same. For each way in which a person was different, he said, he was the same as others in fifty ways. Variations in skin tone, eye color, and size were inconsequential.

Arjun thought about Melinda, and about Ron, Debbie, Sharon, and Sully. He thought about the Finns. They weren't following a rulebook. They were paving the road as they traveled it. They were strays.

The police cruiser blew a burst on its siren, and the crowd parted.

"This is a weird day," Candy said, her eyes settling on the cutouts of smiling actors glued to the Bollywood Eggrolls truck.

"Would you like an eggroll?" Arjun said. "Perhaps a Delhi tea?

"Yes, yes. Please."

"Everything is going to be okay."

"Oh, I know. It's just weird, you know?"

"I know."

"Do you ever wonder if all this could disappear? If all the nice things we complain about could just go up in smoke?"

"Sure."

"Do you worry?"

"No."

"Why not?"

"I just know we are going to be okay."

"How do you know?"

"I just know."

Candy watched Arjun drop an eggroll into the fryer. "My mother used to say I had a guardian angel on my shoulder," she said. "She would say he was watching over me and would not let anything bad happen to me. But I guess even an angel has to sleep sometimes. And my angel kind of came and went."

"I think your mother was right."

"Why?"

41

"Because you are here. You were not rolled over by a trash truck or eaten by a bear. You were not struck by lightning. You were spared."

"I can't imagine why."

"We do not know why. We just know what is."

"Well, that's nice, but… what are we supposed to do with that information?"

"Everything we can."

6 | Annie

"Propane explosion," a police officer muttered into his megaphone. "Nothing more to see." The onlookers dispersed, slowly at first, and finally as a stampede, remembering the work they had to do. A few remained, whispering among themselves, parsing details they believed others had missed. Their conversation grew animated, with furtive mentions of the Twin Towers and Oklahoma City skipping through the lot.

"Listen to those idiots," Melinda said. She looked at Aubrey, who was dabbing her forearm with a hand towel. "Sweetie, you okay?"

"Just a scratch."

"Were you hit?"

"No... I just needed to bleed a little. I feel better now. The pressure builds up and I need to let it out."

"Sweetie, we agreed."

"Well... it's either that or I rip somebody's eyes out."

"You're mutilating yourself."

"Mom..."

"You are hurting yourself. You have to stop."

"Can we go home now? I need Daddy to help me with my algebra. Oh wait, I forgot. He can't."

"I can help you."

"You can put on your Daddy mask? And do a Daddy dance? And let me shave your face with your Norelco?"

Melinda took her daughter's hand and tugged her up the stairs, into the truck. "Listen. I know you're mad at your father, but—"

"I'm mad at *you*."

"What?"

"You drove him away."

"What?"

"You didn't love him!"

"I did love him. You don't know anything."

"Mom, I saw him cry."

Melinda looked into the eyes of her only child. One day Aubrey had been riding her bicycle around the cul-de-sac, singing "Ring around the Rosie," and the next she had locked her bedroom door and thrown "Bring Me to Life" by Evanescence on a loop.

"I beg your pardon," Melinda sang, pausing for a beat the way Lynn Anderson did in the song. "I never promised you a rose garden."

Candy loitered over her eggroll. "I don't want to go back to my desk. They're making us sell stuff over the phone."

"Is it good stuff?" Arjun asked.

"How would I know? I can't afford it."

"Okay. Here is what you must do. Before you pick up the telephone, go to your happy place. Spend a moment in the sunshine of your soul. While you are there, nothing can torment you."

"I'll remember that while they're cussing me out," Candy laughed.

"Yes."

"Could I have another eggroll?"

"I will make you as many eggrolls as you like. Perhaps you will tell me more about your Bobby."

"Oh, Arjun. I think I'm becoming my mother."

"What did she do?"

"She fell in love with a lummox who could barely tie his shoes. But he could open a bottle of Jack. He could buy lottery tickets."

"Did he win the lottery?"

"No."

"I am sorry. But I do not understand why you love a lummox."

"He's sweet to me. And I need sweetness in my life."

"Do you know why puppies should not eat chocolate? Because chocolate can kill a puppy. Free advice."

Candy remembered the advice offered to her by Walt Franklin in the driver's seat of his Dodge Charger: *Don't tell anyone. If you do, you won't get into college.* When she got home, her hair a mess and jeans askew, she had run to the bathroom and thrown up her Starbursts. "People usually charge for advice, don't they?" she said.

"They try," Arjun said.

The Finn brothers were cited for failing to secure a fuel tank. Instead of mounting the tank on the roof, they had put it inside the truck, next to the chicken fryer. A faulty valve had allowed a trickle of gas to escape and linger.

Soon the brothers were back, inspecting damage and checking inventory. They were quiet at first, traumatized by the shattering of a perfect day. But soon they were boogieing to Gnarls Barkley's "Crazy." Casey climbed the ladder to the roof. Chester surfed the windshield. Buddy vamped on the asphalt. Everything was going to be all right.

"Next little infraction?" Eddie said. "Back in the clink."

Arjun thought about his father, who had sacrificed his home and business to police corruption. He had returned to square one in the belief that a new life would be better than the one he had. And he had been right. They were thriving in Tucson. And their son was a Phi Beta Kappa graduate of the University.

America was a land of opportunity. Anyone could start a business. Anyone could become president. But America was also a place where free enterprise rewarded the bloodthirsty and left the rest to forage for seeds.

Every first-generation American, from Myles Standish to Sergey Brin, had fled his home country to put down stakes in the land of the free. Dissatisfaction and flight were woven into the American fabric. Every American was seeking some amorphous better life or following in the footsteps of someone who had.

Every American had, in some wistful moment, looked back at his homeland and thought, *fuck that place.*

"I guess I should go," Candy said, licking her lips in a gesture of appreciation for the chef.

"Duty calls," Arjun said.

"If you see Bobby—"

"I will alert the authorities."

Candy waltzed across the lot. Although her cubicle was a drab and dingy oven, she would curl up on a big, overstuffed chair in her mind and sell an alluring security to people who probably had a use for it. Everyone wanted to be safe. Everyone wanted to protect loved ones.

She thought of washing cars for the Kiwanis Club in Midland, climbing on the hoods of the muscle cars in her tank top and short shorts, teasing the drivers with her smile. She enjoyed the warm feeling she got from helping people. When she rolled out of bed on those sunny Saturdays, she skipped to the kitchen and made a big pan of scrambled eggs for herself and her mother. She gave her mom a hug and talked about the domestic violence shelter that would be built downtown. She glowed with self-esteem.

But Randy wanted her to stop. He didn't like the way the drivers looked at her, and he didn't like the way she looked back. One night, as they argued in the back seat of his car at the Food Lion, he slapped her with the back of his hand, bruising her cheek. She pushed him away and hid her face in her hands.

Now she was sitting in a cubicle in a skirt and blouse. No soap suds, no climbing and scrubbing. And while Bobby was an emotional terrorist, threatening to jump off the rocks at Great Falls if he couldn't see her on some random Tuesday night, he had never struck her. *You can't blame the boy,* her mother would say. *He's just a bundle of raging hormones.*

It was her fault she was mixed up with Bobby, her fault she was scaring people into buying alarm systems. It was her fault she lived in a dumpy apartment in a bad area. It was her fault she lost Randy, that she fell in with the dumb kids at Medford, that she wasn't singing on a stage, doing the one thing she ever thought she was born to do.

She sipped her Diet Coke and nibbled on an Oreo. She thought back to her performance as the titular character in *Annie* in the sixth grade, when tomorrow was only a day away. She remembered stunning her high school friends and teachers as Mary Magdalene in *Jesus Christ Superstar*. She could sing. She could act. She could bring an audience to its feet.

She picked up the receiver and keyed in the next number on her list of new mothers. The phone rang.

"Hello?"

"Hi!" Candy chirped like a young Andrea McArdle. "My name is Annie Bennett with EverSafe Solutions. Do you feel safe in your home? Or when you go to sleep? Or when you return from doing errands? Are you confident that your nest is secure and protected?"

"Well, I suppose... but not really, I guess."

"Well, all you need to do is lock your doors and windows."

"Huh? I don't need to buy something?"

"I doubt it!" Candy said, laughing. "If an intruder can't get in, he can't set off an alarm. But your puppy? He'll set it off just for kicks. And those balloons from your baby's birthday party will float around the house and trip the sensor as soon as you've left your driveway. It'll make you crazy."

"Okay, but... if you're not selling something, why are you calling?"

"To congratulate you on your little bundle!" Candy said, stifling a giggle. A splash of Diet Coke burned her sinuses. Alarm systems were so hard to sell, she thought, she might not sell *any*. She might have to leave this sensitive work to seasoned professionals.

Billy popped a zit on his chin. Clearasil was for amateurs. It didn't work. It just made him look sunburned. It spurred taunts from the other kids. He dabbed the wound with a washcloth. It was oozing blood.

His mother had told him not to apply pressure. It would scar his face. It would make it more difficult to attract a woman if he ever fell in love. He knew what Mom was trying to say: he would not get laid. He would be a sad creep holed up in a dingy apartment, chatting with a dirty old man impersonating a teenage girl on a Russian dating site. He would be ordering pizza every night and getting fatter and fatter. He would be alone.

He texted his friend Justin: *FML*

yeah dude right, came the reply.

we gonna practice?

yeah cool

Billy and Justin had started a small band featuring Billy on guitar and Justin on drums. They had played some parties. They had rocked Justin's family picnic, a multigenerational affair packed with hot cousins from Louisville, Kentucky. Billy was into 3 Doors Down. Justin liked Nickelback. A friend of Billy's dad had met Dave Grohl backstage at the Rock & Roll Hall of Fame. That was their ace in the hole. Someday, when they had fans, they would pull that card and play it.

They rehearsed in Justin's garage, in a little space between the Buick Century and the wall. Justin played a Pearl Roadshow kit with a cracked hi-hat pedal. Billy ran a Squier Stratocaster through an old Peavey amp. The noise was enough to make them dizzy, as Justin crashed his cymbals and Billy climbed onto the hood of the Century for blistering solos. On the wall behind them hung a bed sheet with the words "Quantum Leap" spray-painted in black.

Billy perused the photos on his phone, thumbing through the gallery of images of Candy Carney. *Damn,* he thought. He wondered if she liked guitar players. He imagined her watching him rip into the chorus of "Here Without You." That would be all it would take. She would be all over him.

Swoon city.

He hadn't had a girlfriend since seventh grade. He used to walk her home, carry her books. They rode their bikes around the neighborhood and talked. But when she started riding in the car of that guy with the letter jacket, Billy hardly talked to anyone for all of eighth grade.

When he saw Candy, it was as if he saw his future. Free and knowing. She could teach him, guide him through the maze he faced each day. She could mold him into a man. She could show him a thing or two about partying.

The statue of George Wythe stood at attention, surveying the grounds of the Broadnax County Courthouse. People were categorized by race, class, and gender, yet they feigned blindness to their differences. They pretended they were all equal, although some could read while others were illiterate, and some could buy property while others were penniless.

He rued the fact that he had taught Jefferson too well. The ideals of the republic were aspirational only. Yet the citizens embraced them as reality in a feast of delusion and wishful thinking.

The solemn figure pondered the words on its pedestal: "The Father of American Jurisprudence." Did a child not bear the crosses of his father? Did he not carry the flag of his forebears?

Arjun stood in the open pass-through. He thought back to a class he had taken at the University, The Agrarian Economy in America: 1650–1860. In a capitalist system, risk was spread over all of society, while profit accrued to a select few. The average person worked for subsistence and an opportunity to work again the next day. He was "free" in the sense that he was free to starve or to flee or to embark on a life of crime.

The Founding Fathers had understood the importance of labor. It was why they kept slaves.

Arjun reached into his pocket and pulled out the crumpled yellow sticky note. *To be my bitch.* Was he under someone's thumb? In Delhi, his father had been beholden to a pervasive corruption. He had awakened each day knowing some of his earnings belonged to a shadowy network of others.

Antwaan watched the World Cup on a flatscreen in the basement of his parents' home in Great Falls. Cameroon was playing Mexico. He sipped a whiskey sour left over from his parents' pool party, exhausted from a night of canvassing the DC hip-hop clubs. He closed his eyes and thought of Biggie and 'Pac, gone too soon.

He was living for more than just the bitches and bling. He lived for poetry. He lived for God.

His father was an orthodontist, his mother a corporate attorney. They had met as undergraduates at Yale, a power couple climbing the ladder. Their only child was conceived on the night of the election of Bill Clinton. They tutored the boy in piano and judo and interpretive dance and schooled him in liberal ideology. They decorated his bedroom with Rothko prints and discussed *Gödel, Escher, Bach: An Eternal Golden Braid* at the dinner table. They taught him to appreciate the finer things.

For his part, Antwaan dropped out of high school.

He rolled an ice cube around his mouth, over his perfect teeth, and took a swig of Russell's Reserve. Never say die. What doesn't kill you makes you stronger. Rage against the dying of the light. He thought of Mandela: *To be free is not merely to cast off one's chains, but to live in a way that enhances the freedom of others.*

After a privileged childhood, he had produced an illustrious record of convictions for urinating in public and disturbing the habitats of native species. His transgressions had appeared in the Great Falls community newspaper. His parents had suffered censure, taunted by the averted eyes of the postman, tormented by the whispers of neighbors in the aisles of Whole Foods. His mother had burst into tears in her leather armchair and demanded to know where—*where*—she and his father had gone wrong.

It was all wrong, Antwaan thought. Wrong to arrive at school in a Lexus while Fiddy dodged bullets. Wrong to feast on filet mignon while his brothers waged war in the streets, their fates consigned to cryptic tags on the walls of abandoned buildings. He had read Maya Angelou. He had read Langston Hughes. They pursued no dreams but their own.

He was lucky, he knew, to have parents who paid to produce his club vinyl as the Assassin. He was lucky to have the same vocal rig as Jay Z. He was blessed to be literate and inspired and able to capture the plight of his people in verse and rhyme.

But there was no justice in his good fortune. There was only the thud of the shoe that crushed the inner cities and shipped young people across the seas to be dismembered and killed. Montgomery would always be Montgomery. The powers now channeled the powers that had always been and held the door for the powers that would forever be. Antwaan Jefferson would be just another rich kid in pumped-up kicks until he liberated his soul from bondage.

He grabbed a croissant and slipped out the back door.

Arjun rolled the door into the roof of the truck. The sun was radiant, the air crisp, and the blue skies promised a day of delectable fare and happy customers. He spied a figure on the steps of the courthouse, sprawled like a squid on the cool granite. It was probably the safest place in town to catch a few winks on a summer night, given its surveillance systems. If one passed out on those stairs, he could rest assured his wallet would be in his pocket come dawn.

Pidgey waddled over the asphalt, his head bobbing to some silent rhythm. He pecked at the gravel, searching for seeds. His mother and father were long gone. One day they were beaming with pride at his self-sufficiency and the next they were on the wing, seeking their fortunes in points west. Before they lit out for the territories, they took him to the Museum of American History to see the exhibit on Cher Ami, the pigeon that saved the lives of the Lost Battalion in World War I. Pidgey wondered if he would ever do anything to merit the *Croix de Guerre*. So far he had only foraged for food and wandered around the lot, never taking flight. He hadn't done anything heroic. If he were to die now, stunned by a speeding car or crushed by a zucchini fryer, he would pass into the annals of natural history, an unexceptional bird with pedestrian accomplishments. He would be forgotten.

Arjun watched the pigeon wander the blacktop like some soulful dove—a bird more loved and revered. He wondered if Pidgey was a leader or a follower. He wondered the same about himself. Although he made his own decisions, his fiefdom was small and contained no subjects. Sometimes he wondered if his lands reached only as far as his own mind. If he were to die now, he thought, his obituary would say simply that he was a naturalized citizen with a food truck.

He would be forgotten.

With scarcely a customer in sight, he set out across the quiet lot. He appraised the grandeur of the courthouse and tried to absorb the ideals of the Founding Fathers. Unlike the Parthenon or the Sphinx, the courthouse would likely be leveled one day to make room for an outlet mall or a stadium with a retractable roof.

He mounted the granite steps. America had been a land of dreams, but now it was more like a billboard advertising the charm and allure of such a land. He remembered his father sitting at the kitchen table, sorting through travel brochures, poring over lush, commercial photographs until his eyes came to rest on the desert oasis of Tucson.

"The Promised Land!" his father had shouted to his little family, laughing at his own excitement.

Arjun recognized the young man sprawled on the steps. He tapped him in the ribs with his shoe. "Wake up, friend."

Antwaan did not move.

"They will arrest you."

Antwaan remained still.

"And then they will arrest you again. And then, one day, they will lock you up and throw away the key."

Antwaan forced an eye open.

"They will lock you up so they don't have to look at you anymore."

"Shit."

"As if you do not exist."

"What the—"

"And you will *be their bitch*."

"What the fuck?"

"Are you not their bitch, Antwaan? Help me to understand."

"What you *sayin'*, Gandhi?"

"I am saying it is time for you to get off these steps. I am saying it is time to wake up and look at the world. It is lying in wait for you."

"You think I don't *know* that?"

"And that world is *not* your bitch."

"Whose bitch? What bitch?" Antwaan said, rising to his feet.

Arjun withdrew the yellow sticky note from his pocket. "Does this look familiar?"

Antwaan grabbed the scrap. "You crazy, motherfucker?"

"I am quite sane."

"No, you *not*."

Arjun looked into Antwaan's eyes and glimpsed only confusion and pain. "All right, then, friend," he said, pushing the note back into his pocket, "I was mistaken. Please accept my apologies."

7 | Stray Cats

The car at the edge of the food-truck lot hadn't moved in three days. A skinny young man with jet-black hair and glasses was camped out in the driver's seat, a laptop pressed against the steering wheel, a bag of pork rinds on the dash. He worked with purpose, lost in his own world. He emerged only to visit the porta-john.

Melinda watched him tap on the keyboard, his lips moving, his eyes glowing. He seemed tormented, seized by thought, unaware of the activity in the lot. Hour after hour, his eyes scanned the screen, never wandering. Melinda wondered if he was strung out on caffeine pills or amphetamines. She wondered if he was homeless or insane.

She scanned the screen of her phone for the names of people logged into her wireless router: "BOMBS," "BOLLY," "PIGGIES," and finally, "HAWK." She appraised the wild-eyed young man in the car. Unless he had a permit to sell food out of his little beater, he was squatting. She highlighted "HAWK" and pressed "delete." He slapped his steering wheel in agitation. He returned to working on his keyboard. And then the name reappeared on her screen.

Melinda walked across the lot, toward the rusted-out compact. The fierce countenance of its occupant froze her in her tracks. Was he a hacker? An investigator? She stood before the battered grill and tried to make eye contact with the man behind the bag of pork rinds. But he was locked in, oblivious to the world outside. She noticed a white cord running up his shirt and into his mop of hair. He was lost in sound.

She waved her arms. "Hey!"

He continued working, his eyes riveted to the screen.

"Hey!" Melinda shouted, pounding on the hood with her fist. "I'm talking to you!" She walked to the driver's-side door and rapped on the window. "I said I'm *talking to you!*"

The young man stopped typing, pulled off his earbuds, and cranked down the window. "Whaddaya want?"

"You're stealing my Wi-Fi."

"What?"

"You're logged on to my router."

"So what?"

"So, get off it."

"What, I'm hurting you?"

"It's password-protected."

"Yeah, whatever. I'm not hurting you. I'm a person and you're a person. And we're sharing the air and the rain and the frequencies over which information travels. People don't own the internet. And they don't own the land. They don't own anything but their own bodies. But hey, check it out, they try to own everything they see, even each other."

"Get off my network."

The young man rolled up his window. Melinda's phone buzzed in her pocket. She had a text message:

Thx for letting me hack yr router. When done coding, Ill give u free app.

The young man winked at Melinda through the windshield, tossed a pork rind into his mouth, and resumed typing. Her phone buzzed again.

p.s. u have food?

Melinda's face turned crimson. There were laws about hacking. There were laws about privacy. There were laws about one person assuming the property of another without consent. She stormed back to the truck. This was what happened when she did someone a good turn. Estranged couples didn't thank her after their divorces. Drunks didn't thank her after court. In their warped, infantile minds, they were entitled to everything she gave them.

She pulled a pressed oval of ground beef out of the refrigerator and tossed it onto the grill. The kid looked hungry, she thought, almost emaciated. He reminded her of Aubrey, a little self-satisfied and ignorant of things that would dig his grave.

Somewhere his mother was probably losing sleep.

She wondered what Darwin would have made of him. But then she realized he was locked safely inside a cage of steel, out of the reach of predators. He had found a source of food. And he was propped up in a comfortable seat that reclined for sleep. Darwin likely would have pronounced him fit.

She crossed the lot to the Bollywood Eggrolls truck.

"His name is Jared," Arjun said. "He is working on an app. He said it will help all of us."

"Sorry," Melinda said, "but that sounds like bullshit."

"Everything sounds like bullshit at first."

"That sounds like bullshit too."

"We will see. I am watching with interest."

"Yeah, interest in his imminent trip up the river. He's trespassing. He is squatting on a lot you and I pay to occupy, where we abide by the law. I'm pretty sure the law applies to him too. I'm pretty sure it has a whole section devoted to the misadventures of snarky little shits thumbing their noses."

"It is a beautiful day, Melinda. Full of possibility."

"Okay."

"You were kind to give him a plate of food. I am going to make him an eggroll and a Delhi tea."

"But you know what? It's like feeding a stray cat. Feed him on Monday and he comes back on Tuesday. Feed him on Tuesday and he comes back on Wednesday. Feed him on Wednesday and he starts to see you as the help. And then, *bam*—where the hell is his goddamn food on Thursday?"

"Life is hard for a stray cat."

"Yes, look at him. Doing whatever he wants. Very hard."

"Maybe it is."

Bobby stood at the bar, inhaling Sex on the Beaches, his face red with sweat. Candy and the girls were clustered in the corner, laughing and singing along with Gretchen Wilson. Curly's was rocking hard. Bobby was thinking about the intersection of the past and the future, the precious, fleeting moment in which he occupied a spot that would never be quite the same again. Life was a bitch, man. You spent all your time pretending you gave a shit, just to get close to people and have some kind of life for yourself. And then she still didn't love you. She still told everybody she didn't have a boyfriend. She still waited for some charmed life that was just around the corner, a life without you.

"Birth, school, work, death," Bobby muttered.

The bartender tilted his head.

"That's why babies don't know anything when they're born," Bobby said. "If they knew, they would never come out, you know?"

"Yep."

"My dad says after a baby boy gets pushed out of the womb, he spends the rest of his life trying to get back in."

"Yep."

"Like a stray cat."

"Yep…"

"How 'bout you, bro? Doing the waitress? Got a place o' your own? Saving money for a big cruise or somethin'? What's up in bartender land, man…"

Billy and Justin waited in the Curly's lobby. The bar had recently started hosting live music on Monday nights. It was time to start their ascendancy.

"I'll do the talking," Billy said. He peeked around the corner. Chicks everywhere, partying. He hoped the room would rock as hard on Monday nights as it did on the weekends. There were whole tables of honeys getting wasted, singing along to 3 Doors

Down. Billy imagined them sitting in thrall before him while he shredded his way through "Kryptonite." Curled up in their chairs, whispering and giggling, they would watch him and think he looked like a rock star. They would argue about who got to talk to him first after the show. And he would hit that solo like a falcon on a rabbit, taking what was his, soaring into the night sky. After that, anything could happen.

"Quantum Leap?" a petite woman asked, a blonde ponytail falling down the back of her Curly's shirt.

"Um, yeah," Billy said. "We're here about a show."

"I listened to your songs, yeah. Come Monday. Be here at nine."

"What percentage do we get?"

"You get twenty bucks. Bar closes at ten fifteen."

Billy paused. "We want a cut of the bar."

"You can sell T-shirts," the woman said. "And you'll play in the hallway, right outside the bar, because you're under twenty-one."

"Okay."

The woman disappeared into the multicolored lights.

"It's not about the money, man," Justin said. "It's about the future."

"And our music." Billy peered into the haze of the bar. School was a bummer. Work was a drag. Home was a throwback. He was a grown man now, with a driver's license and an electric razor.

A tingle ran up his spine. He heard her voice ringing out like a bell in Pavlov's steeple. He cocked his head. She was laughing. He slipped into the room and looked around. Bar, hallway, tables. And there she was, curled up in a booth by the wall, her knees drawn up to her chest, pressed against a pink halter top. He stared. She was like Buffy the Vampire Slayer, but hotter to the tenth power.

"Hey," one of the girls said. "Can we get some waters?"

"What?" he stammered, his eyes bugging out. "I don't work here."

"Then what are you looking at?"

"Um…"

"Hey!" Candy shouted.

"Oh, hi…" Billy said.

"Are you stalking me?" Candy laughed.

"No, me and my friend…"

"You are so stalking me."

"I was just—"

The table erupted in laughter as the girl sitting next to Candy delivered the punch line of her joke: "Go on, I'll hold your monkey for you!" Billy teetered backward and staggered into the shoulder of a man seated at the bar.

"What the fuck?" It was a stout man with cropped hair, a petulant drunkard Billy would soon know as Bobby.

"Oh, sorry."

"Isn't it your bedtime?"

"Sorry."

"She's outta your league, son. She's outta my league. She's in a league of her own…"

"Yeah, man…"

"What did you say?" Bobby grabbed Billy's earlobe and twisted it. "That is my *girl*."

Billy was overwhelmed by the sickening aroma of peach schnapps. He wriggled free and sprinted toward the door, his heart palpitating. *She had a boyfriend?* He dashed through the lobby, past Justin, through the revolving doors, and into the night air. Justin tracked him past the empty benches, past the day lilies and hostas, to the space where he had parked his father's Buick Century. Billy stared at the asphalt, his chin in his ribs.

"Dude, what?" Justin said.

"Let's go," Billy said. "Let's just *go*."

The silhouette of Lincoln, sprawled on the asphalt underneath Aubrey's chair, averted his gaze, but accidentally glimpsed Aubrey's inner thigh as she propped up a knee. Mary Todd would scold him for that, to say nothing of God. He refocused on a point in the middle distance, on the statue of George Wythe. It was a solemn vista, weighty with portent.

He thought of Jefferson's declaration of the rights of every person to life, liberty, and the pursuit of happiness. In his mind, it meant everyone had a right not to be killed, not to be enslaved, and not to be impeded in efforts to build a better life. Jefferson had assumed that the meaning of his words would remain fixed, like ink on parchment. But it had evolved. People now thought they could have any life, do anything, and indulge any whim.

Lincoln glimpsed Aubrey's colorful drawers emblazoned with smiling pink ponies. He then apologized to the Lord and bemoaned his humanity. In the modern day, this delightful creature was but a child. But in the time of the Civil War, she would have been a soldier's bride, a comfort to a conscript upon his triumphant return from the rigors of battle. She would have been bearing children.

Lincoln took a deep breath and closed his eyes. The characters on stage stayed the same, he thought, while the sets changed like the seasons. And he had seen more in two centuries than he had ever wanted to.

Aubrey squirmed. She keyed a number on her phone. "Hey, it's me... Yeah... My mom is on the warpath... Not at me... Some kid in the lot... Okay, YOLO, bye." She reached into her backpack and pulled out a worn copy of *The Outsiders*. English teachers had so much respect for freshmen, she thought, that they assigned them books written by sixteen-year-olds. So this nerdy book was written by a bored girl in study hall or whatever. And Aubrey knew there wouldn't really be anybody named Ponyboy. That was stupid.

Everything was just so dumb and pointless.

Aubrey's eyes rolled over the words, but the words did not enter her mind. The door to her imagination was barred by a fantasy in which she climbed fifty flights of stairs to the top of the Washington Monument and jumped out the window. She caught a breeze over the Mall, sailing like a seagull over the Capitol and the

Lincoln Memorial. She glimpsed Jefferson standing inside his little dome, situated off the beaten path, immortal in the incandescence of evening. The city was beautiful and shining and timeless but was stumbling into decay. In all its grandeur, it would leave behind only a hint of the decline and fall, a whispered account of a failed world.

Pidgey pecked at the gravel by Aubrey's chair, searching for seeds blown off the nearby trees. He had little interest in people beyond their propensity for littering. He savored the sustenance of a Bollywood Eggroll, the succor of a Burger Bomb. He treasured the joy of jelly doughnuts and fried chicken and pulled pork. He cherished every bite, an explosion of sensory color more intense than the morning sun. To be free in the world was to sing to the sky and hear choirs of angels harmonizing. It was to live forever within each crystalline moment.

He expelled a burst of gas from his intestines.

"Gross," Aubrey said.

Well, surely her digestion was not perfect, he thought. Surely there were moments, even whole days, when she fought queasiness and feared the censure of her peers. Unlike him, she could not solve the problem on any spot. She had to navigate social norms. She had to observe a code of conduct. Because she was not free.

Pidgey tottered toward the courthouse. When no one cared about you or placed a value on your head, you flew under the radar. You did as you pleased. While the baby pandas and Bengal tigers languished in cages, longing for liberty, the squirrels and rabbits and pigeons had the run of the place. No one was profiting from them. No one was telling them who to be. And there was no greater freedom, he thought, as he mounted the base of the statue of George Wythe, than the freedom to be yourself.

Jared Hawk had been awake for thirty-six hours. *Coders are the new Leonardos. Software is the new cave wall. And I am a genius.* He popped a Paxil. The world was spinning, tilting on its axis of possibility. It was singing and calling and becoming itself, over and over again. And he was documenting it.

He was unmoored, surfing the cosmos like a spirit free of its physical body. Silicon Valley was the perfect wave. He would catch that frothy breaker and ride it all the way to the beach. Nothing could stop him. The world might not know him today, but tomorrow the media would clamor to get a glimpse of him. And he would laugh when *Wired* took notice and called him an overnight sensation.

He stared at the code on his screen:

@interface QuartzBlendingView : QuartzView

@property (nonatomic) UIColor *sourceColor;
@property (nonatomic) UIColor *destinationColor;
@property (nonatomic) CGBlendMode blendMode;

@end

Concept and architecture were entwined like strands of DNA, twirling in his MacBook. He was a vessel for the cargo of the angels. He reached over to the passenger seat and grabbed the last bite of the Burger Bomb. There was nothing new under the sun. Everything that vanished reappeared in some other form. He thought of his breath, his sweat, the food in his hand. He thought of the oil from the fingertips of Steve Wozniak, drying to a matte sheen on the keys of the Apple I. Ashes to ashes.

He popped another Paxil.

He remembered little about school but moldy tales of heroes and villains and battles. They meant nothing to him. He had wasted years in that hog pen, eating slop from the trough. They were only fattening him so they could slaughter him later. Once he graduated, he would be a glistening Virginia ham in some corporate brick oven. He would wind up in a Cuban sandwich, trapped between the pickles and cheese.

His pulse quickened. One foot in front of the other, he thought. One brick at a time. One line of code and then another. Don't think about where it will end. Think only of the path, the mortar, the words.

Think only of transformation.

He had spent twenty-three years in the chrysalis. He had always had ideas. He had always dreamed. But it wasn't until now, as he sat in his old beater, his laptop balanced against the steering wheel, that he was able to envision where it would lead. Need spurred innovation. Supply met demand. The pieces of the jigsaw puzzle found their mates. And the puzzle became a picture.

Every line of code was backed up to a server in Boise, Idaho, and mirrored by another in Fountain Valley, California. If his hard drive crashed, or his laptop was stolen, or his car burst into flames, his work was safe. In the event of his death, his little brother would recover the files and continue the work.

He tinkered with the triangulation routine, leaving a placeholder for the password and coordinates of the satellite. The elegant solution, he thought, turned a wish into a need.

There was a knock at the glass. He stared at the keyboard like a magician at a crystal ball, trying to decipher the next line. He rolled down the window. "What?"

"Are you hungry?" Arjun asked.

"What am I, a stray cat?"

"Aren't you?"

"I don't think about food, okay? I don't even think about girls. I only think about what I'm doing."

"Eggroll?"

"Okay."

In the back seat of Jared's car, Arjun saw a duffel bag, a stack of books, a pile of clothes, and an assortment of fast-food wrappers and drink cups. He saw a backpack stuffed with computer cords. On the floor, he glimpsed a basketball, some sports trophies, and a stack of video games. This was a young man who had left home. This was a kid scratching out a living doing God knows what.

"If you are going to carry the load, make sure you are ready."

"Yeah, okay."

"Otherwise, you will fall. And the load will crush you."

"Uh, thanks."

"1 know you don't want to think about it. But if the engine stops running, the car is dead. And it goes nowhere."

"Jesus…"

Arjun set out across the lot. Melinda was whistling in her window. Aubrey was zoning out in a floppy hat. The Finns were break-dancing, Sully was tending his pit, and Ron was licking doughnut glaze off his fingertips. Debbie had her head in the ice-cream case, breathing cold air.

Candy stood at the Bollywood Eggrolls pass-through, supporting her weight on one hip, smiling behind her oversized sunglasses. "You're not very responsible, wandering off like that," she said.

"Where is your Bobby?" Arjun said. "I dreamed he wandered off and never came back. Poor fellow."

"He always comes back. He's like a dog."

"Shaggy?"

"Loyal."

"Human beings can be loyal too," Arjun said. "And they possess cognitive skills. It could be a win-win for you, upgrading."

"He just needs some time to grow up."

"Dog years are short."

Candy laughed. "Hmmm," she said, drawing out the word, the *m* sound buzzing on her lips. She set her purse on the pass-through. "I don't suppose you'll make me an eggroll now. You probably think I'll just give it to my dog."

"I'm sure your dog is well fed."

"He doesn't seem to think so."

"Well, he is just a dog," Arjun said. "What does he know?" He dropped a pair of eggrolls into the fryer. He didn't understand women, bright and insightful but smitten with cads and lummoxes. The men they chose for their intimate adventures were sure to make the most unreliable life partners imaginable. And yet.

"Can I get mine extra crispy?" Candy said.

"I think that is apropos."

Antwaan turned on the PA. The speakers crackled with life. He touched the microphone to his lips and busted a rhyme about a neighborhood shorty with proclivities. *She was fine, dressed to the nines.*

His parents' basement, underground except for a back-door walkout, muffled his high-decibel rants and served as a womb for his burgeoning ideas. It allowed him to build a world separate from the one outside. Sheets of notebook paper littered the floor, strewn about like refuse from a tornado. The room was an alternate universe, he thought, where the sky cried words.

And his parents only came downstairs to get bottles of wine.

He held the mic and testified. *Sweet as world piece, Beyoncé's niece, biscuit joy for the phat homeboy.* He picked up his pen and added, *that girl got a complex.* He had written hundreds of raps since high school and was gaining a reputation in the club scene for sparkling political rants and character sketches. He simulated a bass-and-drum beat with his lips, his tongue, and the roof of his mouth: *donk-donk, ba-donk-a-diddy-donk, krunk-krunk, junk inside the trunk.* He stared into the far corner of the room and saluted an invisible audience. *Funk in the pink, jammy, funk in the pink.*

He scrawled verse after verse, imagining the stunned and delighted faces of the crowd when he dropped this science like rose petals on their waiting heads. No one could touch the Assassin. He was the coldest. He would win every battle, launching total slaughter like a nuclear missile. He would rise to the top in DC, in the mid-Atlantic, in the USA. He would tour the world.

He thought of the bouncer at Kill City who had noticed his manicured nails while inking the back of his hand with a "21" stamp. *Compton coming up in the world.* Antwaan had glared at him but had to admit truth was truth. He was a kid from Great Falls. He had an Xbox and an Antelope sound system and a pair of Jimmy Choo Belgravias. He drove his mother's Lexus. He could spend the next four years at an expensive private college if he wanted to. But that bourgeois scene was a trap.

He reheated some grilled orange roughy in the TurboChef. He was eating right, like Kanye. He was fortifying himself for the battle to come. He was getting plenty of sleep, training his body and mind to compete on the big stage, to grab the brass ring. By giving himself the best of everything today, and protecting himself from harsh conditions, he would be ready to walk through fire when the time came.

He threw his plate in the sink. He tapped the windscreen of the mic, generated a simple beat from his vintage Oberheim DMX, and began to rap:

Watch for the Assassin as he's passin' through the 'hood
Your fever for the lever is the Devil's firewood
The Assassin is a teacher and a preacher of the Word
A Messiah, not a liar, he is everything you've heard
Watch for the Assassin as he's blastin' through the town
On fanatical sabbatical, a rapper in the round
The Messiah is on fire with a molten megaphone
His desire never tires, he forever must atone
Eye of the Assassin
I am the Assassin
I am the Assassin
A million miles from home.

8 | Intruders and Madmen

Melinda checked her makeup in the mirror. Her cheeks were pink, her nose shiny. Her freckles were like sprinkles of confectioner's sugar. She dusted her skin with quick strokes of her brush. Each year, she thought, her face demanded a little more of her time. Eventually she would be a wilted old woman in a rocking chair, applying concealer from dawn until dusk.

She thought of all the women who had come to her law office with stories of betrayal and humiliation. *He has ruined me for other men. He has ruined me for myself.* She had murmured "now, now" while they seethed. She had nodded in assent while they dissolved in self-pity.

Their victimhood was seared into her memory like the lines on a burger. *Look at me,* they said, *I am scarred.* She glimpsed their pursed lips, their furrowed brows, quivering in rearview mirrors, in revolving doors. They wanted justice. They wanted revenge. They wanted the guy to hurt the way they did.

Sometimes she saw their wounded eyes in the depths of her own. *Look at me. I am scarred.*

Her best friend since junior high had celebrated her divorce by dyeing her hair bright red and getting a tattoo of a red rose just above her vulva. *He scarred me, but these scars belong to me.* She had sent Melinda a bottle of Moët & Chandon. Melinda had sat quietly in her off   with the lights off, sipping the champagne from a coffee
ing to the bubbles.

Sometimes, she thought, you served as the maid of honor at your friend's wedding. Other times you handled the dissolution of her marriage fifteen years later.

It was all about freedom.

Aubrey cut herself to own the pain, to make it visible. Her scars spoke. She wanted her mother and father to know, as they maneuvered for position against each other and their old friends, that she saw them. The witness to their actions was the living embodiment of all they had destroyed.

Sure, Melinda thought, Aubrey was unhappy. But brats were petulant. They thought the world revolved around them and were no more aware of the pain of others than they were of polio in Equatorial Guinea. Dramatizing their dissatisfaction didn't validate it. Melinda thought back to Aubrey in her crib, an *enfant terrible* screaming for her bottle. She had absorbed the fury of this creature and thought, *I surrender.*

Melinda looked at her crow's feet, more prominent when she grimaced or smiled. They had sneaked up on her over the years. And now they were scars of every joy and disappointment she had ever endured.

She spread more blush on her cheeks.

Now that she had established a leadership position on the lot—her father had taught her the value of primacy—she had started thinking about the collective power of the food-truck community. Step one was grabbing the biggest piece of the pie. Step two was making the whole pie bigger. It was all about getting others to listen and follow. It opened doors to bigger and better things.

She looked around the lot. Most of her competitors were lost in their own little worlds, focused on their fledgling businesses, unaware of the perils and possibilities of entrepreneurship. They didn't realize a month of bad weather could send them to the bread line. Without a broader view of the food-truck business, a dynamic vision of its potential, they would be blown away by fickle providence.

Melinda took a deep breath. She needed an ally, a first mate. But everyone she had trusted—her conniving bosses, her deadbeat clients, her philandering husband—had deserted her when it mattered most. And she had promised herself she wouldn't rely on other people anymore.

Melinda looked at Arjun. He had no customers, as usual, but was in his usual good mood. Was he independently wealthy? Or was he just researching a book about the inner workings of the food-truck world? He didn't look like a restaurateur hustling for every dime. He looked more like a laid-back tourist of nondescript parking lots.

Melinda walked over to the Bollywood Eggrolls window. "Hi!"

"It is a beautiful day!" Arjun said.

"Yes, it is. And I've been thinking."

"Oh?

"I've been thinking we could get some more customers."

"Yes?"

"People don't know enough about us to care—to really care—that we're here. They stumble out of their offices when they're squeezed for time. They grab a snack for the drive home. But they don't *plan* to visit us, you know? Maybe that's our fault."

"I have customers who come every day."

"You have two. And one of them is Jared."

"He likes eggrolls."

"But he isn't a customer. He is more of a leech."

"Free eggrolls are good karma."

"Free eggrolls are inventory shrinkage. Wake up. He is eating your food. You are losing money."

"I am okay."

"Is that all you want to be? Okay? Don't you want the world to know the Bollywood Eggroll is an unrivaled, deep-fried concoction? Don't you want to influence a whole generation of food-truck chefs?"

Arjun paused. "I do want the world to know. What do we do?"

"We pull together. All of us."

"How?"

"We work as a team. And that doesn't mean we stop *competing*. It means we start *cooperating*. We could call it 'co-opetition.' We run our own businesses and help each other thrive."

"Uh…"

"When you and I support each other, or Sharon and Sully help the Finns, or Ron and Debbie work together on a promotion, we all benefit. When one of us helps another, the food-truck court becomes just a little more unified and dynamic, and we all do better. The rising tide floats all boats."

"Right," Arjun said.

"So… I have an idea. We throw a big block party, right here on the lot. We plaster every telephone pole and alleyway with posters. We invite everyone we can. We call it the First Annual Gourmet Battle of the Vans."

"They are hungry," he said.

"Famished."

"And we will feed them."

"Yes."

Jared Hawk had spent his childhood absorbing the pronouncements of his parents and teachers and Boy Scout leaders. With their advice and guidance, he had swallowed colorful lies about human history. Columbus had "discovered" the New World, the genocide of Native Americans had been "manifest destiny," and America was the "land of the free." He knew he had been "given" liberty, but someday he would also get death, like everyone else.

People were panting like Iditarod dogs to put food on the table and a roof over their heads. They were about as free as rats in a maze. When they made it through the labyrinth, they received processed pellets and drops of water.

He had stopped attending his psychology class at the community college before they covered megalomania. Consequently, he hadn't read about delusions of grandeur, which explained the narcissism at the root of much human volatility. His fantasies of disruption and domination were likely hallmarks of a personality disorder. But he had told his parents what he thought of shrinks.

His phone buzzed. It was a text from his mother. *Sweetie, I found the lithium in your underwear drawer.* He stuffed the phone in his pocket. He only wrote code when he was off the meds. He wasn't going to go back on them now. They stopped him from crying and from making phone calls to Silicon Valley luminaries at two o'clock in the morning, but they also painted the sky and the trees and the strip malls a hazy, dispassionate shade of gray. They short-circuited his dreams. They helped him accept things as they were, without complaint, as if the need to fix a broken world was no more urgent than the wish to stroll down the street at dusk.

He opened his laptop. The core functionality—the ability to track and display locations on a grid of city streets—was in place. On that he could build the homing capability. The challenge lay in the transmission of video from remote locations to the user. It was one thing to be able to see where something was, but it was another to monitor it in all its high-definition glory.

His phone vibrated again. *Your father says if you do something stupid, you are on your own.* No shit, Sherlock. He was already on his own. He was living in a car. He was subsisting on scraps. He was evacuating his bowels in a malodorous fiberglass box. He was bathing with the pigeons in the marble fountain by the county courthouse. If that wasn't being on his own, he wasn't sure what was. *Your father says only you can save yourself from yourself. Come get your pills.*

His father had wanted him to go out for the high school football team. No amount of weightlifting would have put meat on his spindly frame, but Dad had envisioned him as a flashy running back. It was Jared's job to do the things his father hadn't done, to rise above the gene pool in a heroic climb to social achievement. But he was a quiet boy who didn't make waves, a skinny kid with bad grades. His best friend was his PlayStation. He wasn't exactly in the running for Homecoming king.

Gradually he had withdrawn from the anthill, skipping classes and joyriding and smoking weed in the woods with the other misfits. When his teachers had called his parents, he had sat quietly, as if catatonic, on the stool at the kitchen island, staring out the window. He already had taken a computer apart and put it back together. He already had written software more advanced than the original MS-DOS. Yet the school was trying to teach him about trapezoids and the Boer Wars and subject-verb agreement.

It was around that time he had stopped speaking, and shortly afterward that he had stopped getting out of bed. He brushed by his mother in the upstairs hallway, oblivious to her worry. He looked at his father with vacant insouciance, declining to run the maze laid out for him. It was his life, after all.

He had his own destiny.

Candy sat at her desk and frowned at the little red light on her phone. Somebody wanted something. She picked up the receiver and keyed in her passcode. *Hello, Candy. Mr. Paxton asked that I bring you in for a brief meeting. He is available this afternoon at three o'clock. We will see you then.*

She worked the file over her nails. Her bosses always took an interest in her. Rollie at the Dairy Queen, Hank at the Food Lion, Coley at the car wash, they all wanted to get to know her. Randy would pick her up at work and kiss her in front of her coworkers, just so they knew she was his. She liked the way he shielded her. She liked the way he opened doors for her and held the umbrella over her head, laughing in the pouring rain.

Now she had only a man-child who reminded her of nothing as much as a raccoon rooting through her trash.

Last night she had sat in her cubicle and made fifty-four phone calls to single mothers of newborn babies. And she was no longer veering from the prepared script. She was rewriting it. She greeted her "target" by identifying herself, as usual, as Annie Bennett of

EverSafe, but then explained she also represented a foundation called Healthy Kids. Her role as a "smile associate" was to reach out to new mothers and educate them on easy ways of making their homes safe for their children. She talked about plastic clamps that made electrical outlets and medicine cabinets safe for toddlers on the move. She gave instructions for getting these items free by mail. She explained that by doing nothing but locking doors and windows, a person reduced the chances of a break-in by ninety-three percent.

As usual, her sales of EverSafe Solutions alarm systems on that evening were lower than projected.

Her stomach growled. In the flurry of data entry, she had rolled straight through the lunch hour. Fortunately, she had time before her meeting with CEO Brad Paxton. In a flash, she was exiting the elevator and whirling through the exterior doors. The sun kissed her cheek. The parking lot rang with birdsong. The food trucks gleamed, soft and dreamy in the steam. She approached the shining object of her affection.

"Hi, Arjun! How are you today?"

"I am well, thank you! Are you in your happy place?"

"Not exactly. But I'm sort of nearby."

"Well... are you content?"

"I guess."

"If you have to *guess*, you are not content."

"How do I know if I'm content?"

"You know it if you are not wanting something."

"But everybody wants something."

"Yes, everyone wants something... but not everyone wants something at every moment."

"You are so weird." She laughed.

"Oh? I think *you* are weird," he sparred. "I think you are more weird than anyone on this lot."

"I don't know. Angry Eddie is pretty weird."

"But he is not a denizen."

"A 'denizen'? You are *so weird*."

"And you are not in your happy place because you are *wanting something*. And what is that thing?"

"A delicious eggroll, sir!"

"But what if I am out of eggrolls?"

"What?"

"What will you do then?"

"I will cry. Stop torturing me!"

"I am showing you the way to your happy place. You cannot cry about an eggroll. You cannot cry about a Bobby. You can cry about missiles in Gaza or about the Ebola virus, but only until you measure your power to change them. Do what you can. And then be happy."

"I'm *hungry*, Arjun!"

"Yes, I know. And that is why you must eat a Burger Bomb."

"What?!"

"Order that delightful sandwich with sautéed mushrooms and melted provolone. You will find it tasty and satisfying. You do not need the eggroll. You do not need the Bobby."

Candy grimaced. "Why are you messing with me?"

"To make you happy."

"No, no. I think it is to make *you* happy."

"I am already happy."

"It makes you *happier*."

"It is a beautiful day," Arjun said, a smile spreading across his face. "We will revisit this topic in due time. You do not need to chase happiness. You will see."

Candy carried her eggroll across the lot to the courthouse steps. Maybe Arjun was right. If she hadn't lusted after the golden treat and its spicy, nuanced aroma, she would never have left her desk. She would simply have sat contentedly in that spot, writing new telemarketing scripts, filing her nails. *Maya*, Arjun had muttered as he dropped the eggroll in the little cardboard boat, *steals your reality. It is the thief that visits you in your night of greed.*

She thought of the pastor at the Church of the Redeemer in Midland, a silver-tongued preacher whose flights of fervor were matched only by his venomous rants. All week long, he wandered through the biblical wilderness of his suburban ranch house, rooting out evil. By Sunday he was a pent-up cyclone, roaring over his submissive congregation with little regard for life or limb. As a little girl, Candy had turned to her mother during the sermon and asked, *Why is God angry?*

Because people are bad, her mother had said.

Candy appraised the courthouse traffic, a mix of slick lawyers and panicky plaintiffs, solemn judges and giggling clerks. She studied the statue of George Wythe, a stately gray but for the bird droppings on its skull. For as long as she could remember, she had accepted her country's flattering depiction of itself, the tales of battles won and people saved, the accounts of justice spread like seed around the globe. God hadn't just blessed Jews and Christians; He had also, by request, blessed America. Americans were one nation, under God. No wonder they were pleased.

Candy thought about Arjun's fanciful stories—the ones about George Wythe and Thomas Jefferson and the slaves they were impregnating—and looked up at the sky. Maybe that was why boys acted as if girls existed to serve them—to cook for them, to clean for them, to perform erotic services for them during drive-in showings of *Terminator 2*. Candy knew Bobby would do anything she needed, would be there for her anytime, day or night, as long as she remained, with or without assent, his faithful servant. It was an innate understanding between men and women with its genesis in the birth of the nation, with its DNA in the code of religion and history.

But Candy wanted love, not a transaction.

She licked the eggroll with the tip of her tongue and dragged its flaky, golden shell over her lips. She envisioned Arjun at his stove, sautéing the savory blend of cabbage, sprouts, and Vidalia onions, and spooning the treat into crunchy shells with layers like baklava. He was attractive, she thought, mischievously handsome, and possessed of an intuition that seemed to see right through her. Only after she said something to him did she realize, when she saw his eyes twinkle, that it was funny. He was a winking satyr, a wizard with a wand, spreading sparkles of amusement.

She scrunched the paper bag in her fist and descended the steps. CEO Brad Paxton had a bee in his bonnet, she thought.

Candy sat down in the big leather chair as a large, digital clock framed in fussy gold and quartz chimed three times. Brad Paxton sat behind his desk, his left ankle propped on his right knee, his hands clasped together. He fixed his eyes on the young woman he had summoned to his office.

"My wife would like your shoes," he said.

Candy fidgeted.

"That spaghetti-strap sort of thing," he said. "She likes it."

"On a shoe?"

"Well, you know."

"You normally see spaghetti straps on camisoles."

"Oh."

Candy looked around the office.

"My wife decorated it," he said. "I don't really like it."

"No?"

"Everyone else does, though."

Candy noted the gold watch, the diamond cufflinks, the embroidered silk tie. She often saw Brad Paxton roll out of the parking lot in his BMW 740i, a dashing cipher in Bugatti shades. Until now, their communication had been limited to nods and smiles in the hallways. This was new.

"Charlene showed me the call logs," he said.

Candy dug her thumbnail into her palm.

"Your department is moving a lot of systems," he said. "Signs, too."

"That's good."

"Yes. Very good. But here's the thing."

She drew a breath.

"When you break it down by caller," he said, "you see something interesting."

Her throat tightened.

"You see, this extension—this one, right here—is on an amazing losing streak. The person making calls from this number hasn't sold a single alarm system or yard sign during the entire promotion. She has made three-hundred-twenty-two calls in less than two weeks with no sales. What do you suppose she's up to?"

"Evening gowns can have spaghetti straps, too, sometimes," she blurted.

He looked across his desk.

"Just saying."

"Maybe you should be selling evening gowns?"

She sat silently.

"You see, Candy, I got a phone call yesterday. It was from a young mother who, it so happens, is friends with my wife. She said she had heard from the most delightful woman at EverSafe. She said the woman had congratulated her on Aiden—her baby—and shown a surprising amount of compassion and concern for her. She added that the woman, who called herself, I believe, 'Annie,' had given her some helpful advice on home security. But she couldn't understand for the life of her why 'Annie' hadn't tried to sell her any products or services."

Candy bit her tongue.

"It was as if 'Annie' wasn't a salesperson at all."

Her heart pounded. She just wanted a simple job in which she could help people. Most people didn't need high-tech alarm systems. They just needed someone who would look out more for them than for shareholders.

"Are you a salesperson?"

"I'm an Administrative Assistant II."

"I'm going to let you in on a little secret," he said. "We are all salespeople. Do you realize that? We all represent something. And we all have a responsibility to spread what we represent as persuasively as possible."

"Okay."

"Now, my wife is visiting her poor, sick mother in Denver. She flew out of National this morning. So unfortunately, she will not be able to accompany me to the Chamber of Commerce gala this Saturday night. I would like you to join me in her place."

"As, like, part of my job?"

"Of course."

"I'm pretty sure galas aren't in my job description."

"I'm pretty sure deviating from the sales script in three-hundred-twenty-two straight sales calls isn't in your job description. I don't think filing your nails is in there, either. Do you? Sometimes we have to be flexible. Play our roles. Sometimes we have to set aside our selfish priorities for the good of the team."

"I wasn't being selfish."

"We never *think* we're being selfish, Candy. But if we really think about it, we can see how we benefit from everything we do. We can see how we wake up every day with the goal of making our lives better. We are pursuing happiness. For ourselves."

"So…"

"When I was a young man, I received a notice in the mail requiring me to register for Selective Service—in case the army needed me to protect the freedom of the United States. I told my parents I didn't want to join the military. I didn't want to kill anyone. But my father sat me down and gently explained to me what I have just explained to you. It's not about us, Candy. It's about a larger principle. It's about the greater community. It's about a world of human beings in grave danger from intruders and madmen. We each have a role to play."

"Did you join the army? Did you kill anyone?"

"Just be a good soldier, Candy. Do your part. Make amends. And wear something nice, with spaghetti straps."

9 | Seiko

"Arjun!" Melinda shouted, sprinting toward the Bollywood Eggrolls truck. "The *Post* wants to talk to me! About this!" She skidded on the gravel, her lungs swelling, her blonde hair whipping in the breeze. "Listen!" she said, reaching through the pass-through and handing him her phone. "Press 1!"

Arjun held the phone to his ear.

"Melinda, it's Tim Samsara. I've been hearing a lot about you. Must say, I'm intrigued. Do you think I could drop by when you have time? I would love to try a Burger Bomb and hear your story."

"See, Arjun? See?" Melinda said. "A rising tide!"

The food critic Tim Samsara was respected and feared. Last month he had praised the sashimi of a lunchroom in Tenleytown, launching it into the culinary stratosphere. The month before, he had slammed an Italian kitchen at Gallery Place with an unflattering comparison to Olive Garden. Restaurants came and went, a carousel of concepts and cuisines and florid, ephemeral buzz. The dedicated, hard-working people who operated them smiled at the daggers and bled out in private. And the critics, cleaning one plate after another, lived to write another day.

"Wow!" Arjun said.

"Rising tide! Floats all boats!"

"You did it!"

"*We* did it."

"Well," Arjun said, "you know I love a good Bomb. But I did not invent it. I did not spread it like a rumor. Of course, I wish Mr. Samsara was dreaming of my eggrolls, but he is primed for USDA prime. He is a carnivore!"

"Well," she laughed. "I hear he loves sashimi."

"You should make a sashimi Bomb!"

"I should make what people like best," she said. "That is how it works. You listen to them, and they tell you."

How quickly success altered one's priorities, he thought. He was doing what he wanted to do, what he dreamed of doing—not what somebody else asked him to do. A chef who took direction from customers was called a short-order cook. "Yes, do what they ask, and they will love you for a moment," he said. "But do what you must, and maybe, just maybe, they will love you forever."

"Keep dreaming." She smiled. "Soon we will all have jet packs."

"We will!"

"You think?"

"I believe so."

"Oh, Arjun. Lose the Don Quixote act. Lose the Bollywood thing nobody understands. Start waking up in the morning with the idea that you live in the real world, where real people live. Those people are your customers. Do you see them chasing windmills? No. They are the same boring people you see everywhere, doing the same boring things all day long, and they are hungry."

Arjun looked away.

"Do you see, Arjun? They don't need a hovercraft or a time machine. They don't need a robot to replace their dog. They need the things they love, the things that bring them comfort. Make a perfect version of one of those things, and you will see a line of hungry people stretching from Broadnax to Georgetown."

"Look at that sky," Arjun said, his voice ringing, his eyes clear. "It is perfect. Do you think people don't love a perfect sky? They do love it."

"Oh, sweetie," she cooed, draping an arm around his shoulder. "You know what people love? The grist. Big Macs, Budweiser, pickup trucks. Simple things."

"The sky is simple."

Melinda laughed. "Well, maybe it is. So, what say you hang a shingle and sell them the sky?"

Antwaan was having a fitful dream. His body pitched like a fish on the deck of a boat. His blankets lay in an unruly heap. Wherever he flew in his reverie, he saw the same creatures on the ground, answering doors, manning counters. He floated above buildings and streets covered in sawdust, anthills that stretched from the Monument to the Beltway. His wings dripped wax on the world below.

Soaring above the subdivisions and strip malls, he watched the creatures emerge from their hills, carrying their payloads, seeking their targets. Like performers on a stage, they ran through choreographed routines, greeting one another, *les bon vivants avec les joies de vivres*. Keep on working. Keep on fighting. Sow your seed. Carry the baton. Love your life, your liberty, your pursuit of happiness. Be humble, good soldier. Repeat until you are dry and brittle in the cool Virginia clay.

He observed the ants in their joyless waltz. He felt the breeze swelling beneath his wings, taking him higher, separating him from the scripted dialog and stage direction. He shouted to the clouds. *Don't they know? Don't they see?* He had risen to a weightless realm from which he could regard every detail on the planet's surface. It was the way station of the wise, the berth of the dreamer.

He turned his head west, soaring over a patchwork of green and tan, squinting into the haze of a faraway land. He felt the weight returning to his body like a drum being filled with oil. His heels dug into the mattress. He perspired under the ceiling fan, his bones moist and pliant. He prepared to answer the door, to man the counter. He flapped his arms and clutched his pillow to his chest.

What did the birds know? More than the ants.

He closed his eyes and counted spins of the fan—*whoob, whoob, whoob*. His mind threw pictures on the insides of his eyelids. *We wanted you to have a French name,* his mother had said. And he had changed the spelling from Antoine to Antwaan. He looked at the battered, old picture she had given him, hanging on the wall by his closet. It was a pen-and-ink drawing of Thomas Jefferson, circa 1803, the year in which the president had bought a tract of land of nearly a million square miles from France. It lay west of the Mississippi River and stretched from modern-day Louisiana to Montana, scraping the face of the Rockies. The new territory extended the American frontier by more than a thousand miles.

His mother's ancestors had been driven out of Nova Scotia by the British during *Le Grand Dérangement* and had traveled down the Mississippi, settling as Acadian-Creoles, or Cajuns, in New Orleans. His great-great-great-grandfather had later hitched a ride on an eastbound train to serve in the kitchens of the US Congress during the first administration of President Grover Cleveland.

His father's people had been slaves, and later landowners, in the town of Charlottesville, Virginia.

Antwaan picked up his tablet and tuned in to the livestream of a protest in a small Missouri town. A police officer had fired six bullets into the body of an unarmed young man on the street. Antwaan watched the crowd milling around on the median, their hands raised over their heads, chanting "don't shoot" as police in riot gear sprayed them with rubber bullets and tear gas.

"What the fuck?"

A photo of an African-American kid wearing a pair of Beats headphones filled the lower-right corner of the screen.

"What the actual fuck?"

He turned on CNN. Michael Brown apparently had run afoul of the law before. He evidently lived in a bad part of town. He reportedly wasn't a very good student. It was a shame.

He threw his pillow at the wall. Who was he to sip Old Fashioneds by the pool while his brothers were getting murdered in the streets? Who was he to curl up on silk sheets while his sisters were being raped in their cells? He scraped his forearm with his nails, a domesticated animal safe in his den of creature comforts. He *owed* that kid.

He had a score to settle.

Your fever for the lever is the Devil's firewood.

He envisioned an eagle soaring over the Mississippi, cutting a noble figure against the sky. He thought of his mother's French family chased out of the Maritimes, searching for a place to alight on a wild and untamed river. America was a land of power and wealth, of exploitation and servility. It was the land of the free.

He had been born into affluence, a safety net of privilege and the finer things. His ancestors had fought for the comforts and opportunities he now enjoyed. They had died for those things.

He bolted upright and vomited on a stuffed animal.

Angry Eddie opened the umbrella on his silver cart. He picked up his tongs, turned up the flames, and counted the buns in the warmer. He needed to sell some dogs. He wasn't afraid of the police or the courts. He wasn't afraid of Melinda McCoy. Sure, he wasn't hip like the other chefs, or enthusiastic or charming or even palatable. But he had rights.

"Look at 'em," he muttered. "Too good for an American classic. Too good for baseball and apple pie, too…"

Arjun smiled. "Maybe they are counting their calories."

"Uh-huh."

"I would like a hot dog," Arjun said.

"Don't patronize me."

"When I was a boy, my parents took me to an international food festival in Delhi. The Chinese food was eggrolls. The Greek food was gyros. The American food was hot dogs."

"Yeah?"

"I had a dog and a Coke."

"No eggroll?"

"No eggroll. I was eight or nine. I liked simple things."

"But you don't anymore."

"I do. I would like a dog, please. And a Coke."

"Sure thing, Mahatma." Eddie threw a hot dog on the flames.

"I am not Mahatma."

"Yeah, I know that. I know you're not M'hat-m'coat. Hey, why didn't you bastards kick the British out like we did?"

"My parents were born into an independent India."

"The Brits left on their own, man. Didn't want you no more."

"They were weakened and dispirited by war."

"Fucking limeys."

"You could be more pleasant," Arjun said.

"Sure."

"Are you unhappy, Eddie?"

"I'm happy, Gandhi. You know what? I have set fire to villages. I have dropped napalm on women and children and cuddly dogs. If I'm not happy at this moment, sitting in the sun and talking to Macaca, I don't know when I would be."

"I think you have PTSD."

"Fuck you."

"Eddie, it is okay."

"Fuck you."

"There is help available."

"Shut up, jackass. Right now. You want mustard?"

"Yes, thank you."

"Here."

"It looks delicious."

"Yeah."

"Eddie, I know a counselor. A therapist. She has worked with hundreds of soldiers who have suffered trauma. She can help you to grow and be happy."

"Jesus Christ."

"I will call her."

"It's been forty-odd years, moron. I'm past saving."

"Just try, Eddie. Let me try."

"Fuck."

Candy slid into the bathtub. The warm water raised goosebumps on her legs. She pulled the razor over her calf, careful not to catch the soft skin around her knee. Bobby didn't like stubble. She wondered if Billy, his cheeks downy with fuzz, had ever run his fingers up a woman's leg. Boys were braggarts and fabulists, possessed of less experience than implied, unskilled in the art of love. Most, with the exception of the prodigious Randy, were about as adroit in the sack as a chimpanzee in a quilting bee.

As a woman who had spent whole summers sprawled over the hoods of pickup trucks, Candy had developed a keen sense of carnality. She had observed all sorts of men through the safety glass, their pupils dilating, their temples quivering with sweat. She had feigned obliviousness as they tried to engage her in conversation. *How long have you been washing cars? You're really good at it.*

She ran the razor over her inner thigh, following it with the fingers of her other hand to make sure it was doing its work. She thought of Brad Paxton, who seemed like a nice enough person, well-spoken and well-coiffed, but who also seemed, just under the surface, to be a creep preying on a powerless subordinate. For years she had thought her innocence was lost, that she was no longer the naïve girl from Midland, but she had been shown, time and again, the error of her presumptions.

She remembered learning about the Bushmen of the Kalahari in her middle-school anthropology class. The men in the tribe were hunters, the women gatherers. The propagation of the species depended on killing and nurturing.

She remembered the day she had said goodbye to Randy as he curled up, hungover, on the bed in their room at the Motel 6. He had moaned and whined as she packed her bags, savaging her while pleading with her to stay. *Look what she does, y'all, when the chips are down.* He had leapt from the couch to launch a blizzard of throw pillows over the balcony as she drove away.

Bitch!

She remembered her mother's warning: *People don't change 'til they hit rock bottom.* She didn't know if ten hours in a fetal position, during which Randy had peed himself in a vodka-induced stupor, spelled rock bottom for him, but she knew the cheeks of her own ass were chapped by gravel. *At the bottom of the sea,* her mother had said, *the little fishy got nowhere to go but up.* Candy had driven her car to the ramp of Interstate 20, flipped a photo of Randy into a ditch, and headed east. She had seen his face spinning in the tumbleweed.

Brad Paxton knew of none of this, of course, and didn't care. To him, she was a fresh face with a quick laugh, a piece of twangy tail haunting the hallways like some alluring apparition of his youth.

She slid into the tub, the water rising over her chest to kiss her lower lip. There was a higher world than the realm of Brad Paxton. There were sturdier dreams than the fantasies of a needy Bobby. There was a greater passion than the hard-on of a hormone-addled Billy. There was a dream of the heart, a destiny of the beautiful, battered soul. And that dream was as real as could be.

Jared was out of pork rinds. His stomach growled, gripped by nausea. He needed a big box of something imperishable he could keep in the back seat—Twinkies or tuna fish or SpaghettiOs. What had Steve Wozniak done when he was coding through the night and the refrigerator in the garage was empty? He probably slapped Steve Jobs upside the head and sent him out for a bag of Egg McMuffins. He probably barely spoke to Jobs while erecting his tower of code. He had little to say, but much to write.

Jared tapped his laptop and read the screen:

```
// Restore the previous drawing state and save it again.
CGContextRestoreGState(context);
CGContextSaveGState(context);
```

His app was called Foodstr. It combined recipes, foodie culture, and social networking. He sent the latest edit of the code to his phone. And there it was—the framing, the graphics, the menus.

Everyone wanted functionality, but they wouldn't swallow the castor oil without the sugar. Jared thought about the boys from Apple, slaving in secret in their suburban cave. Wozniak made the software useful, but Jobs made it necessary.

If the best things in life were free, he wondered, where was the free food?

He dug through the laundry on the floor of the car, tossing socks and Jockeys and T-shirts to the shelf under the rear window. He tore through fast-food bags and hamburger wrappers: a sliced pickle with mustard, a stray french fry, a scrap of stale bread. His stomach roiled. He bent over and drew a breath, his forehead pressed against the wheel. He could go home to retrieve his lithium. He could ask his mother to make him a sandwich. Maybe she would even make him a few for the road.

No, no, no.

The lot sat empty in the light of dawn. He opened the driver's-side door. He walked toward the food trucks, surveying the grounds and the courthouse steps. He tried the door at Burger Bombs. Locked. He pulled on the handle of the sliding window. Sealed. He tried the doorknobs of Bollywood Eggrolls, Doughnut Hounds, and Saturday Sundaes, but none of them budged. The Three Bucketeers truck, streaked with soot, was padlocked. Resigned, he tugged on the window of the Pig Rig.

It moved.

He dug his foot into the truck's running board, pulled himself up, and slipped through the window. The refrigerator was purring. He opened it. On the top shelf sat a tray of pulled pork, split into portions and covered in Saran Wrap. He turned the tray upside down, dumped its contents onto the plastic wrap, and twisted the wrap into a makeshift bag. The aroma, tangy and sweet, buzzed in his sinuses.

He pushed the door open, swung it back into its frame, and dropped to the pavement. The courthouse was quiet, the campus peaceful. He walked by the trucks, power cords running to a large steel cube on the grass, and noticed a shiny object in the gravel by Burger Bombs. He stabbed at it with his toe.

Normally he would laugh if he saw someone pick up a penny. But not this time. He snatched the coin and stuffed it into his pocket.

"So, the rumors are true," Tim Samsara said, his cheeks round with ground beef, his eyes watery from the jalapeños. He crossed his legs and appraised the colorless tableau of the courthouse and the EverSafe Solutions building. "The most delectable hamburger in the Washington area comes from a step van in an office park."

"Sounds like an angle," Melinda laughed. "No correlation between first impressions and quality."

"Some of the worst dreck I ever had," he said, "was on a rooftop in Adams Morgan where the martinis were thirty-five dollars. Some of it was at the White House. Now tell me… what is *in* this?"

"Oh, you know."

"Nothing unusual?"

"If I told you, I would have to kill you."

"Oh, that's good," he said, scribbling on his pad. "And your friends? Are they as secretive as you are?"

"They don't really need to be."

"Why is that?"

Melinda laughed. "Well, they all have tasty food. I *love* it. But it isn't exactly, you know, different."

"And yours is."

"The proof of the pudding is in the eating."

Tim Samsara took another bite of his Bomb. "Is it fresh garlic I'm tasting? Something in this absolutely *addicts* me."

She smiled.

"Well, you're on to something, Ms. McCoy. This is a real hamburger—from the real McCoy."

"Sounds like a headline."

"Yes, yes. It's *real*."

"Well, I'm all about real."

"And the others? Are they real?"

"In their way."

"Because the guy with the movie stars on his truck... you know, he kind of seems to be focusing on glamor and illusion."

"No, no. He's a real, Americanized Indian."

"Real?"

"Real."

Tim Samsara held up his phone and snapped a photo of the Bollywood Eggrolls truck. "Weirdly real... and really weird."

"Want some photos of me?"

"Sure. What is a Bucketeer, by the way? Is that fried chicken?"

"Yeah."

"And barbecue too? Dancing pigs. Funny."

"Hey, you could get some shots of me in front of my truck holding up a Burger Bomb. Or I could put on my daughter's roller skates."

"Wow, doughnuts? And ice cream? Paradise."

"Would you like some sautéed mushrooms?"

"No, no. I'm stuffed. But thanks again for your time." He walked between the trucks, snapping photos of each of them. As he turned to leave, he shouted to Melinda, "Fresh garlic! From the real McCoy!"

Arjun's phone buzzed on the nightstand, rousing him from sleep. "Hey, Bhagwan," he mumbled. He had been dreaming of dancing with Sonam Kapoor, their cheeks pressed together as they strutted across a stage in the moonlight, the actress and the aspiring restaurateur professing their love before a slavering crowd in the Garden of Five Senses. As he opened his eyes, he lost sight of the couple in *I Hate Luv Storys* and felt Sonam slip away.

He pulled the phone to his face and read the text: *Seiko is asking for you. Martha Jefferson Hospital.*

What? *Is Seiko hurt?*

You need to come right away.

He tumbled out of bed, banging his knee on the corner of the nightstand, and stumbled into the bathroom. A strange cry burst from his throat. *It must be bad,* he thought. *She is sick or hurt. Or she is already cold in her bed. Something horrible has happened and I will never see her again.*

He splashed water on his face, pulled a shirt over his head, and slipped into a pair of Levi's. He had been meaning to drop Seiko a line, to ask her how things were going at Jiyū, to seek her advice. He needed her to remind him why he was doing the things he was. Before he had waltzed into her restaurant on that first day, he had been a young man with more potential than focus, a ball of energy without purpose. Seiko had shown him who he was. And he had never properly thanked her.

Fool.

He grappled with his key in the car door, jiggling and reinserting it several times before the handle would budge. Charlottesville was a hundred miles away. He would arrive by dawn. He started the engine and turned on the radio. Sports talk, infomercials, religious programming. Noise to fill the silence.

Seiko was a Japanese expatriate. Her only family in America was the kitchen and wait staff at her restaurant. She lived for them and for her customers and for the idea that food was communion. Arjun wound his way down route 29, across the foothills of the Blue Ridge, through the cornfields, past the unpainted barns and decaying roadside motels. He had been thinking of her. He had been speaking with her in the recesses of his mind, the hidden place where he kept the people he loved but rarely saw. She was always there, smiling and encouraging him, reminding him that his dreams were taller than the walls. *Never let them change you. Never give up.* He squinted at the highway and wiped a tear from his eye. As a boy, his father had told him God was always near, watching over him, making sure he did not lose his way. He had remembered those words when he came to America, when all he encountered was alien, when everyone he met was a stranger. *He is watching over me. He is watching over Seiko.* He spun the radio dial, through the hip-hop and the smooth jazz and the pizza commercials. He rolled past a farmhouse gutted by fire. He saw morning's first light on the rolling hills, banishing the shadows, sweeping away the nighttime.

He turned off the radio and sang along with a song echoing in his mind: *Are you wandering in the forest? Are you lost among the trees? Are you following the North Star? Are you down upon your knees?*

Martha Jefferson Hospital sat on a sprawling medical complex on the east side of town. He spun onto the access road and followed the signs. The brick-and-glass buildings projected a reassuring air of permanence and authority. They allowed the angels in the white coats to work their miracles.

He parked in the lot and passed through the main entrance. The lobby was a large, open space filled with designer chairs, the aroma of coffee, and the silence of dawn. He passed through the hallway, his heart pounding, his stomach grinding. He turned the corner and stopped at room B-29. He felt dizzy, disoriented, as if the world had changed. He wondered what he would say. He steadied himself on a nurse's cart, drew a deep breath, and peered through the door.

He entered the room.

A man sat next to the bed, his head bowed, his hand clasping the pale, limp fingers of Seiko Okuhara. She lay motionless, her eyes closed, her bed a tangled maze of tubes and wires. *Beep, beep.* The man looked up. "I am Watanabe. The sous chef."

"I am Arjun. What—"

"Seiko has been under stress."

"Stress?"

"She has been unhappy."

"About what?"

"Everything."

"Everything?"

"The Chinese restaurants, the Thai eateries, the Vietnamese places... they do not understand modern tastes. They are losing business to Seiko. They are failing. They hold on to the past and they lose customers. Then they add a fusion dish... and they lose even more customers." He began to cry. "They released rats into our kitchen in the middle of the night. They burned her car."

Arjun looked down at his mentor, as still as dawn in her bed on wheels. "Seiko…"

"They spread vicious lies about her."

"Seiko…"

"She does not hear you."

"Seiko, please."

"She will not hear you."

"Wake up, Seiko!"

"*She cannot hear you.*"

Arjun hid his face in his hands. "But she is *alive*, isn't she?"

"She left a note."

Arjun held the card up to the light and recognized Seiko's handwriting.

Dear Arjun,

This has been happening since before we were born, since before our parents were born. I am tired now. I cannot fend off the slings and arrows for one more day. We do not live forever. We are born and we fight and, if we succeed, we move the boulder an inch up the hill. But we can't change any of it. We can only fortify ourselves and put locks on our doors and post the phone numbers of the police and the paramedics for when it is time to face the real world. We fight and we move on.

Watanabe will give you a signed, notarized letter that covers the dispensation.

I moved the boulder a little, didn't I? And it doesn't look so bad. I am tagging you, friend. You're it.

Love,
Seiko

10 | Quantum Leap

Antwaan slipped the microphone into its travel case. He avoided the skanky mics in the clubs, battered SM-58s slobbered on by every rapper within twenty miles. Who knew what microbes hid in their windscreens? Itzhak Perlman didn't grab just any violin off the shelf. He played only his Stradivarius.

Antwaan thumbed through the stacks of vinyl by his bed: Kurtis Blow, the Sugarhill Gang, Grandmaster Flash and the Furious Five (twelve-inch of "The Message"). *Testify*. Life was a party, but the celebration was a matter of life and death. Run-DMC took what was theirs and spread it around the world. Russell Simmons listened and led. And the Beastie Boys borrowed every inflection, like Elvis in the fifties, like Benny Goodman before him.

Antwaan hated himself for hiding out in Great Falls, for vacationing with his parents on the beaches of Anguilla. He was weak and selfish and afraid of his destiny. He was a layabout welded to comfort and security. Wasn't rap about resetting the scales? Righting the wrongs? His life was perfect. He appeared to have everything.

He thought of his father's shiny patent leather Italian shoes, whispering a message of assimilation as they slid across the carpet at L'Auberge Chez Jacques. He thought of his mother's pearls, as snottily regal as Queen Elizabeth's. His parents didn't talk about their origins. They talked mostly about jobs and politics and charity balls. They told neighbors in the Whole Foods about the carriage ride they took on the Mall with the Chief Justice of the Supreme

Court. They shared their dream of becoming space tourists alongside Richard Branson.

Antwaan didn't care about money or fame. He wanted only to affect the people. *The arc of the moral universe is long*, he remembered, *but it bends toward justice.* Sure, they might dismiss him today. They might ignore him tomorrow. But someday his voice, seasoned by years of shouting into the wilderness, would ring over the clubs and the streets and the tenements.

Antwaan's job was to preach the gospel. He had been retained to spread the word to the wayward youth of the DC area. His position paid little, but the Lord had provided for him through the largesse of his parents, who covered his expenses as he trekked through the dark forests of discovery. Sometimes the words filled his mind like a great flood. All he had to do was pick up his pad and pencil and transcribe them in a glorious fever. He was a vessel, a tool in the hands of the Maker.

Testify.

He grabbed his mic and slipped out the door. Mom's Lexus was parked out front, waiting. Tonight he would open for Baby D and Luther Madness, the duo from Anacostia who had snared a profile in The City Paper. They were his brothers in the battle for the hearts of DC youth, his compatriots in the quest to refocus the media on social issues. They had spent time in juvie. They were ordained ministers. They were well known at the intersection of MLK Avenue and Good Hope Road.

He ran over the set in his mind. He would open with "Rage in the Cage," move into "Funky Maritimes" and "Dripping Wax," and close with "The Assassin." He would thank Fat Gene for giving him a spot at the Annex and cede the stage to a thunderous ovation for Baby D and Luther. And then he would work the room, chatting up the skillets and shorties, leaving tent cards on the tables. He was nobody tonight, but he would be somebody soon.

The silhouette of Lincoln languished in the lint, lost in the pocket of Jared Hawk. The darkness reminded him of the time leading up the Battle of Gettysburg, days of fear and dread punctuated by hope. Although he was the commander-in-chief of the Union Army, he was more spectator than general, safe in the White House with Mary Todd and Tad while Meade held Cemetery Ridge and Grant plotted the capture of Vicksburg. While running the government, the president waited in the dark for news. Although he was the architect of the strategy to defeat the Confederacy, he knew little of the movements that would preserve American democracy.

Jared hadn't washed his jeans in weeks. Lincoln blanched at the aroma. There could be a war raging outside those pants, and the most powerful man in the Western Hemisphere would know nothing. The Union could be falling at the hands of Lee and his Army of Northern Virginia, withering in the advance of Pickett's Charge, and he would be oblivious.

Why the young man wasn't donning a uniform, protecting the land of the free, Lincoln had no idea. But a failure to fight was an abandonment of morality. Without an ideal to defend or an enemy to destroy, the people were robbed of purpose, of their pursuit of happiness. And life, so rife with pleasure and pain, was devoid of meaning.

Justin jammed the bass drum into the back seat of his father's Buick. Billy wedged his guitar case between the two front seats and threw his amp in the trunk. After weeks of after-school rehearsals, Quantum Leap were ready to launch their assault on the Curly's bar. *Take no prisoners.* Billy checked his complexion in the rearview mirror.

"Think she'll be there?" Justin asked.

"Hope so. I had a dream we were playing and she started dancing on the floor right in front of us. You were all, *fuck yeah* behind the drums, and I wailed on this flaming solo for, like, five minutes. And she just stared at us with that smile she gets, like she's about to say something but never quite does."

"You are screwed."

"Nah."

"Derp."

"It's like she's a hot teacher or something. Like she doesn't even *know*."

Justin navigated route 7, craning his neck around the bass drum in the mirror. "You need to shine 'er up, man. You're the dude. She's waiting for you to make a move."

Billy's stomach turned. "I'm gonna be chill, see what happens." He watched the strip malls roll by, brittle tumbleweed on the suburban prairie. "She seems so free," he said, "like nothing could hold her." He caught sight of the pigeons on the telephone wires, balancing, surveying the scene below. He thought about school and his parents and his job at the Walgreen's. He thought about his guitar, a tool in his quest to build a future, a weapon in some cryptic war he had been born to fight. It was all bleeding and sweating and crying for a dream, for a life, for a girl.

Justin parked in a spot by the dumpster. His eyes were fixed on the steering wheel. When they performed in the garage, nobody saw him but Billy. But tonight, there would be secretaries and waitresses and cougars on the prowl. There would be contractors and guys in business suits, appraising him, judging him. He felt sick. He remembered his first drum lesson, when he mishandled the sticks and his instructor laughed at him. *Colonel Sanders might hold a drumstick like that, buddy.* As the beat had fallen apart, he had withdrawn into himself like a flower into the dark. His instructor had mussed his hair and chuckled. After that he had attacked his kit every day after school from the time he got home until Mom called him upstairs for dinner.

He threw open the car door and vomited on the blacktop. His eyes filled with tears. "Shit, man."

"Let's rock," Billy said, a smile spreading over his face. "This isn't Madison Square Garden, but it's people partying and that's what matters. *We* are the partiers supreme. *We* bring the party!"

Justin forced a smile.

"You think Jimmy Page never puked? Come on, man, the dude *heaved*. You know he stood backstage at Wembley and saw the crowd that went on forever and wondered how he ended up there as, like, the total dude of the moment. He was scared shitless, man. Jimmy Fucking Page."

"No…"

Billy extracted his guitar case from between the seats. He needed his bandmate to recover quickly, to rise to the levels of confidence and showmanship he displayed in the garage. "Just think of Jimmy, waiting in the wings before the intro, his double-neck hanging from his shoulders, chucking into a little bag. Nobody sees him in the shadows, but he barfs his shepherd's pie into this little paper sack. He's shivering like a little girl. And then he's ready."

"Dude, that is bullshit."

The duo moved equipment from the car to the bar, squeezing past the hostess stand and piling their gear by the restrooms. The room was packed, a carnival of drinkers and talkers and antisocial loners. Billy felt the adrenaline course through his veins, unsteadying him as he squatted against the wall and tuned his Squier. Justin jammed his drum stool into the corner and pulled the bass drum up to his feet, allowing just enough room in front of the cymbals for someone to get to the bathroom. Quantum Leap had no contract and no rider. They had no stage, no lights, no roadies. They had no sound man. They had only their energy and their passion for the oeuvres of Nickelback and 3 Doors Down and Puddle of Mudd.

The lights dimmed. Out of the corner of his eye, Billy caught sight of a couple stumbling through the door. The woman had her arm draped around the man's neck and was hanging on him as if unable to stand on her own. She was kissing his ear and laughing and waving at people around the bar. Bobby nuzzled her and spoke to the bartender, who poured two shots of Cuervo. Bobby handed one to Candy and threw the other down his throat.

Billy plugged his guitar into his little Peavey combo and dragged his pick over the open strings. *We bring the party.* He twiddled the tone knob on his guitar and turned up the amp volume, coaxing a distorted shimmer from the single speaker. Justin played a machine-gun triplet on the snare, announcing to the patrons at the Curly's bar that Quantum Leap were about to enter their world.

"Hi," Billy mumbled into the mic, his eyes peering into the room. "We're, like, new here and everything, but thanks for coming out."

A voice split the air. "White Stripes!"

"Um, yeah..." Billy laughed nervously. "Are you ready to—"

"But the drummer is a dude!"

"Heh, heh," Billy responded. "Heh..."

Justin sprayed a light roll over the cymbals, his eyes fixed on Billy's right hand, waiting for a cue. Billy froze at the mic, pale and mute.

"Dude," Justin whispered. "*Dude.*"

"Hey, dudes," Billy said, regaining his composure. "And girls..."

He grabbed the neck of his guitar and dug his fingertips into the fretboard. His hand fell into an open E chord. He muted and plunked the low strings, making a booming sound like an elephant walking across the floor of a soundstage. *Bump, bump, bump.* Justin tried to double the notes on the bass drum, but just missed each on its attack, creating a quick echo: b-*bump*, b-*bump*, b-*bump*. Billy slashed at the strings, his fingers tearing as they had so many times before. The little amp exploded, too loud for the room.

"Turn it *down!*" the bartender screamed.

Billy cranked the volume on his guitar and pivoted toward the amp, coaxing a shriek of feedback from the speaker, seizing the attention of everyone in the bar. The crowd erupted as Billy and Justin launched into an FM radio staple. Billy shouted something about walking around the world and leaving his body "in the sands of time," his eyes burning with missionary fervor, the veins in his neck pulsing, his foot stomping in lockstep with Justin's snare. He saw Candy throw back a shot of tequila and screamed into the mic, a falsetto squeal that surprised even him. Justin grinned and drove the song into its break, pushing the pace like a wind-up toy gone berserk. Billy sneered, kicked his volume pedal, and dove into a sloppy, distorted, viciously loud solo that sent hands over ears from bar to booths. The bartender shouted and slammed the mahogany. A squat woman in a Curly's shirt burst out of the back office, her ponytail swinging as she ran past the men's room to the floor in front of Quantum Leap. She jabbed her finger into Billy's chest and juked to her right, sending Billy teetering into the cymbals and throwing the song into chaos. She kicked the amp away from the wall. With a dramatic gesture, she held the electrical cord in the air and yanked it out of the socket.

Gasp.

Murmurs, titters.

Silence.

"Get *out!*" she screamed, her hands trembling. "You will never, ever, *ever* play this venue again!"

Billy and Justin froze, their mops of wet hair dangling. Billy leaned over and unplugged his guitar from the amp. Turning around, he encountered a young woman stumbling into his path. Pinning him against the wall, she buried her lips in his ear, laughing and tugging at his belt buckle. It was Candy, her face glowing, her hair a fetching mess of sweat and tangles. She threw her arms around his neck and planted her mouth on his like a stopper on a drain.

His knees buckled, his eyes twitched, and he fell to the floor. He heard the scrapes of barstools over the hardwood and squinted into the lights. His jaw throbbed. He looked up. Bobby loomed over him, sneering, kissing the middle knuckle on his right hand.

"Yeah, fucker," Bobby said.

Melinda smiled. Aubrey was in bed, the cats were on the sofa, and the tea was steeping in a cup on the kitchen counter. She unrolled the map of the parking lot, a blueprint of a Gourmet Battle of the Vans™ to be run by Burger Bombs and sponsored by EverSafe Solutions. There would be food, music, jewelry, and games for the kids. There would be appearances by a local TV meteorologist and members of the Washington Redskins. There would be hundreds of hungry visitors bonding with the chefs and food trucks and culinary creations of Broadnax County.

She drew a big, puffy cloud over the lot and scrawled "Drop the Bomb" inside it in block letters. She had planned the holiday parties at Worthington Fairchild, boisterous affairs held in the banquet rooms of local restaurants, gaudy shows fueled by rum punch. She figured if she hadn't become a lawyer, she would have become an event planner, a conductor of bashes and blowouts. If she hadn't simply fulfilled her father's dreams like a good little girl, she might actually have done something she was suited to do. But that water had rushed over the dam long ago, part of a flood of calamitous relationships and broken friendships and a marriage to a man who never stopped circling the human buffet table. The price of lessons was high. She was brittle now. Her angular cheekbones protruded from her face like a car bumper, protecting her from accidents.

If her father had taught her anything, it was to give everything. *If you don't want to win,* he said, *get out of the game.*

She wanted to win. She wanted to help others, too, but only if she could lead them, only if she could make them grateful. Nobody remembered the silver medalist unless she later starred in a sitcom or got caught in a tryst with a presidential candidate. And nobody cared about the bronze medalist at all.

Everybody had to start somewhere, Melinda thought. *They couldn't just roll out of bed and hoist the Stanley Cup over their heads.* But she had started more than once, more than twice. She had started over every time a school or a job or a husband went sour. Again and again, she had failed to pass Go, had failed to collect two hundred dollars.

She thought of Aubrey, fragile, vulnerable, oblivious to reality. As angry as Aubrey seemed, wielding her Exacto knife like some Arthurian sword, she still believed in people, still maintained hope inside some tinkling music box that people were basically good. But Melinda knew the damage was done. There could be no starting over. It had become a salvage operation. Everyone was a wounded warrior, she thought, convalescing in a bed in her own Walter Reed. Some wounds showed, and some didn't, but there was no regenerating a limb, no turning back time. Sometimes there was simply no atoning.

The only option left was to change the game.

She thought of her father, pacing the sidelines of the soccer field as she took a pass from the wing, alternately exhorting and excoriating her in earshot of all the parents and players. *Poor Melinda*, they would say. *Why doesn't he just let her have fun?* She smiled at his approbation and withered in his censure. Her exploits were his exploits, just as his had been his father's. She existed to repeat his achievements while transcending his failures, to take the baton from him and run the fastest leg of the race. If Mom had harbored her own ideas on childrearing, she had left them in the maternity ward when Dad pulled the Rambler American up to the front door of Sibley Hospital. If she had harbored her own hopes for her daughter, she had boxed them up with the booties and the blankets and the diaper pins and stuffed them in the attic with the old photographs.

Melinda had her father to thank for her ability to stand up to and defeat any man who crossed her path.

She had outperformed the boys in high school to become valedictorian. She had outmaneuvered the male attorneys at her firm to claim the corner office. She had pummeled the philandering husbands of her friends and beaten her own husband into his sad submission of wine, women, and song. She shuddered to think what sort of life she would be leading if she had never learned to aspire, to compete, to win.

11 | The Lost Battalion

The motel air conditioner sputtered. The window sported a hairline fracture, the carpet a stain of unknown origin. The faded bedspread reeked of smoke. Arjun turned on the scratchy sheets, his eyes fixed on the streetlamp outside. The room reminded him of a dirty school bus, belching exhaust over the potholes of Delhi.

He considered relocating to the bathtub.

The clerk at the front desk, an unsmiling woman with a bouffant hairdo, had handed him a brochure highlighting points of interest in the Charlottesville area. These included Civil War landmarks and monuments to Thomas Jefferson. They also included a water park and an outlet mall. A "hamburger emporium" cast in the mold of Monticello featured in its parking lot a thirty-foot statue of Jefferson holding a scroll, presumably of the Declaration of Independence.

Arjun heard a thumping behind the wall, insistent and rhythmic. He jammed a finger in each ear, but soon felt the headboard shaking with each beat, punctuated by grunts. He curled into a fetal position, racked by nausea.

Seiko wasn't coming back. Caught between life and tunnel-light limbo, she was breathing and eating with the aid of machines. She wasn't thinking or laughing or talking. She wasn't teaching anyone how to mix chili into pad thai or whispering a dumpling recipe to her sous chef. She was simply functioning, like a computer at rest.

Arjun leaped from the bed, dashed into the bathroom, and vomited in the toilet.

When dawn broke, he showered and threw on a polo shirt and khakis and drove to Martha Jefferson Hospital. He found Seiko alone in her room, breathing shallowly under the buzzes and beeps, a fallen angel in a purgatory of machines. He sat in the chair by the bed and took her hand in his.

"I have been putting Amma's curry into the eggrolls," he said.

The machines whirred.

"I make the curry just like she does, in just the way Grandmother did. And everyone asks me what wonderful thing is in the eggrolls. But I do not tell them."

Bleep. Blurp.

"Remember that time you sautéed the vegetables in plum sauce, and your pan was filling the room with smoke, and we could not see the burners or the switch for the fan? I was panicking and you were laughing and the peppers smelled like sugar and the stove light was glowing like a beacon on a lighthouse…"

Dee-dee-deet. Blap.

"And the cook pulled the alarm and all the customers bolted for the door." He stroked her hand. "The firemen were so stern with you, as if you had nearly killed someone. They were asking you if you had stopped, dropped, and rolled—or something—and you were just giggling. And then I started laughing, and the cook, and the server…"

Seiko was silent.

Spaghetti straps were less popular this year than last, but Candy found a trio of suitable dresses hanging on the formal rack at Neiman-Marcus. The red was too strong, too clearly defined. The purple was awkwardly frilly, as if her chest had sprouted a bed of flowers. The black was simple and straightforward, and in the way of all black garments, silent on its wearer's state of mind. Given her reluctance about the event, and her mixed feelings about CEO Brad Paxton, she chose the black.

Candy took the bag and exited the store. She wound her way out of the garage, slowing for a wheelchair, stopping for a small child in flight from his mother, and deferring to a klatch of well-dressed older ladies. She had left Midland to *stop* explaining herself—to Randy, to her mother, to the leering creeps at the car wash. She had left to escape their expectations that she be what they wished or imagined.

Of course, she hadn't left everything behind. She liked to dance and she liked boys, and she liked to cavort in the company of boys, and she still dreamed of waltzing through a colorful, glittering life on some metropolitan stage. With boys. An office was not unlike a car wash, with slavering predators around every corner, ogling her, pursuing her in some genetically coded tango of carnality. Every man she met was potentially the one who would give her what her father never did. She didn't know what that was, exactly, but she knew she could feel the spot where it *wasn't*, like a phantom limb.

Bobby was a petulant child, a boy impersonating a man. Billy was a walking hormone, a blank slate seeking the chalk of experience. Brad Paxton was a predator, an architect of entrapment. She daydreamed she and Bobby were wasted at a rave, and Bobby beat up Billy in the parking lot of the club, and Brad Paxton roared by in his BMW and scooped her up and wooed her with champagne and caviar in a dimly lit room at the Ritz-Carlton. She swooned. She wanted their wild stares, their crazed obsessions. She wanted to be their quarry, intoxicating, irresistible, but just out of reach. She wanted all of it and nothing, all the time and never.

But she found only portions, served occasionally.

Billy's kiss lingered, sweet and sincere and spiced with the cinnamon from a fireball. She flashed back to his eyes, fiery as she plunged into his mouth. She remembered his wonder in the moment before Bobby exploded in rage and clocked him like an inflatable clown.

She thought of Brad Paxton, cloaking his approach in professional decorum. She had seen his expression on the faces of countless other men, and it was usually followed, within a period of one to three days, by an invitation to drinks or a brush in the hallway or a pass in the elevator as it descended to the lobby.

She squirmed in her seat, dewy with the dreams of a grown-up girl aging at the speed of light. If it wasn't Brad Paxton in a suite at the Ritz-Carlton, it would be Bobby in a trailer or Billy in a van, or some other nondescript male who caught her in the right place at the right time. It was her life. She could seize the moment or let it ride.

She pulled her car onto route 50, turned on the radio, and wondered where Arjun had disappeared to.

The umbrella cast a shadow on the lot, its frame clanging in the breeze. Angry Eddie sat on his folding chair, his foot balanced on his knee, sipping lemonade and thumbing through a book called *PTSD and You: Reclaiming Happiness*. He frowned at a photo of a figure in a wheelchair, a slumped, legless man in a US Army uniform crying on the shoulder of a physical therapist. Eddie read his story of enlistment and deployment and meeting a landmine in a vacant lot off an Iraqi highway, a tragic tale of duty and the wounds of war. Upon checking into Walter Reed, the man learned of his wife's suicide by ethylene glycol. After months of treatment, he walked on prosthetic limbs and fell off a treadmill, breaking his jaw.

Eddie thought back to his time in the 198th Infantry Brigade, when his status as a high school dropout without dependents had rendered him an ideal conscript. After seeing his best friend's skull blown apart by a stray round during a lunch break, he had deserted his battalion, stolen some civilian clothes, and disappeared into Saigon. There he had hidden out and smoked opium until the fall of '71.

Like Eddie, the soldier in the book had killed children in the performance of his duties, and spent the subsequent years seeing their ghastly, contorted faces in his nightmares and waking dreams. The clarity of those images exceeded that of all others, like an insect pressed under a microscope, still and dead and magnified for closer inspection.

There was always a good reason for war, Eddie thought. And the reason changed all the time.

He looked at the food trucks, at the cars, at the high-heeled women in skirts walking across the campus. It reminded him of his unit. Everyone was working toward a common goal, keeping his head down, trying to survive. A stray bullet could whistle by at any time. It only took one, he thought, like a cancer cell or a meteor or a van careening through a festival crowd. A chicken bone could get lodged in his throat. A rock from a jackhammer could catch his temple. A newborn baby in an upscale pram could roll over his foot on the sidewalk, sending him tumbling into the path of a speeding Harley-Davidson. How he had survived to the vaunted age of sixty-five he had no idea, given the perils. His brother had died in his sleep. His sister had fallen down a staircase. A trio of cousins had perished in Vietnam, victims of hepatitis C, Agent Orange, and friendly fire, respectively. His aunt had died in a house fire in Staten Island on Christmas Eve.

The CIA, Monsanto, and Dow Chemical ruled the world, he thought. And the commies and gooks—Ho Chi Minh, Pol Pot, Kim Jong-un—were always jockeying for position. He smirked. His hands still trembled at the thought of HO, numbing his nerves until they forgot how to respond, how to function, how to care or even to calm down. He could still smell the napalm, glistening on the grasses and the roofs of the thatched huts, waiting for a spark to incinerate it and flush the women and children into the streets, screaming and crying and expecting somebody to give a shit.

But shits were seldom given, considering the power and real estate involved.

Eddie pulled a hot dog out of the basin and wrapped it in a roll. People killed pigs and cows and cut them up into Virginia hams and marbled ribeyes, ground the unused ends into a mixture of fat and internal organs, and used what remained to make sausage and, finally, when the vat contained little but blood and cartilage, to form hot dogs. It was all part of the bounty bestowed by God. Eddie dressed the dog in mustard and ketchup, kissed it, and took a bite.

What happened in Vietnam had changed him, made him angry, loosened his grip on the ballgames and bike races and family picnics that receded now into the darkness of his memory.

Aubrey was sick of Pocahontas, John Smith, and John Rolfe, tired of the idea they had anything to do with her. History bored her, and having to sit through it every day during third period, before lunch, while her stomach raged, infuriated her. She questioned the accuracy of accounts spun by historians over centuries. They were about as enlightening to her as Disney movies.

Her bestie, Amber, had sketched a comic in the margins of her notebook in which Pocahontas solved crimes in tandem with Diana, Princess of Wales. These tales included cameos from Batman and Hello Kitty.

Aubrey stewed and stared out the window. She ran her fingers over the scars on the inside of her forearm, her mind whirring over thoughts of her parents and their arguments over how to raise her. Her father wanted a curious daughter without preconceptions. Her mother wanted a model child with a plan. Instead, they had produced a brat who was, in the parlance of athletics, resistant to coaching. Whatever they suggested, Aubrey was sure to embrace its opposite.

Amber had drawn Pocahontas and Princess Diana eating lunch, chatting about the advantages of hooking up with British nobility and royalty. Underneath the panel, she had scrawled, "BUT IT KILLED US BOTH." This provoked explosive amusement in both girls.

"So great," Aubrey said.

Pidgey pecked at the pavement. He was a bird with needs. He required food, as without it he might find himself in the beak of another. He needed robust plumage, as otherwise he might end up in a storm drain. Sex was helpful too.

He pondered ways to soothe his restless legs or treat his acid reflux. He grumbled about his hemorrhoids. He thought of ways to keep himself safe in the middle of the night, when feral cats prowled the courthouse grounds in search of snacks. He worried about the link between deep-fried treats and heart disease.

In carefree times—and there were stretches when the sun warmed his wings, lulling him into a sense of invincibility—he dreamed of lost friends and family who might one day return, or of the cozy familiarity of his brothers and sisters, beaks open and waiting, packed in the nest as their mother fed them. He thought of his father, tall and fearless, leading him through the campus of EverSafe Solutions in search of June bugs and caterpillars. He conceived of idyllic evenings with his childhood comrades, gathered around a block of suet or a seed bell.

Once satiated on succulent morsels and libertine females, he dreamed of becoming a bird who might inspire his peers with courage or brilliance, who might be known for his generosity or compassion or contributions to avian society. *What a bird can be, he must be,* he thought, surveying the grounds and skies and the creatures crawling and soaring through them. Whoever Pidgey truly was inside his plump torso, he needed to summon the DNA that differentiated him from other birds and rendered him able to do *that thing.* There were many pigeons on the lot. But there was only one Pidgey, only one spinner of glowing, nourishing Pidgey dreams.

He thought of Cher Ami, laying her life on the line for the Lost Battalion, soaring over the carnage of the Battle of the Argonne to preserve a shred of sanity in a world gone mad. As the bullets grazed her wings, she carried a message to the allied forces ahead: *We are along the road parallel to 276.4. Our own artillery is dropping a barrage directly on us. For heaven's sake, stop it.*

Pidgey looked around the lot and wondered, from his beak to his tail to the flesh of his fluttering heart, when he would receive the call.

12 | Fly into the Sun

The massive bridge rose to the sky, standing against the sun. It had to end somewhere. Melinda shuffled over the concrete, counting the cracks on the sidewalk as it turned toward an apex only the birds could see. She rushed up the grade. Would she ever get to the top? Or would she just run until her heart surrendered? She ran harder. Eat it, you sons of bitches, jump in the drink and drown. I am stronger than you are. I don't need your secret handshakes. I don't need your country clubs. Fuck you. I don't believe in you or in anything your dead father built. She pressed on. Papa was a rolling stone. But where he laid his hat was anyone's guess. Mama was a crying child. But why she sobbed no one knew. Except that it was his fault. The stone in descent, the victim in tears, together they worked their child like a marionette on an elastic band, launching her at the stars like a rocket. Except higher. Closer. Fly into the sun. Play with the big boys, but you'll never be a boy, ever. She winced and pushed forward, upward, toward the head of the span, to the camp on the hill where her father and Jim fished in a pond and talked about the women they had loved and left. Life was good for the man who knew himself. Life was perilous for the woman who followed him, for the little girl who threw away her dolls and played football with the boys. Cool girl, strong girl, beat them at their own game. Make them love you. Call Daddy on the phone. Follow Jim in the car, see where he goes before he comes home. Climb to the top of the pyramid where you can be alone and see it all—every ant crawling and eating and fucking on the ground.

Run.

Melinda shivered and wrapped her body in the covers. She had Aubrey's flu. There was nothing to do but endure it. She saw Jim at the altar, at the family picnic, bouncing baby Aubrey on his shoulder and singing a lullaby. She saw Aubrey on her trike at Christmas, wearing a circle in the rug around the tree. She watched her mother in the rocking chair, knitting booties. She envisioned her father's postcards, hastily written and sent, collecting in a bowl in the kitchen. She saw her brother falling from a branch in the weeping willow, his face twisted as he plunged to the ground. She regarded Jim laughing and pulling her close as the sun set behind the sycamores. She remembered the bed at the Four Seasons where they collapsed on their wedding night, too tired for anything but sleep.

She thought of how Aubrey had laughed when she asked her about the poster of Lady Diana Spencer on her door. *That's, like, before she was a princess,* Aubrey had said, smirking. *When she was still happy.*

Melinda wiped the sweat from her forehead. Princess Grace had been the same way, hadn't she, before she married Ranier? Life in the palace became death on a hairpin turn. Be careful what you wish for, missy.

The airwaves were jammed with Viagra commercials and sports talk and music that sounded as if it came from an industrial drum. Arjun scanned the dial for something to take his mind off Seiko. But everything reminded him of death. It was like a recipe he didn't want to follow. She was leaving. She wasn't coming back. And he would soon be gone too, along with his mother and father and everyone else. He would rise to the heavens or fly into the sun or simply cease to exist as his soul decayed into dust for new souls. The awareness of his heart and mind and of other people would recede into the ocean of space.

There was no past, he thought, and no future. There was only today. But how could that be? He remembered the past. He remembered home and school and the sounds of the city. And his dreams—of people enlivened by art and community—were just a step away. He was working toward them. Yet this dull moment of driving home was all he had. He could not change the past. He could not see the future. He could only pass through life like a hamster through a tube, slipping and sliding and looking out the tinted plastic, until somebody pulled him out and buried him in a shoebox.

Then, in a moment, he saw it. It blotted out the sun. He slammed on the brakes. The airbag exploded. The windshield shattered. He felt the trickle of blood, warm and sticky on his cheek, cleaving his face to the seat like an ant to the floor of a glue trap.

"Seiko?"

Billy stocked the feminine pads. There were the ones with the deodorant and the ones with the wings and the ones with the extra-absorbent shields. Every customer who passed through the aisle found their day brightened by the sight of a pimply teenage boy stocking feminine products.

"Stay fresh," a young man said as he squeezed by.

Billy was no stranger to humiliation, what with the acne and the emaciation and the compulsive masturbation his mother discussed at every opportunity. But he glimpsed potential in the mirror. He had seen pictures of Gavin Rossdale as a kid in school, hiding behind the hem of the headmistress. He had seen the dork from Maroon 5 transform into a heartthrob. Billy knew he just had to hold on a little longer and he would become a man. His complexion would clear, and he would put on muscle, and he would find a girlfriend. And nobody would know he had spent hours, days, even weeks, unpacking and stacking boxes of feminine pads.

His mouth watered for Candy.

He wondered what it would be like if they hooked up. Would she stay? Would she move on? He sorted through visions of her trembling thighs and long, flowing wedding dress and legs spread as she pushed out a bald little Billy Jr. He saw himself at the door of a suburban ranch house, briefcase in one hand, coffee cup in the other, kissing her goodbye as a passel of toddlers tugged at her skirt. He felt her tongue linger in his mouth, just as it had that night at Curly's.

He wondered if Candy would make him stop playing music with Justin, if she would redirect him toward a life of wage slavery and household chores and trips to Crate & Barrel. He wondered if she would dispatch him to Walgreen's when she ran out of feminine products.

He shuddered.

He was beginning to see there was more to becoming a man than turning the pages on a wall calendar. There was so much more, in fact, that he was blinded by a sudden awareness that he knew nothing, a fear that his ignorance would flatten him like an ant on the perilous road to manhood. He looked at the box of pads, festooned with colorful graphics of winged creatures flying toward a smiling sun. One by one, he stacked the boxes on the end cap, balancing them as they rose toward the ceiling.

"Punch?"

"Sure," Candy said, appraising her boss with a wry detachment. She could get through this. She could smile and nod through the evening and be charming enough to satisfy but not to mislead. She caught her reflection in the glass doors, a winsome blonde in a fetching party dress, a Texas honey with a wink and a smile. She had cast herself in the mold of his expectations, or what she imagined his expectations to be, and needed only to sustain the charade until midnight, when her carriage would turn back into a pumpkin.

She watched him press through the crowd, shaking the hands of the men and grazing the shoulders of the women. He was a natural operator, concealing his guile in an armor of guilelessness. *Yes*, she heard him bellow, his laugh reverberating across the room. *I know!* She clasped her hands behind her back and rocked on her ankles. The Broadnax Founders' Ball reminded her of prom, with a roomful of strivers emulating the height of style and a caste of observers lining the walls. She wondered if she had been mistaken for Brad Paxton's daughter. Or worse, for his escort. She felt the eyes of the men upon her, wolfish squints softening when they caught her gaze, plotting, calculating their chances of "mentoring" her. She felt the acid stares of their wives.

She remembered Randy's hand in hers as he had led her onto the dance floor, squeezing too tightly, tugging too insistently. He had dipped and spun her in a show of possessive bravado, a would-be Astaire guiding his Ginger through a sea of oafs. She had pirouetted from the dais to the snack table, a princess in frills, a comet streaking across the mirror-balled sky. Randy loved her and she loved to be loved, and everyone in the room could see where she was headed.

She wondered if they remembered now.

She wore a red wig to play Annie. It transformed her, as if she was not just a girl in fake hair, but another girl altogether, a girl who believed in tomorrow. She didn't know then that tomorrow often turned out a lot like today. Sometimes something bad happened, or something good, and then, after a few weeks or months, things returned to the way they were. *You take your mirrors with you*, her mother said.

Candy felt the same inside as she had as a little girl. She was always waiting for her father to ring the doorbell on a Daddy Sunday. Sometimes he showed up and sometimes he didn't.

She spied Brad Paxton across the room, his teeth gleaming as he chatted up a matron wearing a diamond brooch. She noted his receptivity, the ease with which he listened. The woman beamed, certain Brad Paxton found her irresistible. And then Brad Paxton moved on, to the next couple and to their friends, to friends of their friends, and finally to their garrulous acquaintances in line at the punch table.

Brad looked around the room and spotted the plumbing guy, the roofing guy, the painting guy. He saw the guy who operated all the McDonald's franchises in West Broadnax, tan and trim and fit as a health-food fiddle. He saw the wives, mannered ladies with facelifts who hadn't drawn a paycheck in thirty years.

"Hey," a man at the table said. "You're the home-security guy."

"That's right. Brad Paxton."

"Penn State guy."

"How did you know?"

"Seen the little Nittany Lion on your car antenna."

"Good eye. What is your line of work?"

"Undertaker. At the Cacumen Home."

"Oh, yes. I've seen you. Met you, in fact, when my wife's father passed. You were greeting folks in the lobby."

"It's a living."

Brad paused.

"Get it? *It's a living.*"

"Yes," Brad said.

"It's a living *until you're…*"

"Got it."

"So, you're in home security. You keep people safe from me, eh?"

"Well, I…"

"That name—EverSafe. It sounds kinda like NeverDead."

Brad fidgeted. "I need to get back to my date."

"Your date? Where's your wife?"

"She's out of town."

"Gotcha."

"No…"

"Here's my card. For when you need me."

"Thanks."

"I'll give you a call too. Need some security cameras installed. Damn teenagers keep breaking into the embalming room."

"Yes, yes, thanks."

Brad shook his head, held a pair of cups in the air, and slipped through the crowd. People were freaks. This was true whether they were educated or not, rich or not, or from a good home or not.

They were simply odd, full of traumas and eccentricities. Get to know anyone well enough, he thought, and you would learn they used to be a taxidermist or covered their house in doll heads.

Brad spotted Candy in the far corner by the door. She was standing still, lost in thought, and Brad felt a sense of relief at the prospect of a simple conversation with a simple person.

"Well, hello there," he said, presenting the cup to her like some rare gem.

"Having fun?" she said.

"I wouldn't say that."

"You look pretty excited."

"Do I?"

"Yep."

"Did you hear about the new Whole Foods?"

"No."

"It's a grocery store."

"I know."

"Well, they built a new one on Broadnax Boulevard, just down from the courthouse."

Candy sipped her punch.

"So where do you think birds go when it's cold, anyway?" he said.

"Where it's warm, I guess."

"Yeah... but where? Florida? New Orleans? Costa Rica?"

"Yeah, probably."

"Which one?"

"I don't think the pigeons go anywhere."

"Well, they're not very smart."

"Maybe they're smarter."

"It's not smart to freeze to death."

"Um, yeah, everywhere you look... frozen pigeons."

Brad laughed. Was she flirting with him? He thought he caught a glimmer in her eye. It was more fun talking to her than fishing for nickels with the ladies from the American Legion Auxiliary. She didn't seem to care about mingling with the people around her, or about currying favor with the boss. "So, what does a woman like you do when she isn't having fun at a fundraiser? Or *fun*-raiser?"

"Oh, I don't know. Feed the pigeons?"

"What do you feed them?"

"Whatever I'm eating, I suppose."

"That could get expensive."

"They need to eat too. Everyone does. Did you know that?"

"Yes. But it's not your job to feed every living thing."

"Whose job is it?"

"I'm going to call you the pigeon girl."

"Okay."

"I'll be the home-security guy and you can be the pigeon girl."

"Okay."

Brad felt the vodka sprint through him, a tilt and blur that rolled him back on his heels. "More punch?"

"Yes, please," Candy said. "Punch me some more."

Brad returned holding an oversized Washington Redskins cup in each hand. "Grabbed these from the pantry! Leave it to your boss, Candy. He's a guy who gets things done. He's a go-getter."

"Impressive."

"It's all about conservation of energy. Fewer steps, more sips. I won the science fair competition in eighth grade, you know. The other kids had papier-mâché volcanoes too, but mine spewed *edible lava*."

"Amazing."

"Tapioca pudding."

"Nobody eats that."

"Right, but they could. They could eat it if they were starving."

"Pigeons don't eat tapioca."

Brad looked into Candy's eyes. Maybe she was messing with him. Maybe she was just passing the time. Or maybe she was luring him into her web. He caught his breath. Surely others were noticing them. Surely they were whispering about the home-security guy and the pigeon girl who wasn't his wife. He felt the sweat on his cheeks. His ears burned. "We should probably call it a night soon."

"Yep."

"Early day tomorrow."

"And you're an early bird."

"But I'm not flying south. I'm staying right here."

"It's better to stay. I left Midland. Everybody I know is in Midland. But I left and now I'm here."

"You can always go back."

"I doubt that."

"You can do whatever you want. This is America."

"Okay."

"Free country. Free as a bird."

"Hmmm."

Brad glanced at his watch. He didn't want to be seen leaving early. "You know," he said, "there was this guy at the punch table. A mortician. He started talking to me while I was getting you a drink."

Candy looked at him.

"He was making these jokes… about death… and watching my reaction. I don't know, maybe it was sport for him. But it was pretty weird, I'll tell you that."

"Were the jokes funny?"

"Not really."

"He was probably just bored."

"But he should know better than anyone…"

"Know what?"

"He should know people don't think death is funny. It isn't funny to be in a situation you can't control. It isn't amusing to be in constant danger. You have no security. You can't be happy. You're in a state of alert, paralyzed by fear. You need to keep death at bay. Keep it away from your door."

"I don't think we can do that, can we?"

"We can. I wasn't eaten by a tiger today, was I? I wasn't attacked by a street gang. I didn't get shot by a sniper or strangled in the park. No, I'm standing here in a lovely ballroom, talking to a charming young woman, enjoying myself in a safe, secure environment."

Candy laughed.

"You think that's an accident?" Brad said.

"I'm pretty sure there aren't too many tigers around here."

"Well, one could escape from a circus or something. It could break out and chase you down Columbia Pike."

"You think so?"

"Stranger things have happened. The DC sniper picked off people while they were pumping gas. A maniac on bath salts ate another guy's face. These things happen. Your security is never total. You always have to be afraid."

Candy laughed again.

"So, you think death is funny too? I promise you, it isn't. I've seen what happens to people who leave their doors open. They think they're trusting others. They think they're showing faith in humanity. But they're dreaming. They're just putting a big target on their back that says—"

"Okay, okay. Let's relax now."

"It's why I'm in home security. To protect people. To keep them safe. So they can live full lives and be happy."

"And I'm sure they are."

"That damn guy at the punch table… what was he doing? Why would he make jokes? I don't know what death is like, but I think it might be like getting on a train as a kid to go live with your aunt and uncle. You're leaving your friends behind and everything. You don't know anything about the new place. If you could avoid going, you would. You would stay with your friends and play dodgeball forever. And that is why I went into home security. To make it safe for people to do that."

"But they still die, I think."

"Yes…"

"I think it's like you're a balloon drifting through the clouds," Candy said. "You float around for eighty or ninety years. You float higher and higher. It's cold up there, so you soak up all the sunlight you can. You lie in the gondola and absorb the rays. And as time passes, you get less afraid of everything. Because it doesn't matter what you don't see. You're above it all. And then one day, when the sky gets so bright you can't see where you're going anymore, you reach that thing that keeps you warm. And you just kind of fly into it."

"Hmmm…"

"I always tell myself stories like that."

Brad slipped his arm around Candy's shoulder. "Well, we're okay now," he said. "And I aim to keep it that way." The ceiling lights were being turned off, section by section. Brad and Candy walked through the lobby, past the front desk, and through the revolving doors to the valet stand. He noticed the softness of her hair, the glow of her skin. She was more beautiful than before, as if his vulnerability had brought her spirit to the surface. He saw her fragility, her openness. In her eyes he saw himself, a child who had traded his Matchboxes for a BMW, his tree fort for a McMansion. He saw a man who had replaced his dreams with plans.

The valet pulled up in Brad's 740i. It was a sleek predator, a pouncing cat. Brad felt a twinge of excitement as he opened the passenger-side door. He was the king, the master. When the house was on fire, he rescued the sleeping occupants. When the damsel pled distress from the tower, he set her free.

"Are you cold?" he said.

"I'm always cold," she said. "I'm from Texas."

He turned on the heated seats. "There you go."

"So… why do you do what you do?"

"What?"

"Why do you do it? To be in charge of things? To be in control? I always wonder why people do the stuff they do. It's nothing personal."

"Sounds personal."

"Sorry."

"I don't answer to others."

"Why not?"

"Because they are not above me."

"So you are above—?"

"Yes. I am. Okay?"

"Okay, okay… sorry."

Brad pressed the accelerator. The engine roared. "That's five hundred and forty horses. Think of all the generals who could have used those. Think of the soldiers in rows, their feet liberated from the ground. Like dogs and cats, clawing at each other. Who lives? Who dies? You ask why I have the reins. But everyone knows why. Everyone." He pulled the car onto a quiet suburban street. "They all know. *You* know, right?"

"Not really…"

He parked by the dead end. He held the wheel in both hands. "She's going to leave me," he said.

Candy bit her lip.

"She's going to divorce me and take half of everything. You know the drill. It's what parasites do." He pounded the wheel with his fist. "You give them everything, and they just want more." His voice cracked. The tears ran down his cheeks, off his square jaw, and onto his pressed collar. "Christ."

Candy placed a hand on his shoulder. He seemed a broken man. But in a flash, he was on her, his tongue in her throat. He pinned her down with his knees, grabbed her hair with one hand, and snapped the spaghetti straps off her dress with the other. He tore the silk across her chest and buried his lips in her neck.

With all her strength, Candy yanked herself free and punched his throat. She tumbled out of the car and onto the gravel. Brad leaped out the door, pleading, crying, and hurling apologies.

"Wait!"

"Get away from me."

"Let me explain!"

"Get away from me."

Brad grabbed her arm, spun her around, and squared her shoulders to his, his face soaked with tears. "No one understands," he said. "No one cares. No one is there when you need them.

They're only there when *they* need something from *you*. They're parasites and freeloaders and *takers*. Damn it, Candy, I am so tired..."

He relaxed his grip. His chin fell to his chest. Candy took a few steps back, her heart pounding, her dirty dress a vision of sackcloth and ashes. She answered in a whisper, "Then get some fucking sleep."

13 | A Hundred Battles

"Seiko?"

Arjun watched the windshield give way to an avalanche of watermelons. He felt a melon split open on his skull. He dug a seed out of his mouth.

"Seiko?"

He heard the truck hissing, its bed wedged on top of the hood, its axle bent over the bumper. He tried to wriggle free, to reach the door latch, but he was pinned to the seat. He smelled burning rubber.

He feared he was going to die in a freakish way.

He felt as if he had been lowered into the ground and was watching shovelfuls of dirt fly into the hole. Nature was reclaiming his body, recycling the carbon for worm food and watermelon fertilizer. It was releasing his mind into the atmosphere, splitting it into playful little quarks for future minds.

It was taking inventory.

He sensed his brain reading his DNA and executing instructions. Scan the senses. Fight or flee. Kill or be killed. Save the body. Climb to safety. Find love.

Know yourself. Respect yourself.

Escape.

Jared counted the change: two dollars and thirty-eight cents. With the exception of a US savings bond given to him at birth by his uncle Mort, his beater, his laptop, his clothes, and some vintage

Zelda comics he had picked up at a yard sale, his hand held his net worth. Dollar store, dollar menu. A penny saved was a penny earned. He examined the profile of the sixteenth president, the countenance of a freedom fighter. No worries, he thought. Dude has it under control. He's worth less than a gumball and is known mostly for throwing car sales on his birthday, but there is bigger stuff in life than money. Like liberty. Jared was free to chase any dream, to code a visionary app whenever he felt like it. Somebody said freedom was just another word for nothing left to lose, but that didn't make much sense if you considered what it would be like to be in prison.

He figured he could land in prison for stealing food.

He thought about sneaking into his parents' house in the morning, before his mom brewed the coffee, before his dad got in the shower, and grabbing snacks from the pantry. Pilfering a few cans of tuna fish to ward off starvation would be forgivable. *Sorry, Mom, you won't be able to make that salade niçoise. But I'm still breathing, so there's that.*

He would grab the lithium too.

Antwaan flopped on the sofa and grabbed the remote. Kanye, Diddy, and Jay were ballin'. They didn't daydream about boosting Cristal, they just did it. They seized the day. Dre surveyed the kingdom and set his sights on the next mountain. Snoop saw around corners.

He took a bite of orange roughy. He thought of all he had been through—the classmates who laughed at him, the teachers who suppressed his creativity, the coaches who sat him at the end of the bench. The world had decided, in its tree forts, lounges, and locker rooms, that he was not special, that he would not be receiving the keys to the kingdom.

There was a place waiting for him, however, in the field of title loans.

Kanye didn't need to beg for a slot at the Annex. He didn't need to turn up the PA to quiet the bar. He just walked in and blew up the spot. He spoke by the authority vested in him and took what was his.

Antwaan's set at the Annex had gone well enough until the sound man left his perch for a smoke. And then the shrieks of feedback and the blown speaker and the pulling of the plug by the stage manager had obliterated his signature song, leaving him cursed and laughed at by an inattentive crowd. *Get off the stage.* He had slinked into the wings, packed his bag, and slipped out the back door. As if it was his fault.

He thought of his Christmas recital in sixth grade, when the last note—high C—on his run over the piano had stuck as if glued, producing an audible *flapt* followed by a chorus of snorts and giggles. His parents had retrieved his coat and ushered him out a side door. He had sobbed in the back seat on the way home. As if it was his fault.

Maybe they thought he lacked the character to overcome obstacles. Or that he was weak and stupid and incapable of sidestepping the pranks of fate.

What assholes.

They would be surprised to hear about the promoter who had taken an interest in him. They would congratulate him halfheartedly, skeptical of his success. His father would nod without making eye contact. His mother would give him a little hug. They would wonder, with visions of lucrative orthodontia and high-stakes corporate lobbying dancing in their heads, what had gone awry in the rearing of their progeny. And they would appraise him with detachment, as if watching a bad movie.

As if it was his fault.

Melinda thumbed through the permits—alcohol, waste management, parking—and dropped them into a manila folder. The lot was approved to host up to a thousand guests. There would be food and drink and music and games, and unprecedented exposure for Burger Bombs. She had secured a temporary injunction that allowed food sales from licensed trucks only. No carts.

She had identified staff and support. EverSafe Solutions would take an exhibit booth in exchange for surveillance. The logistics were coming together.

She thought of the text she had received from Tim Samsara: *Show me a wine to pair with a Bomb?* She had responded with a smiley face. He was attractive—piercing eyes, full head of hair—but his rakishness unnerved her, made her wonder what sort of man lurked beneath the raves and putdowns. He was obsessed with food, a feverish scribe with an insatiable hunger. She thought of the spark she had seen in his eyes as he bit into his first Bomb. Had it burned for the Bomb or for her?

No one else on the lot—least of all Arjun—was likely to attract that degree of attention from Tim Samsara. She had him in her back pocket. The way to a man's heart, her mother had said, was through his stomach. And the way to his newspaper column was through the pairing of a nice Cabernet with a premium cut of beef. She would wine and dine him. She would wrap him around her pinkie.

Forget me not.

Her boss at Worthington Fairchild, a full partner and compulsive golfer who spent just two days a week in the office, had kept a little book on his desk: *The Art of War.* Its author was a sixth-century-BCE Chinese general who held forth on methods of attack, maneuvers, and espionage. Melinda's boss had shown her the book while planning the divorce strategy for a client whose husband had been caught laying the maid. *If you know both yourself and your enemy, you can win a hundred battles without jeopardy.* The successful attorney, like a champion prizefighter, won because he took only cases he knew he would win. Examples included those with damning correspondence and photographic evidence. Cases lacking slam-dunk support, such as those based on alienation of affection, landed on the desks of the junior litigators.

Arjun was benign, oblivious to the race between them, blind to the percolating conflict that would someday bubble to the surface. She could eliminate him as easily as she could a housefly. She could play ally or adversary, even when using the same words. Traffic was the rising tide that floated all boats, but the bounty of the tide—the nets of squid and sardines, the whale oil and the treasures of old shipwrecks—belonged to her. She knew herself and she knew Arjun. And she would take his lunch money every time.

She walked to the window, a panoramic bay that overlooked the path into the woods. Sometimes she caught deer loitering in the garden, nibbling on her blooms. When the neighborhood kids bounded through the yard, chasing a wiffle ball or waving butterfly nets, she noted their resemblance to wild creatures. She thought of the Angus cattle and the corn in the fields and the scars on her daughter's arms. Everything in life was free, she thought, until someone figured out a way to make people pay for it.

Eddie looked at the Bollywood Eggrolls truck, quiet and locked up tight. He hadn't seen Arjun in days. As much as he rued the young man's Pollyanna disposition, it beat the ill manners of the rabble that tormented him every day. *A dollar! When I was a kid, a hot dog was twenty-five cents.* Yeah, well, he thought, when you were a kid, you should have had the crap kicked out of you. You should have been shot in the clavicle on your first day in Nam.

He thought of how these runts ran in packs, driving down the prices at yard sales and Goodwill and food carts. *I would never pay you a dollar.* Yeah, well, I wouldn't feed you if you were starving. I wouldn't call 911 if you got hit by a truck. Broadnax was packed with cocky punks, drunk on entitlement. He provided delicious food at competitive prices. And all they did was complain.

He thought of the great anthills in Spain and Portugal, vast colonies working together to build a world. When one colony spilled into the territory of another, it would kidnap and enslave its rivals and sacrifice half of its own to save the other half. Nature had programmed its creatures to eliminate the competition through bloodlust and oppression. There could only be one king of the hill.

Arjun was like an ant, he figured, wandering through a meadow, basking in the sun as it warmed his thorax. It was only a matter of time before a wasp or beetle devoured him. Nature played no favorites. Eddie had been taught as a child that the meek would inherit the Earth, but he wasn't so sure. The meek would more likely be enslaved, raped, and eaten by predators unburdened by moral issues. But maybe, he thought, these benign souls would rule over all creatures in the next Disney blockbuster.

Eddie's father had been an amateur boxer in Maine. His mother had been an amateur boxer's friend. They had married and taken jobs at the Portland wharves, where the haddock and cod were plentiful. Early Americans could have remained on the Atlantic coast and eaten like kings forever, but they pushed inland, to the unknown, to a land of dreams where they died in the deserts. Although Nature had already provided for them, these plaintive pilgrims chased mirages into nothingness, imagining saints and spirits who beckoned with promises of immortality. Stupid fuckers. Seeking music on the wind, they stumbled in the dark and became morsels for jackalopes and chupacabras.

And now they were pushing further, into the vacuum of space, disappearing into cosmic silence.

The callowness of humanity was boundless. If humans were not busy committing suicide, they were plotting genocide, killing one another in their beds. They were swarming over the land, securing territory, burning forests, poisoning bodies of water, extracting and exhausting natural resources that had taken millions of years to form, creating weapons of mass destruction, and pissing on their neighbors' lawns, all to prove to the gods they were now ready—after discovering fire and inventing the wheel and mastering the delivery of lethal chemicals from helicopters—to colonize the stars. Well, they were fucking up. They were not ready.

Eddie and his unit had spread napalm over the rural settlements of North Vietnam for six weeks in the summer of

1970. Peanut butter and jelly. *Come get a sandwich, kids. Eat right.* He remembered the piercing screams of the innocents who had no idea why they were being roasted like marshmallows. They didn't know it was because the most powerful nation on Earth had work to do. They didn't understand it was because of democracy. To them it just looked like a horrifying act of boundless cruelty. Of course those dumb gooks didn't see the bigger picture, the one the US Army had access to.

Sometimes, Eddie thought, a man had to do what he had to do. Without order, there would be mayhem and murder. This was true, he knew, because humans were bloodthirsty animals. And no matter how many hungry children they tried to feed or deadly diseases they sought to eradicate, they would always return home to slaughter the pigs and beat the slaves and impregnate their neighbors' wives.

It wasn't bad. It just was.

"Hey, do you hear me in there?"

"Seiko?"

"Sir? Are you all right? We're here. We're going to pull you out of the car."

The Toyota rolled from side to side. EMTs were pulling watermelons off the hood and roof. Arjun caught a glimpse of sky through the shattered glass. He had been driving up route 29. The morning sun had blinded him. He had lost sight of the truck ahead. A violent jolt had tossed his head like a bowling ball. His body had twisted and spun, as if weightless.

"Seiko…"

"Sir?"

"I have to get home…"

"Can you hear me, sir?"

Arjun spotted a face through the window. "Yes."

"Stay still. Sit tight. We'll have you out in no time."

Arjun ran his fingertips over his cheek and found a sticky goo of watermelon juice and blood. His lap was full of rinds and seeds.

His mother wasn't going to be happy, he thought. Why had he not returned to Tucson after graduation? If he had gone back home, he would be working with his father at the Foot Locker at Park Place, learning retail management, mastering the finer points of sports footwear. He would be training in an established profession. He would be spending time with the people who loved him, fortifying the family bond with the little things, like eating dinner together and watching television and going to high school football games. He wouldn't be living alone in a tiny apartment, talking to himself like a tropical bird. He wouldn't be sitting behind the wheel of a mangled car, his face in an airbag, a forklift dangling the Jaws of Life over him. He thought of the parade of Tucker sedans winding through Chicago, gleaming in the soft light of the harvest moon. He felt them disappear.

Everything had changed.

"Amma?"

An enormous steel claw dug its nails under the brim of the roof. It peeled away the frame, bolts flying, glass cracking under the crush of the hydraulic crane. The operator worked the valve as the jaws ripped their way around the roof, lapping it like a can opener prying the lid off a tin of beans. Arjun sat still, his hair goopy, his eyes stinging. *Hey, Bhagwan.* He saw the sedans in their promenade around the circle, engines humming in harmony, chrome shining in the neon. He saw their creator standing on a patch of grass, his eyes beaming like headlights. He heard the crowd erupt in applause. "Amma? Seiko?" He gripped the wheel. *I cleaned my room. I cleaned the kitchen.* He sobbed, his chest heaving into the melons. *I gave the homeless lady a dollar.* He saw the crane looming over him. *I am not an accident. I am not forsaken.* He saw the operator's eyes gazing down at him, smiling.

"We've got him!" the man shouted.

He wiped the tears from his face, saltwater mixing with his blood and sweat and the juice of the fruit, a breeze caressing his skin as it rushed through the cabin. He tasted the nectar on his lips, sweet and sour, yin and yang, good and evil clawing each other's eyes out in a gambit to the end.

He saw the sun wink.

I am here and I am listening.

JANUARY 2015

14 | Sometimes You're the Bug

Candy toddled across the EverSafe Solutions parking lot, her heels clacking on the asphalt, her skirt rippling in the breeze. She hoped she didn't encounter Brad Paxton on the way in. She hoped she didn't see him all day, and preferably all week. She wondered if she could give him the slip forever, timing her entrances and exits around his, avoiding the parking garage, proffering colorful excuses for being unable to play volleyball or attend the next office party. If she never ran into him again, she would never have to look at the shame in his eyes. She would never have to endure his clumsy, agonizing apology. She would be able to go on as before, whistling while she worked, as if nothing had happened.

She crossed the lobby to the elevators. Monday mornings were always eerily quiet, as if everyone was in mourning. Staff clutched their coffee cups, taking refuge in the aroma, steeling their insides for another week. No one said a word. They just stared at their reflections in the steel doors, ghostly images of the present and future.

Candy stumbled down the hall, her purse bouncing off her hip. She passed Charlene's desk, the kitchen, and the empty office where the productivity consultant camped out twice a year. She walked by the rows of gray cubicles, tiny fiefdoms presided over by the keyboardists and telemarketers. She saw the coats and scarves scattered on the credenzas, sloppy closets in a warehouse that would never feel like home. She wondered if she should turn around and walk out, pack a couple of bags and drop off her apartment key and head west. She could ask her mother to let her sleep in the half-bedroom. She could see her friends again. She could drop by the car wash, chat up her old boss, and get her old job back. Everything could be as it was before.

Horrible.

She turned the corner. Everyone seemed especially quiet this morning. Must have been a wild weekend. Maybe Charlene and the ladies of the data pool had rented a limo and gone gambling in Charles Town. Maybe they had hit a strip club. Maybe they had gotten trashed on Dirty Shirleys and jammed some bills into some briefs. She smiled at the thought of Charlene marching her charges into a den of iniquity. Maybe they had all passed out, hairdos a mess and bras askew, and spent the night in the drunk tank. Maybe they had all gotten sick in the fountain of the Hollywood Casino.

Candy felt the eyes upon her, watching her as if they expected her at any moment to trip and fall or burst into song. She detected a frown on the face of one, a flat affect in the voice of another. She noticed others rising just far enough above the cubicle walls to catch a glimpse of her. What was that about? She wasn't late. She wasn't disheveled. She wasn't trailing toilet paper from her heel. Yet she suddenly felt she was the center of attention. Her stomach turned. Her cheeks burned. She glared. *What?* She checked the buttons on her blouse, the snaps on her skirt. *What are you staring at?*

She skidded into her workspace, dropped her purse, and took off her coat. More calls to make today. More sidestepping. She wondered if she would ever escape the twirl of the hamster wheel. She caught a glimpse of herself thirty years down the line, typing memos, stapling papers, making phone calls. She saw herself in a jaunty bouffant, filing her nails in a loud Christmas sweater, digging through her purse for a Virginia Slims. She saw her varicose veins and cellulite packed in a girdle.

She looked at her desk. It was empty.

"I have your things."

She turned around. It was Charlene, stern and still, holding a large EverSafe Solutions box across her chest. A security guard stood behind her.

"Put your coat on. Get your purse."

"What? Why?"

"Follow me, please."

"You're moving me to another cube?"

"Follow me."

Candy retraced her steps, trailing Charlene back up the hall, past the cubicles, the copy room, and the kitchen. Again the eyes of the room landed upon her, peering like sun through a magnifying glass. They all knew. They knew where she was going, and they had opinions about it, as they did about everything. The silence brought its own weight, highlighting the sound of a dropped pen and a sniffle and a steno chair sliding across the floor. Candy teetered on her heels, nearly toppling the water cooler. She felt faint. She shouldn't have stayed up so late with Bobby, drinking mudslides and watching *The Voice* and dancing to Nicky Minaj. She shouldn't have let him stay.

Charlene pressed the elevator button and stared into the doors. Candy saw her furrowed brow, her clenched teeth. It was as if she was standing at the edge of a battle, raising a sword in defiance. Candy remembered a night when she had dropped off a customer file at Charlene's apartment and found her boss fevered and sneezing in a tattered bathrobe. The living room had been littered with tissues and pizza boxes and cat toys. A little television had glowed in the corner, playing *The Beverly Hillbillies*. Candy had wondered if Charlene's life, seemingly so small and suffocating, was typical of ladies of a certain age, and if her own life was already on that track.

By the time one figured out what was happening, it was too late.

Charlene marched out of the elevator and into the lobby, her heels clacking over the stone floor. "The company has decided to make a change," she announced, her voice echoing in the multistory atrium. "Thank you for your work. Your efforts are appreciated." She pushed through the revolving door. "Remember the agreement you signed on your first day. It prohibits your speaking publicly about your employment at EverSafe or accepting a job from a competitor for eighteen months. Failure to comply will result in legal action. Do not apply for a job with EverSafe in the future, as your application will not be considered. If you have questions, you can email them to human resources. Again, EverSafe wishes you the best in your future endeavors."

"What?" Candy stammered. "Why?"

Charlene pressed the box into Candy's chest. "Well, you know, sometimes you're the *windshield*," she said, winking in reference to a philosophical song that was popular among the members of the data pool. "And sometimes you're the *bug*."

The statue of George Wythe watched Candy falter on her heels. Without range of motion in his neck, his peripheral vision was poor, and he perceived little but what passed right in front of him. But he recognized the leggy blonde. She reminded him of Ann, fresh and dewy on their wedding day, healthy and glowing before she died. *Secundis dubiisque rectus*, he had engraved on the gate after her death. *Upright in prosperity and perils*. He later inherited the family plantation and its slaves and married the daughter of a wealthy planter.

He watched Candy tilt, her cargo crushing her bosom, her hips gyrating in an effort to remain upright. Surely she needed a man to assume her burden. Surely her training in cooking and childrearing had not prepared her for this. He saw her ankle turn. He saw the box slip and fall to the ground, its contents spilling across the pavement.

He watched her sit down on the curb, bury her face in her hands, and begin to cry. It was the blessing and bane of women, he thought, to tend emotions close to the skin, to soften the cruelty of the physical world. Women, their flaws aside, were important tools. Men could not propagate the race without them. Perhaps a man had discarded her for a woman whose father could assist him in his career, or for one with a large dowry. Or perhaps she was simply menstruating. In any case, her foolishness and weakness undermined her. This was why women, like slaves, did not vote.

He thought of Lydia Broadnax, her smooth, dark skin hot against his, her tongue wet on his neck. She was earthy and real and beautiful. When his second wife passed away, he chose love. He built as many little houses on the plantation as were needed to hold the children. And the first of his line with young Lydia was a boy named Michael.

Michael Brown.

Arjun pulled the padlock off the door and hung it on the hook. The truck was as he had left it. The lot rang with the clatters of pots and pans. Melinda sat in a folding chair, a pencil in her teeth. Debbie licked an ice-cream cone while Ron painted a dog eating a jelly doughnut on his van.

Arjun stretched his facial muscles, still sore from the impact of the airbag. He scrunched his nose, still swollen. Everything looked a little strange, as if something had changed while he was away. He thought maybe the shadows were falling differently or that the sounds of traffic were muted. Even the aromas seemed unfamiliar. The clearest voices in his mind—of his parents, of his childhood friends, of Seiko—were echoing down a tunnel somewhere, blending with the rush of water and the songs of birds, dissipating in the air like smoke rings. They were mixing like the memories of school years and sports teams, like the perfume of coriander and ginger and garlic.

He picked up the newspaper and read the headline: "Missouri Unrest Enters New Phase." He thought of Michael Brown and the officer who shot him. America was a nation of immigrants, of outsiders and expats, of outcasts and fugitives fleeing their homelands. It was a land of backbenchers building their own private Alamos. In America, he thought, there were no preconceived notions, no caste hierarchies, no states of being that could not be rearranged or reinvented.

It was a free-for-all.

He wiped down the countertop. Life had gotten messy. Seiko wasn't dead, but she wasn't alive, either. He remembered his grandmother, shriveled and tiny in hospice, squeezing his hand while the morphine dripped into a clear tube. She had whispered his name, her eyes twinkling, and reminded him of when she and his grandfather took him to the fair in Lajpat Nagar. He had won a stuffed Godzilla and carried it around all day under his arm. *Sometimes you're Godzilla,* his grandfather had said, a smile spreading across his face, *and sometimes you're Tokyo.*

He heard a bump and rustle behind him and turned to find Pidgey waddling over the pass-through. "Hello, friend!" he said. "Where have you been? Oh, wait, what is that you say—it is I who was absent? Yes, I am afraid so. I expected to return and find you with a family of your own, honing your talents and forging your way. I expected you to have made something of yourself. But, but. Think about that. What does this say about my expectations, friend?"

Pidgey stared.

"It says they are unrealistic."

As much as Pidgey dreamed of a meaningful life filled with joy and adventure, he found precious little evidence of it in the physical world. In his mind, he was like Cher Ami, a bold avian with a higher purpose, a knight of the round nest. To others, he was a doddering fowl pecking at seeds, never flying, a rat with wings poaching mushrooms from a stir-fry. He expected the visions to match. Yet they were as different as the statue of George Wythe and the boy Antwaan.

"Hey there," a woman's voice rang from the pass-through. "Back from vacation?"

Arjun turned to find Melinda munching a rice cake, her sleek cheeks bonier than ever. "Not exactly."

"Well, Happy New Year, eggroll man. Things are looking up. Tim Samsara stopped by again. Jim got the Christmas spirit and dropped the custody case. Aubrey has been almost tolerable. And I'm selling a boatload of Bombs."

"That is nice."

"Yes, it is. I'm going to the gym again too. Three times a week." She flexed her right bicep. "Might makes right."

"It does?"

"Only if you believe history, paisan. Or anything else you see. Nice guys finish last. A strong guy is better than a nice guy. A strong guy is actually *nicer* than a nice guy."

"Oh?"

"Leading the way is the nicest thing you can do for somebody who can't get out of their own way."

"I see."

Melinda smiled. "Hey, the Gourmet Battle of the Vans is coming together. When the warm weather hits, *bam*, we'll be ready. It will be our coming-out party. And the world will see what we're all about."

"What are we about?"

"Meeting a need, hello! Every morning when I wake up, I think, 'people need me today.' And that inspires me. It gets me out of bed. It keeps me going."

"Going where?"

"What are you, a fortune cookie?"

"I am just wondering."

"Yeah, well, wake up. You're selling weird eggrolls to weird people, and that might not be your Holy Grail, you know? Who puts curry in an eggroll, anyway? And who eats eggrolls without Chinese food? A smattering of people. A *smattering*. You need more than a smattering to grow. You need a stampede."

"A stampede?"

Melinda fixed her gaze on Pidgey. "And this? Health-code violation. They'll shut you down in a heartbeat if they find this guy roosting in your roof. Here is my advice, eggroll man. When life gives you pigeons, make squab."

Candy sat on the curb. She checked her bank balance on her phone: seventy-six dollars, even. Sprung from captivity by her officious boss, and by her boss's predatory boss, she was finally free to starve to death and evade bill collectors and be evicted from her apartment. She stared into the bleak sky.

It was one thing, she thought, for CEO Brad Paxton not to replace the dress he ripped, or to leave her half-clothed and stranded in the middle of West B.F., Virginia. It was another to send her to the end of the bread line. With a wave of his hand, he had stolen her security. And there was no one—at EverSafe or in the courthouse or in the court of public opinion—who could save her. She wrapped her arms around her ribs, closed her eyes, and remembered what her mother had said, drunk and stumbling through her smoke-filled trailer. *Life is sweet, baby, but here come the bastards.*

Sure, she had thought, I'll keep my eyes peeled. Do the bastards have nametags? Do they wear a scarlet "B"? Brad Paxton was a respected businessman and a hollow husk without a soul. Was he a bastard while he was raising funds for battered women? Or only while he was actually battering women? Did he rape his wife or just his employees?

She wondered if Brad Paxton's dark whims were the compulsions of a psychopath.

She thought of Bobby and Billy, dueling for her affections. She had delighted in their animal antagonism. She had allowed their desires to soothe her sores, to make her complete. She was abominable.

She felt sick.

Was that Arjun across the lot? She smelled the curry in the recesses of her brain. Her forearms erupted in goosebumps. Her cheeks glowed with delirium as she thought of the deep-fried, golden shell, flaky and satisfying. Just a bite would soften the pangs in her stomach.

She set out across the lot, leaving the box in a heap. "Hey!" she shouted, waving her arms. "Hey! You're a sight for sore eyes!"

Arjun turned. "Shouldn't you be at your desk, threatening homebodies by phone with the prospect of a home invasion?"

"I don't have a desk anymore! My desk is that little pile of stuff over there. See?"

"That is your desk?"

"That's it! Isn't it great?"

"Is it?"

"Yes! Arjun, if I sing a little song for you, will you make me an eggroll? I'll sing any song you like."

Arjun mulled it over. "Well," he said, measuring his words. "I was thinking this morning was a hard morning. Things have not gone well this holiday season. I was thinking, 'Hey, Bhagwan, there is no place to go but up.' I thought if I could get past the morning, the afternoon would be better. And tomorrow would be fine."

Candy saw the sadness in his eyes. "Well..." she sang, a trill of notes spilling from her lips. "The sun will come out tomorrow... I'm betting my bottom dollar, here in squalor..." She laughed and kept improvising. "Just thinkin' about tomorrow... clears away the rain and rapists 'til they're gone... When I'm wrestling in a beamer with a clean-shaven psycho, I throw out my knockers and say, 'I'll get you, you horny, dumb bastard, tomorrow... *come what may!*'"

"Bravo!" Arjun shouted. "To Broadway!"

"To the Alvin Theatre!"

"Andrea McArdle *wishes* she was you!"

"Thank you!"

"But what is this about a rapist? A psycho?"

"Yes! You missed so much. That's what happens when you go away."

"I had to go see my friend."

"Oh?"

"Yes, she taught me all about food. And about thinking of everything at once… instead of just one thing. She believed in me."

"She's your girlfriend?"

"No."

"But you like her."

"She is in a coma."

"What?"

"She is brain-dead."

Candy froze. "What do you mean?"

"I mean she is lying in a bed but does not know she is there. At least that is what the doctors say."

"I'm so sorry. I didn't know."

"I did not tell you. I did not tell anyone."

"You can tell me, sweetie. I'm no longer employed. I can be a full-time listener. All ears."

Arjun looked up at the sky. He steadied himself on the countertop and drew a breath. "I remember all the things she taught me," he said.

Candy walked to the side door and looked inside. Arjun was staring into the fryer, tending the eggroll. She entered the kitchen. "What did she teach you?" she asked, placing an arm around his shoulder. "Tell me and I can know her a little too."

"Oh, just everything," he said, tracing circles in the oil with the tongs. "When I was little, I thought love was romance. Hearts and flowers and rings. I thought it was for adults who wanted to be like people in the movies. But I know now it is not that. It is not a feeling. It is what we do. It is how we live." He wiped his eyes. "I have a food truck. I make eggrolls… and they are better if I make them with my heart. Not just curry or spices. When you love what you do, it loves you back. And it never stops."

Candy squared his frame to hers. "I am at a crossroads," she said.

"And?"

"And I want to get out of the truck I'm in. I want to unload it and get myself a new truck."

"And go where?"

"Someplace that has, you know... what you said." She wrapped her arms around his neck. "Nothing I ever see is like that. It's mostly just people chasing things... I don't know what they do with the things when they catch them. Put them in a safe-deposit box, I guess. What happens to all those boxes?" She drew his face close to hers. "Do you ever think about accidents? And fate? And why people meet? I think about that stuff all the time."

"A little."

"My mom thinks she was Mae West in a former life," she said, laughing. "But she was born before Mae West died."

"So, she is not Mae West."

"I guess not!"

"Maybe she is Clara Bow?"

"She definitely sees herself as the 'it' girl."

"Okay."

Candy frowned. "So... every girl thinks she's the 'it' girl?"

"Um, yes?"

"Well, I don't think I'm the 'it' girl. I never made it to Broadway. And nobody ever discovered me at a soda fountain. I can't even keep a job selling squares of laminated cardboard on a stick. I can't even carry a box."

Arjun smiled. "We all have a job to do."

"I don't."

"You know... on my way home, after I saw Seiko, I was in a traffic accident. I was driving into the morning glare when I came around a bend and over a hill... and I lost myself in the steam rising. Before I knew it, I ran into the back of a truck and was crushed by bounteous watermelons."

"What?"

"A man in a crane cut me out of my car. I had to go to the hospital."

Candy looked into his eyes. "You were hurt?"

"Not really."

"You were crushed?"

"Maybe fate crushed me."

"Why would it do that?"

"Maybe it was talking to me."

"So fate... let you live?"

"I don't know. Did you quit your job?"

"Charlene fired me."

"Well, you look none the worse for wear."

"Oh?"

"You look... even a little better than before."

"I doubt that."

"I think you look nice. I see a little spark shining in your eye. And your hair has a fetching little wave."

"'Fetching?'"

"Yes."

"So... why *do* people meet, Arjun?"

"I don't know."

"Is it an accident or fate?"

"Yes."

"Which?"

"Whichever one you think."

Candy pressed into his chest. She was hungry. The eggroll sizzled in the fryer, throwing droplets of hot oil into the air. "Is it ready yet?" she asked.

"It might be," he said.

"What do you mean?"

"It depends what you think."

"It depends on *me*?"

"Maybe it is fried to a golden brown, maybe it is frizzled to a shining bronze. You decide if it is right yet, if it is ready."

She looked into the fryer. "It looks delicious."

"It does."

"I think it is ready."

"Are you sure?"

"No, I'm not sure!"

"You will never be sure."

"But you're sure, aren't you?"

"I am not sure," he said, pulling her close and kissing her. "We cannot ever be. But I know one thing. Sometimes we are the eggroll... and sometimes we are the oil."

15 | The Walk Nonstop

Billy stood in the garage, tuning his Squier Strat. He needed to confront the crowd, to grab people and shake them. Make them see. Loving and losing were the arteries of life. And music was the blood.

He thought of Candy and the taste of tequila.

He watched Justin tuning his snare drum with a silver key. The dude who sat behind the kit, he thought, was forgotten. He blended into the background like a painted tree in a school play. He was the butt of jokes about drug use and dumb girlfriends and diner food. He was never around when the big decisions were made. Yet without that badass doing the heavy lifting, driving the song forward, a rock 'n' roll band had about as much raw power as a barbershop quartet.

Justin's dad had parked the Buick closer than usual to the wall, leaving Quantum Leap with barely a postage stamp of space in which to hone their craft. Billy sat down on the hood of the car and rested his foot on the bass drum.

"I wrote a song, man," he said.

"Dude."

"It's about a girl. And freedom. I was just sitting on my bed, and it came to me. I was stoked."

"That is awesome."

"It's called 'Girl in a Car.' It goes like this," Billy said. He fingerpicked a simple figure alternating between an A-minor chord and a G and began to sing. It wasn't quite Nickelback, but it was a start.

Jared tweaked the palette to make three shades of blue. The first was a deep, ocean blue, a strong blue like a corporate logo. The second was the same hue with thirty percent less black, and the third was the same with fifty percent less black. Layered, the shades produced a monochromatic rainbow, a soft blue over a basic blue over a rich, signature blue, each a harmony of the other two. Jared filled his logo with color, fading from dark to medium to light and back to dark, spelling out the word *FOODSTR*. The dark blues on the edges created boundaries. The pale blues in the middle suggested emptiness. The hungry user, Jared imagined, entered the app, compelled to fill his stomach with something delicious, to make the empty blues full again.

He popped a Paxil. He could always tell when he had forgotten to take his medication, as he started to get really good ideas. Instead of thinking about stealing food from the trucks, he dreamed of how all food was like color, illuminating other foods, as vivid and alluring as a Monet canvas. He envisioned food as music, a symphony roaring in sympathetic harmony, filling the concert hall of the world with a unifying passion. He thought of his app as the Sistine Chapel, as *The Great Gatsby*, as the Beatles at the Hollywood Bowl. He saw it as the divine code that answered the call, the mystical, sacred charter that filled the hole inside every person.

His cheeks turned pink, releasing the heat as it rose inside him. Van Gogh had cut off a piece of his ear, and Jared knew why. No creature could endure the gift of sight if it never abated, if it played twenty-four-seven like some torturous marathon in his mind, revealing a million doors that never stopped opening. Nature wrote its code to preserve the host, and allowed only glimpses of the Gorgon, fleeting exposures to the unknowable, the unspeakable. Jared felt his tears protecting him, softening the acuity of perception. He rolled down the window and breathed the cold air. He felt his heart skitter.

Jesus Christ, I am so hungry.

He closed his eyes. What was happening? Was he just going to die here? For the first time since fifth grade, when his dad had the heart attack and fell off the stool at the kitchen island, he put his palms together and said a prayer.

Help me out, man. I'm sorry.

There was a knock at the window. It was Angry Eddie, shaking his fist. "Go to school or get a job or go see Uncle Sam! Go see Uncle Sam and jump a plane to Nam!"

Jared had noticed this weird old guy in the lot but hadn't paid much attention to him. With the gray beard and ruddy cheeks, he looked a little like Uncle Sam.

"Bouncing Betties! Nibblin' on your kneecaps!"

Jared rolled down his window. "Dude. Do you think you could, like, move along?"

"I've *been* moving along. I moved along to the recruiter's office. I moved along to Andrews. I moved along to the barracks and the bedbugs and the bombs, got it? Don't tell me to move along!"

"Okay, dude. Hey, let me ask you a question."

Eddie stared.

"If people could easily find your cart when you're pushing it around—and hell, I don't know when you push it or where you push it, or even why you push it—would it help you to sell more?"

"You mean if people knew where I was parked?"

"Yeah."

"Well, sure, I guess. It would help."

"I can do that for you."

"Bullshit."

"I can."

Eddie sized up this insolent punk condescending to a man three times his age while living in a rusted-out 1991 Nissan Sentra. "You know, I can kill a man with my bare hands."

"Dude, chill. I'm offering you a piece of something big. It will change your business. It will change your life."

"Uh-huh."

"You give me two squares a day and I'll give you more customers than you've ever seen."

"Any funny business and I will kill you in your sleep."

"Well, awright!" Jared said, rubbing his palms together in anticipation of his first meal in days. "Two dogs. With relish!"

Melinda ran the scoop through the tray, forming half-pound balls of Angus and lining them up in rows. They looked like soldiers, standing at attention, awaiting instructions, fighting under the proud banner of Burger Bombs. *One, two, three, four, I love the Marine Corps.* She grabbed a portion, flattened it in her palm, and worked in sautéed mushrooms and onions and goat cheese. She then laid it on the grill like a baby in its cradle.

Once a customer bit into a Bomb, she thought, he was a lifer. He would never eat another hamburger without comparing it unfavorably to the best burger he ever had. He would never again be happy with fast food. He would only pine for the unforgettable burger he had tasted once, at that place, remember, over in Broadnax... until he wracked his brain for the location and returned to it. Melinda knew the drill. The better the food was, the more space it occupied in the mind of the famished.

Sun Tzu knew all about it.

Aubrey had been cutting herself again. She was failing algebra and breaking up with boyfriends, suffering in silence, and retreating to her bedroom right after dinner to dig little canals in her forearms. *Mom, if I taste my own blood, is it cannibalism?* It wasn't the scene Melinda had imagined when tying pink bows in the hair of her toddling little Shirley Temple. It wasn't what she had foreseen when Aubrey sat her dolls at the kitchen table for tea. *They never tell you*, she thought, *what it's really like.* They only smiled and shot you out of a cannon, blindly confident, it seemed, in your ability to breathe oxygen in the reaches of deep space.

Each truck, Melinda thought, should be the same model, with the same windows, same headlights, same tires. They should work as a team. How could they market themselves if each was doing her own thing, following her own muse? Who would understand why they were together? She thought of the recruits at Fort Bragg, marching in lockstep, radiating unity into a world poisoned by narcissists. Human beings were pack animals. They lived in families, in clans, in communities. They defended the perimeter. They protected the queen.

Melinda looked at the Bollywood Eggrolls truck, its panels plastered with faces she did not recognize. Why bother? If something didn't make sense, it was gibberish. Why not get to the point? Arjun was a person like any other. Yet he acted as if he was different.

Each truck, she thought, should be the same. It should be painted a sanctioned color. It should be parked parallel to the other trucks. It should not play music or break into dance routines or otherwise call attention to itself. Only then would it reach its potential, its natural place as a cog in the machine. Only then would it know that the sun, the stars, and the streaking comets, suspended like mobiles over a crib, did not revolve around the Earth.

Antwaan parked his mother's SUV at Starbucks. He opened the hatch and pulled out his trail bike. He would become known as the rapper on two wheels, jumping curbs, crossing over street and sidewalk. That rapper could aspire to bigger things. That rapper could become iconic, like Tupac and Biggie, like Jay. He could feel the ground through the pedals, every bump and contour, informing his next move, teaching him. He could sense his place on the planet, the ever-shifting spot where he was, sometimes, perfectly balanced. Everything he saw, everywhere he went, every face that crossed his path in a blur of urban hurry, was a sign guiding him. In the next moment, he wrote the next song, and in the next song he was someone new, someone better.

His mother had been prodding him to get a job. *You can work in the mailroom. Climb the ladder.* He wondered how one clung to that edifice, rung after rung, as the winds whipped up and threatened to throw it off its moorings. Play your role, they said, and the world rewarded you. Behave and the benevolent took note—*such a good boy*—and looked out for you. But whatever remained of human decency, he knew, had been lost long ago. You either climbed the ladder, white-knuckling each rung, or you stayed on the ground.

He tilted the bike backward, onto its rear axle, and rode a wheelie down the sidewalk. His heartbeat locked into a pounding rhythm. Like a scientist in a lab, he saw the possibilities, aware of who he was and who he could become. The words echoed like a mantra. *I am the assassin, a million miles from home.*

He thought of the bouncer at the Annex, posted up by the door before the show, rolling his eyes and scanning the list of performers. *Ain't no "assassin" on the mic tonight. Come back another night.* Antwaan had grabbed the clipboard and pointed to his name. The laughter in the line had rung in his ears long after he had slipped backstage. He had stood alone in the hallway by the green room, watching the other rappers come and go, sipping their purple drank from plastic cups. They had laughed while vetting his Diamond Supply sweatshirt and Kamikaze sneakers. *Yo, somebody been to Karmaloop. Somebody been to Metropark.* When he had gone onstage, he had felt less like the next coming of Jay than like an affluent poseur in a tracksuit. He had felt naked.

And then he had stood and delivered.

He careened around the corner of Wythe and Broadnax and coasted down the hill toward the courthouse. He saw the statue and the steps and the pigeons on the lawn. He saw the food trucks in repose, puffs of smoke rising from their vents, lines of customers winding around their fenders. He saw the stenographers and executives in transit, heels clacking, eyes fixed on objects in the middle distance. He rolled to the patch of asphalt in front of Bollywood Eggrolls, slammed on his brakes, and threw out his back wheel in a showy announcement of his arrival.

"Yo, *Ar-joon!*"

Arjun looked out the pass-through. "Ho! Where have you been, friend?"

"Ballin'. Dodgin' the popo."

"I saw you driving a very nice car the other day."

"Oh, yeah… I's like, 'boost that ride.' Joyridin'."

"I hope you are careful. One man's joy is another man's criminal activity. Would you like an eggroll? Perhaps a Delhi tea?"

"Shit, no! Can't be seen like that. Maybe for my last meal, before they strap me into the electric chair."

"May I ask you something?"

"Break it down."

"If you had a great idea, but it wasn't like most other ideas… how would you explain it to people?"

"Talk is for wankstas. Walk the walk nonstop."

"I see."

"You see?"

"I think so."

"You see, Ar-joon!"

"Thank you, friend. I will speak with my actions, not my words. I will walk the walk nonstop."

"Throwin' bolos."

"Yes."

"Hey, how's about one of them eggrolls."

"I knew you would come around someday."

"I's hungry, skillet."

"Melinda says you are the Assassin."

"Whassat?"

"You know, the Assassin. The rapper."

"Maybe I am."

"She is looking for musical performers for the food-truck carnival, the Gourmet Battle of the Vans. You should talk to her."

"Shit. Carnival? You think I'm gonna blow up *that* spot? Buncha white people with their 'problems,' like a cracked iPhone. Buncha wankstas thinkin' they's assed out."

"Just talk to her."

"They see a boy on the mic, and they say, 'he buggin'.' Or they scared."

"Yes, and I thought that very thing when I opened Bollywood Eggrolls. I thought, 'the people are afraid of an eggroll like this.'"

"And they was!"

"But they are curious."

"No, they's not!"

"Some are."

"Shit."

"People want something special, Antwaan. Give them something that changes them a little. They will thank you later."

"Is that what they doin'? Thanking you? For *this* wack?"

"Some are."

"You funny."

"I am glad I amuse you."

"You amusin'. What's in them eggrolls? Elephant eggs?"

"Secret recipe," Arjun said.

"Like a secret weapon?"

"Yes."

"Ooh."

"It is actually quite nutritious. All fresh ingredients."

"Farm-to-table, yo!"

"And prepared with great care. I do not buy anything in bulk. I do not freeze anything. I do not have a conveyor belt."

"Organic, homes!"

"Well, my friend taught me everything she knew."

"Now you talkin'."

"She taught me all this—the food, the preparation, the dream. She taught me to follow it, no matter what people say."

"Haters gonna hate."

"But *you* are not a hater."

"I hate things that's for hatin'."

Arjun pulled the basket out of the fryer. "Well, I believe you are going to love this, my friend." He dropped the eggroll into a cardboard boat and handed it to Antwaan.

"How 'bout it."

"Enjoy."

Antwaan inhaled the aroma. "Now *that* is fine," he said. He closed his eyes and bit into the flaky shell. "Damn, that is like somethin' somebody's mama would make. Mmm-mmm. You down by law."

"Yes."

"You my ace."

"Yes, I am."

Antwaan looked into the lot. Haters were going to hate, it was true, but there was a lot out there to love.

Pidgey waddled through the grass. Nobody was hunting, nobody was gathering. Nobody was burning the midnight oil, not even Jared, not even the silhouette of a drone in an office window at EverSafe Solutions. The point, he thought, was not the seeds. The seeds were just fuel for the task.

He traced a circle around the statue of George Wythe, lapping the Father of American Jurisprudence with a gait that led him by the same scenery again and again. Straightaway, curve, straightaway, curve. Doppler effect. *And it's Pidgey on the inside, making his move.* Someone up there, he thought, was tallying the laps. Someone was paying attention. What was the point in venturing elsewhere? The loop was home. *Hello again, yes, I'm still right here, looking out for you. I'll see you again on the next pass.* There was no better world waiting out there, no shining city on a hill. There was only this lawn, shot through with edibles, cool on his feathers. He had seen the birds who dreamed of a better place. He had watched them leave the lot. He had wondered if they ever found anything. They never dropped a line.

He figured they were all dead.

Of course he would be dead someday too. And he wouldn't be able to run his loop or wander through the lot, prying seeds out of crevices. He wouldn't be able to watch the comings and goings of other animals. But those creatures wouldn't go unappreciated. Somebody else would be watching them, acknowledging them, affirming them. Somebody else would be wearing little paths in the grass and holding down the fort, praying without ceasing, dreaming a dream of the track.

MARCH 2015

16 | Hungry?

The apartment was cold, but the blankets were toasty. Arjun tickled the bottoms of Candy's feet with his toes. He watched the blades of the ceiling fan spinning. He thought of the seasons cycling, warming the world before sinking it into a desolate sleep. *I remembered the beginning, but I never saw the end. When I saw the end, I forgot the beginning.*

Candy nuzzled his neck. She was hungry. There were benefits of going home with a chef. "Do you eat eggrolls at home or just at work?" she said.

"I do not eat eggrolls," he said.

"What do you eat?"

"This and that."

"I eat crap, mostly."

"You should not eat crap."

"You're funny."

"And you are implausible."

"Most women are deadly dull, trust me."

"Not charming and unforgettable?"

"Nope," she laughed.

"Well, happy Saturday, Ms. Implausible. It is a beautiful day. I am ready for some hours away from the lot."

"What, you don't like your lot?"

"I like my lot."

"It's not a *lot*, I know. But it is *your* lot," she giggled. "My lot is being hungry."

"Okay, then, I will make eggs. With cumin and coriander. And paprika and pepper. And garlic potatoes."

"My chef in shining armor."

"I thought your Bobby was your Galahad."

"Tsk. Knights don't worry about such things."

He smiled. "I am not worried. If I were worried, I would fall to my knees and cry, and beg you to forsake all others. Instead, I am just laughing at how implausible you look with your bedhead."

She slapped the top of his skull. "Oh? Maybe you should worry a little more. Maybe you are too comfortable."

"Perhaps so."

"Maybe I should dump you and make you pine for me."

"Perhaps."

"Maybe I should get a protective order against you and force you to break the law to see me."

"But then you would have to wait," he said, whispering in her ear, "for your delicious breakfast. And you would be so hungry. You must learn to think things through. Otherwise, those things will outthink you."

The prototype gleamed in Jared's hand. The vector animations were functional. The GPS was engaged. Soon the Foodstr app would launch on phones around the area, guiding hungry people from their offices and family rooms and idling SUVs to the best food in Broadnax County. Jared watched the montage, stylized photos of Burger Bombs, Bollywood Eggrolls, Doughnut Hounds, The Pig Rig, Saturday Sundaes, and Three Bucketeers, dissolve in a virtual art show.

He pressed the red button on the home screen: "Map My Route!" He watched the line snake its way from his parking space to the area where the trucks were parked. Wherever people were located, whatever they happened to be doing, they would have a map from the spot where they stood to the lot where they would eat.

"Hungry?" their phones would ask. "Follow me!"

Jared had watched with fascination when a famous dad-rock band, in a fit of ambition, had given people an album that seized their phones without warning. And now Jared was giving people an app. On his command, a simple hack would download Foodstr to every phone in the metro area. Foodstr would appear on every screen, nestled among the social networking icons, beckoning to be explored. Compulsive eaters would be swept into the land of food trucks like fish into a net.

He smiled. By the time the app police had rooted out his malignant code, the lot would be exploding with customers.

Antwaan answered his phone. "Yes, Mom."

"Where are you, baby? I need the Lexus."

"I am in town. Seeking employment."

"Tonight is the Beaux Arts Ball at the Kennedy Center, remember? I am overseeing the donations. You said you would join me."

"Apologies. I did speak with a man at an agency on K Street. We discussed opportunities. He said he liked the cut of my jib."

"Lovely, dear. See you soon."

"Goodbye, Mom."

Antwaan stuffed the phone in his pocket. He was not to blame for his circumstances. He was not responsible for the expectations of others. All his life, he had taken counsel from his parents and teachers and coaches. And they had reinforced what they had been told as children. They had echoed conventional wisdom, rooted in tradition and prejudice. But he was no mere fortunate son. He wasn't a servant or a slave, a cog or a pawn. He was a prophet, an interloper left on the banks of the river in swaddling clothes.

I am the Assassin, a million miles from home.

He walked up Broadnax Street, past the coffee shops and vegan restaurants, past the Metro, to the parking garage at the corner of Glebe Road. He watched a woman push a tandem baby carriage over the crosswalk, her cashmere coat whipping in the wind. He saw the walkers on their phones, heads down. He looked up at the towering, glass condominiums, reflecting the sun back and forth across the street in a volley at the speed of light. Who would fix this? Who would fight for the lost, in their tattered shoes and scarves, in their addictions and delusions and unanswered prayers?

All human beings were created equal. But that changed right around the time they were born.

His father had some white blood in his veins, he knew that, but his parents never talked about it. They just called themselves "proud African Americans" and paused for a split-second afterward in reference to some nuance of lineage. "Descended from slaves?" they asked. "No. *Ascended.*" And Antwaan liked that part, free of power and privilege, free of guilt. He liked knowing he came from hard-working people who seized their freedom, who "pulled themselves up by their bootstraps," as his father said, and created liberty out of bondage.

He unlocked the door and slid behind the wheel. A woman across the row watched him, no doubt wondering how a Black man in an army-surplus coat had come into an expensive SUV. He glared and ducked into his collar. In any situation, it seemed, he was either a child of privilege—a cornball brother disconnected from his roots—or a bad element, a threat to public safety. He thought of where he would be in five years, blowing in arenas, rolling in Bentleys, swigging Cristal from the bottle. He thought of the rappers at the Annex saying they knew him when. They would text him and beg for slots at festivals and downtown jams and stop him on the street to take snaps and talk about old times. *Yo, stop grillin' me*, he would say, and throw an arm around their shoulders, a superstar who never forgot his roots. He wasn't about the paper or the shorties. He was about the juice, the pull that came with being a truth-teller. He was far from home, like John Rolfe holed up in the log cabin, maps on a table, a burden on his shoulders. He didn't know if he would ever see his loved ones again. He dreamed of them putting a candle in the window and killing the fatted calf when he appeared over the crest of the hill. He saw their faith. He saw their love.

He saw everything that was lost in the world.

Melinda grabbed the stapler from her coat pocket and threw it open. She slapped flyers on telephone poles and pine fences and the backs of park benches, tacking multiples in each spot as if to drown out the din of scraps calling for misplaced cats and dogs. Melinda figured they were all found by now, alive or dead, so she covered their faces with flyers, mournful eyes hidden by fresh print. She shrouded them with images of balloons and food trucks and cotton candy on a stick. *Gourmet Battle of the Vans™. Sat., April 4, 2015. Courthouse Lot. Free Admission.* She hit battered doors and window frames and the plywood sides of newsstands. She slipped flyers under the windshield wipers of parked cars.

She stapled a flyer to the door of the Cathedral of St. Francis, then opened the door and slipped inside. She remembered her mother, serene yet terrified of the unknown, praying in desperate ecstasy as the sun streamed through the stained glass. She thought of her father, monolithic in his skepticism. *There is strength in numbers*, he said, *especially when you are number one.* She walked up the aisle, past the pews, to the lectern and the altar and the sacristy. She thought of the day Jim had waited for her on that spot, beaming in his rented tuxedo. She had grown up dreaming of her wedding day, and when it arrived it was no more real to her than the dream had been. Someday, she knew, Jim would get the upper hand.

He would find a way to control her.

The hot dogs glistened, fat and appetizing. It was another slow day in late winter, another stretch of hours that was not going to pay for itself. Angry Eddie surveyed the lot, as quiet as church on a Thursday afternoon. What, they didn't need to eat? They were probably sealed in their cubicles, eating cheese crackers from the machines.

He noticed a flyer tacked to a dogwood in the median. He tore it off the bark. *American and International Cuisine in a Carnival Setting.* What dumbshit had dreamed this up? With little kids? And clowns? He snickered. The food-truck court was like a meadow of cows waiting to be slaughtered. They just stood around grazing, enjoying the sunshine, making the dumbest faces imaginable, while some higher authority checked his calendar for the date of their butchery. He looked at his metal cart, gleaming in the sun. No gasoline, no electricity. No internal combustion engine that failed at a critical moment. No windows to clean, no expensive, all-weather tires to maintain. It was like an infantryman's backpack, light and versatile. When the bullets started flying, the soldier needed to move. He couldn't go throwing three packs on his back and pulling a festive wagon. Anything else on his mind—his wife, his children, smoky nights playing poker with the boys—was window dressing, like fantasies of Caribbean cruises and models slumming in the casinos on a Saturday night.

Eddie clutched his chest. Sometimes his stomach forced a gas bubble under his lungs, wedging it there like a little heart attack. He grabbed the Pepto-Bismol. *Don't get upset,* his mother always said. *You'll get an ulcer.* Really? Just waking up in the morning, knowing his faith in humanity had died in the streets of Saigon, was enough to sour his stomach until lunchtime. The simple fact that he had left home with good intentions and returned without them was enough to disrupt his sleep for decades. *Don't get upset? Okay, Mom, I'll just shoot smack for the duration of the Carter administration. That'll keep 'er under control. Then I'll get hooked on methadone and end up in a halfway house where they steal my wallet and sell my ID. Then I'll get a job cooking eggs at Waffle House and live in a Motel 6. I'll drink Aristocrat all day long and get fired because I'm not the right guy to fry potatoes. Or to qualify for disability. Or to convince a tight-fisted bureaucrat that I need some extended time at Walter Reed. Thanks for the workfare, Clinton, 'cause it's been really restorative for me. I can drag my ass to the bus stop and freeze to death on the corner while my heart pounds like a jackhammer. Shit, Mom. I'll just start a food cart. Set my own hours. Dream my own dreams. Hang on to this misery for as long as I can.*

And then Obama will restore my faith, like a wizard. And I'll believe again, like an altar boy who got raped by a priest but decides years later that the priest is really a good guy, after all. He meant well. Everybody did. Fuck you, LBJ. You could have gotten us the hell out of there when I was in high school. Fuck you, Robert McNamara. You bloodthirsty pricks, you waved the flag in our faces. We were never going to put flowers in our hair. We were going to stand up for the good old U.S. of A.

Fuck you, Henry Kissinger.

He watched the food-truck owners ease their way into another sleepy afternoon. They were building lives of purpose, despite everything, just like he was. They still had hope for this moldering purgatory. His anger drained like blood from a corpse. He looked at the flyer.

Fuck it.

"In my dream, I am walking by this dock," Arjun said, "by a big lake. And my parents are sitting in folding chairs, next to each other, looking out at the water, and they are talking. Heads close together. My father looks upset. My mother is stroking his hand. They notice me walking by and my father says angrily, 'Could you just go get us some ice cream?' He does not look at me. I say, 'Please do not speak to me in that tone of voice.' He glares. I continue down the dock. I see a building, like a mall or a department store, on the other side of the lake. I think there must be an ice-cream shop in a place like that. I walk around the banks and through a field, and into the parking lot. But when I get to the entrance, there is furniture piled on the sidewalk, blocking the door."

"So, what do you do?" Candy asked, pulling the blankets up to her chin.

"I climb over desks and chairs and grandfather clocks. I am fifteen or twenty feet off the ground, way up high. The furniture is shifting under me. I look down and see the tiles of the floor under a china cabinet. I slide down the pile, brace myself, and slip through this big, open door. There are little shops along the outside walls. There are people everywhere. A guy in a baseball cap stops me and asks, 'Why are you here?' I say I am just a kid looking for ice cream. I am going to buy two cones and leave. He says, 'They will stop you.' I look around and see people in uniforms. They have walkie-talkies. They are watching me."

"Why?"

"I don't know. It is a dream."

"So, what then?"

"They start following me. And I start walking faster. They act like they are not chasing me, but they are. I go up the escalator and crawl along the top of a wall that surrounds a garden. They cannot catch me. I keep looking around, but there is no ice-cream shop."

"No ice cream for you. Poor baby."

"And they are closing in. They are talking into their radios and cutting off the exits. I see the guy in the cap, and he says, 'You need to get out, but you cannot.' No, I say, I got into this, so I can get out of it. I slide down the guardrail by the escalator. I land on the tile and walk toward the front of the mall. There are guards standing at the doors and putting backpacks on conveyor belts, like at an airport. I run through a gap in the glass wall, and into the parking lot. The security people are shouting. I break into a sprint. I look over my shoulder and see dogs chasing me. I run harder. They get closer. I can feel them on my back. And then, at the edge of the property, they just stop running. I walk down the banks of the lake and back to the dock."

"And that's it?"

"Well, I find my parents, who are still sitting in the same spot, watching the ducks swim by. I say, 'They did not have any ice cream,' and I keep walking down the dock. My father does not look at me."

"What the—"

"It is a dream."

Candy kissed his neck. "Your father wanted you to please him. And you didn't. But you tried harder than he knew. You did a lot!"

"My father is usually quite nice."

"But you disappointed him."

"He is not usually disappointed."

"That's good," she said. "But didn't he want you to come back home? Didn't he hope you would work with him in his store in Tucson?"

"I suppose."

"And you didn't."

"I do not think he *expected* me to."

"But you grew up in his store, right? Watching him? Learning from him?"

"Yes."

"Okay, then."

"What about you? You have dreams?"

"I usually dream I'm flying above the clouds. I see everything. Little boxes, tiny ants. Everything moving, nothing changing."

"And what does that tell you?"

"Well, in these dreams, it's as if I already know everything."

Arjun laughed. "Life would be dull if you knew everything."

"It's as if I don't need to worry about anything. And that's nice, you know? It's like I'm dead or something. I'm just watching from above."

"That is a little creepy," Arjun said mischievously.

"No, it's not!" she said. "It's peaceful."

"And a little creepy. And weird."

"Stop it!"

"Weird, creepy girl with wings. Glad to be dead."

"You are cruisin' for a bruisin'," she said, pinching his arm. "You need to stop dreaming about your father and start dreaming about the sky."

"Hmmm."

"My dad asked me why I didn't go to New York. He said, 'How come you never went to Broadway? Always wanted to see my little girl in a Broadway show.' And I thought, 'Gee, I don't know, it never occurred to me. Thanks for the idea.' As if I could just walk into the Neil Simon Theatre and start singing 'Tomorrow.' He took off when I was five. He hardly ever came around. Mom said he was playing slots and screwing around. Sometimes he dropped by to borrow money. She would go to the cookie jar and give it to him. I don't think he ever gave any back."

"I am sorry."

"So, I don't dream about him."

"Your dream is very good. You are floating on the wind, not fighting it. You are free. I would like to have that dream."

"Close your eyes."

He squinted and leaned into her.

"Think of an open sky," she said. "You are riding in the gondola of a balloon. You hear the sounds of the city. You watch the eagles, flying alone, each aware of the paths of the others. You see what they see. You know what they know. Nothing on the ground matters. It's like a TV in the background. You open your memory. The moments are still alive. They are there to remind you. Don't give up, they say. Don't let yourself forget. Remember the letter your friend wrote you. Remember the girl who kissed you. Remember the afternoons you spent on the playground with nothing to do, with no place to be. Remember that feeling. Put it at the center of you. Watch the eagles and do what they do."

Arjun felt her lips on his, warm and wet. He was half-asleep. The scenery rolled by. Everything was as it was meant to be. He thought of the hopes and dreams of his ancestors, alive in his DNA. He thought of the love of his parents, of his aunts and uncles and cousins. They were passing along what had been given to them. Pay it forward. Leave this place a little better than you found it. Save the world from the crushing cannibalism of the human race. Evolve.

He felt his body fall away as she climbed on top of him, his heart pumping blood. He floated up to the ceiling and came to rest in a corner. Everything moving, nothing changing. He saw the roof over his head and the food in his belly, preserving him, sustaining him, extending the play until he could complete it. He would live until it was over. And then he would live in someone or something else, somewhere.

She vanished into his embrace. The air shivered, little bombs bursting in the heat. *Love thy enemy as thyself.*

Surrender.

17 | The Sous Chef

The sky looked a little brighter than usual. The grass looked a little greener. The lot was cleaner, the buildings more pleasingly arrayed, the sounds of traffic more melodious. Everything had upped its game, Arjun thought, like a tennis player at match point. Everything mattered just a little more.

He spotted a flyer taped to the side of his truck: "Gourmet Battle of the Vans™. Music and Fun and the Best Burgers in Broadnax." Clip art of a hamburger and an electric guitar and a young family crowded the margins. And in tiny print running across the bottom ran the words: "Chicken * Ice Cream * BBQ * Doughnuts * Eggrolls." Apparently, Melinda had obtained the required permits.

He walked over to the Burger Bombs truck. "Hello!"

"Oh, hi," Melinda said, pulling her head out of the sink. "Scrubbing these pesky mustard stains."

"I see you have been busy."

"Oh, yeah. A busy bee. Taking care of business. TCB."

"April 4 is the date of the carnival?"

"Didn't I mention it before? Sorry if I forgot. I've been so *busy*, you know. Marketing, red tape, City Hall..."

"Do the others know the date?"

"Oh, I think everyone knows. It's on the flyer! We'll all be together, meeting new customers, getting on the radar of foodies all over town. You know the rule: *a rising tide floats all boats*. Good times ahead, starboard side!"

Arjun looked at the flyers on the trees and telephone poles. "I will try to attend."

Melinda laughed. "Well, I didn't have time to get everybody together. It's been a *whirlwind* in McCoyland. Contracts, provisions about the GMOs... and Aubrey! I love her to death, but she is a pain in my rear end."

"She is a good kid."

"A good kid with issues. Many issues."

Arjun saw a handwritten list taped to a spot of steel over the pass-through: "Eggs, cayenne, garlic, yellow peppers, goat cheese, Vidalias." It looked familiar. He stared at the red ink, the rounded letters, the hard loops at the end of each line. He had seen this handwriting before. He reached into his pocket and pulled out his keys and a pile of change. Mixed with the metals was a wadded-up scrap of yellow paper. He unfolded it and read the question he had written on his first day at Bollywood Eggrolls: *Why am I here?* And then he examined the odd reply: *To be my bitch.*

He clenched his jaw. "Do you see yourself as a leader?" he asked.

"Well, I try," she laughed.

"It must be hard to lead our motley group."

"Don't worry, Arjie. It's a dirty job, but somebody's got to do it. I don't mind. I *love* our food-truck family."

Billy stood before the mirror and touched the zit on his cheek. Candy saw him as just another pimply kid, some gangly boy mopping floors at Walgreen's. There wasn't much he could do about the way God made him. He kicked the vanity. When he was little, he had been pigeon-toed, causing his knees to knock together like bocce balls. And then he had lost his two front teeth when he fell down the stairs. He was perpetually afflicted. Everything about him was wrong. He would never be good enough. He would never be normal.

He popped the zit.

Well, he thought, *that wasn't so bad.* She might love him yet. He was much smarter than that dumb ox she called a boyfriend.

Maybe he would go out driving and look for Bobby. When he found him at Curly's, he'd sneak up behind him, wrap a foot around his ankle, and send him crashing to the hardwood floor. And Candy would see what kind of man Billy really was.

And then he would show her a thing or two about love.

Jared balanced the notebook computer on his knees. The burger lady was always changing the W-Fi password, which slowed him down, but guessing it was about as difficult as divining the days of the week. First it had been "AUBREY," then "AUBREYGIRL," then "AUBS2000." When it came to passwords, people were about as creative as soldiers in rows. And that was their downfall.

Too bad Aubrey was only fourteen. Cute face, nice rack. Teenage girls seemed to exist to ripen indefinitely, he thought, without ever being picked and enjoyed. And that was messed up.

He hacked into Melinda's server and stumbled on a directory called "IMPORTANT." *Clever name, genius.* Inside he found folders called "FINANCIALS" and "SUPPLIERS" and "CARNIVAL." Each was crammed with files sequentially numbered with the word "IDEAS." He started opening files at random, scanning the thoughts of his internet provider. "Personality Profile," the first read. "Finns are fun-loving, but not the sharpest knives. Threat level: 0. Ron and Debbie are less fun, might bite if provoked. Threat level: 2. Sharon and Sully have restaurant experience. Threat level: 3. Angry Eddie is unpleasant and unpredictable. Threat level: 4. Arjun is a wide-eyed lamb with a Galahad complex. Threat level: 5. RECOMMENDATIONS: Outmaneuver Arjie, neutralize Eddie, roll the rest like dough. And BOOM."

Other files contained background on local meat markets and bakeries and fresh-vegetable stands. Some stockmen pumped the cows with antibiotics. Some bakers used packaged yeast. Some farmers soaked their food in pesticides and hosed it down after it was picked. Each organic business hid a shadowy margin where profit thrived.

A file called "HOTWORDS" was stuffed with terminology for use in promotions—expressions such as "fresh" and "local" and "farm-to-table." Others included "pure" and "simple" and "like Grandma used to make." Each was color-coded—green for organic, blue for familiar, and red for hot-button. Under the red word "juicy," she had added "sex sells!" Jared wondered why she didn't just wrap her daughter in a tight T-shirt with a picture of two tomatoes across her chest.

He remembered his first job in high school, when he donned a Statue of Liberty costume and waved a sign offering help with tax returns. His boss instructed him to dance along the sidewalk to get the attention of drivers. Sometimes motorists honked and waved, sometimes they flipped him off. He figured it was just a matter of time until some sweet old lady, disoriented by the cavorting of a patriotic icon, plowed into a packed Metrobus stop. Wags would remark on the Statue's role in the hospitalization of those huddled masses.

He scrolled through the folder. Tucked in a list of customer names, he found a file called "JARED." He opened it. "Little jagoff hacked into wifi," it read. "Doesn't have anywhere to go. Sleeping in his car. Eating scraps. Smoking weed in porta-john. Staring at Aubs. Caught him on cam stealing BBQ. At our mercy." He snorted. He had plenty of places to go. And he had a job. He was an entrepreneur. He might not have money or food or clean underwear, but he would get them soon. He would get all the cool things they had in Silicon Valley.

He popped a Paxil. The anxiety was washing over him like a wave. The app was groundbreaking. It solved a problem. It was fun to use. Everything he had absorbed—from the philosophy of Steve Jobs to the TED speeches of Tim Berners-Lee—was encoded in his software, strands of digital DNA entwined like lovers. He had left high school to write it. He had dropped out of community college to finish it. And now he was living in his car without food or water and wondering if he had created Foodstr in spite of his panic disorder or because of it.

It isn't too late, he thought.

His mind drifted to the girl from class, the one who laughed at his awkward code and showed him the architecture of the app. *It really isn't that complicated if you know this one thing.* Suddenly, a world had opened inside him. It wasn't just about being able to write code. It was about what you said with the code.

He had slept in her bedroom at her parents' house every night for four months. Then he had driven to Denver in an unbroken forty-hour episode, dizzy and hallucinating, racing over the prairies with his brain starved for serotonin. When passing through Kansas City, the glare of traffic blinding his sight at the edges, he had seen the food and the trucks and the people glowing like plutonium under the streetlights. He had envisioned in a flash the app that would liberate them from their inertia. He had seen it in the safety glass, under the rearview mirror, blinking and calling to him.

He had seen it before. Love.

Antwaan stretched out on the basement sofa, grabbed the remote, and began scanning the channels. Shorties in the club. Melo for three. A fat guy on a skateboard in a half-pipe. He lifted the bottle of Basil Hayden's to his lips. Drown out the noise. Calm down. Mom and Dad understand. Everything is going to be all right. Life is about using time, not marking it. It's a mission, not a movie.

The rappers at the Annex were posers. They were so wrapped up in their cred and their bling that they missed the big picture. There would always be fads and flavors of the month, splashed across magazine covers, injected into the media streams of smartphones and digital billboards. Images faded as quickly as the light used to create them.

He thought of a quote he had seen on social media. *Darkness cannot drive out darkness, only light can do that.* He wanted to wrap the world in a warm embrace. He wanted to heal the pain. *If you're not the master, you're the slave.* Why? Hadn't Jefferson made it plain?

Everyone had the right to life, liberty, and the pursuit of happiness. No masters, no slaves.

Yet still there were kings and pawns, bosses and drones. *Lead, follow, or get out of the way.* He took another swig of bourbon. Joshua led his people to the Promised Land when they failed to find it on their own. But Antwaan was different from the four-star generals and the corporate titans.

He was a servant.

He thought of the bus drivers and the cooks and the government clerks, rising each day, making small differences in a world that ran on service. They grabbed the baton and advanced it a lap. They served.

He thought of his songs of freedom, ringing around the Annex, driving him from morning until night and thumping in his heart as he slept. He remembered the look on the face of the young man who wandered into the club for a malt liquor but stayed for the fervor of the Assassin. In every city, on every street, there was someone who cared enough to compress a lump of coal into a diamond, who loved enough to take a risk, who persevered in the face of astronomical odds or the censure of peers or the way things just were. That person mattered.

A servant was not a slave. A servant was a king.

He took one more gulp of the brown liquor. *Fuck the haters.* He wasn't some wild child domesticated by Ritalin. He wasn't a follower of some guru. He was a solitary man untainted by influence. He was a servant and a king.

He was an assassin.

Hate cannot drive out hate, he remembered, his eyes blurring. *Only love can do that.*

Friday evening had stretched into Sunday morning. Candy sat on Arjun's sofa and scrolled through her messages. Most were from Bobby. *Where r u? Y u not @ curly?* She felt a twinge of guilt. She envisioned Bobby standing alone at the bar, slamming Bud Lights, checking his phone like an automaton. She saw him staring into his suds, his eyes filling with tears. Was he worried about her safety? Or just about whether she had stood him up?

"You are texting to your Bobby?" Arjun called as he loaded the dishwasher.

"No... but he was texting me, I guess."

"He is upset?"

"He was, I guess."

"You are guessing a lot. Do you know anything for certain, Little Orphan Annie?"

"I guess not."

"I am thinking you should stay," he said.

"I don't have any clothes."

"Krishna and his maidens in the Dance of Divine Love, they did not worry about clothes. They did not worry about worldly things. They sang and danced in the light of Vishnu. Have you read the Bhagavata Purana?"

"I've barely read the Bible."

"No matter. I think you should remain here, where you can eat and sleep and recover your strength."

Candy laughed. "You'd like that, huh?"

"And you would not?"

"Well," she said, tilting her head and affecting an exaggerated drawl. "I have always relied on the kindness of strangers."

"I do not recommend that."

"Of course, *you* are not a stranger."

"No."

"You are a sweet boy taking advantage of me."

"Perhaps."

"I won't lie," she said. "I've been living paycheck to paycheck. And now I don't have a paycheck. So, I guess that means I don't have a life."

"You have a life. But it is on life support. You are in a money coma. You cannot function normally. But you are alive. You can do things."

"Like what?"

"Well... you can work for me. In the truck. You can be my sous chef."

"Sue?"

"I will pay you a salary. But we need to sell more eggrolls. We need to grow. We need to talk to the customers and figure out what kinds of eggrolls—"

"Burritos," she said.

"What?"

"*Burritos*. With chicken and steak and shrimp. With weird blends like Hollandaise and habaneros. Trust me. Your customers are Americans, raised in the land of the free. And by 'free,' I mean free to indulge themselves."

"Oh?"

"Yes. I love your eggrolls, baby, you know that. They're wonderful. But the dum-dums don't want them. To them, eggrolls are, like... Chinese carryout. They're the crunchy things that come with sweet-and-sour pork. People don't know what Bollywood is. They don't recognize the faces on your truck. They don't *get it*, you know? They just walk right past you. They go over to Burger Bombs or Three Bucketeers or the Pig Rig and feed their faces. Then they stuff their fat mouths with doughnuts and ice cream. It's what they do."

"Mother of Krishna, I did not know you had so many opinions."

"Do you love me less now?"

"Maybe a little."

"Que sera, sera."

"You think we should switch... from eggrolls to burritos?"

"Yes. Make three of them at first—a simple one, a traditional one, and a really unusual one that changes every month. And lose the Bollywood thing. No more movies that nobody knows. No more weird faces. Paint the truck with cowboys and horses. Paint a dusty little town with a sheriff standing on the corner. And wear a cowboy hat."

"A hat?"

"Trust me."

"I am not mistrusting you. But I do not understand how you know so much about all this."

"I'm a Texas girl. America is a Texas country."

"I did not know that."

"Right. You thought America was a big melting pot of people and cultures and cuisines. And it is. But everybody wants to be a cowboy. They want to be cowboys because cowboys are free. Cowboys do whatever they like."

"And they eat burritos?"

"Yup."

"I see."

"You thought you were helping a damsel in distress. But you were empowering a pain in your ass."

"Yes."

"I'm sorry."

"Do not be. I was not selling enough eggrolls. They are like opera. Respected but not popular."

"Opera is beautiful."

"Yes, cactus flower, it is. Just as the fields and the streams are beautiful before people defile them to erect a Laundromat. Just as a snowfall is magnificent before someone relieves himself in it. I was not born yesterday. I realize what I am doing is foolish and stubborn. But I understand why I am doing it."

"You do?"

"I am doing it for love. Of my family. Of my country. Of Seiko and what she taught me. I love that we matter, each one of us. We each bring something to the oil."

Candy shivered. She thought of her moments on the stage, the only times, she knew, when she had ever been completely visible to other people. "And it is up to us to show who we are."

"Yes. And not just for us, but for them."

She stared. "Yes."

Arjun wrapped his arms around her. "You are smarter than I thought."

"Thanks, I think."

He nuzzled her neck. "You are like a little rabbit Einstein. You will make a brilliant sous chef. You know your cowboys and foodies. You require no instruction in the finer points of hospitality. You are a natural, like Rachael Ray. One day you will survey your product mix of burritos and fryer oil and low-salt chicken stock, and realize you are the queen of an empire. Yes, I think you will make Martha Stewart flee like a frightened squirrel into the Connecticut woods. And I will be glad simply to have known you."

"Arjun..."

"Yes, you will see me one day on the street and say, 'How have you been, boss? How are the eggrolls selling?'"

Candy slapped his chest. "Stop."

"Yes," Arjun said. "I see momentous developments on the horizon for you... with mustangs and spurs and ten-gallon hats... and cowboys and foodies lying down together like the lion and the lamb. I see more accolades than there are horsefly bites on a cowpoke's behind. Is it not exciting? It is!"

Candy pinned him to the refrigerator. "You need to be taught a lesson," she said. "You need to be taken out to the woodshed. You need to walk out to the weeping willow, see, and pick a switch. And you need to be whipped."

"Oh! And this is what *TMZ* will report about Candy Carney! She is beautiful, yes, with gleaming teeth and an alluring carriage, but under her comely curls and silky skin lurks a monster!"

She slipped her tongue between his lips. "You have a mouth on you," she said, "and it's time somebody shut you up." She growled and bit into his ear.

"Hey, Bhagwan!" he said. "Predatory behavior!"

"Self-defense!"

"Assault!"

"Grrrl power!"

"I like you, cactus flower, even if you are implausible."

She grinned. "I like you too."

"As well you should. You have leapt from homelessness to panhandling to gainful employment. You have left your life as a waif and become a sous chef."

"I am in your debt, sir."

"And that debt will be amortized over a long period of time. It might take many years for you to be free of it. Maybe forever."

She stared into his eyes. "I don't want to be free of it."

"You just want to be free."

"Yes," she said.

18 | Throw the Net

"Sweetie, we're going to be late!" Melinda crowed through the foyer. "Aubs?" She packed her satchel—a laptop, an apple, a tiny hardcover of *The Art of War*. She dropped to one knee and retied her Reeboks. Weekday mornings were like fire drills in which she and her wayward child sprinted to safety. Every day, she pulled up to Lydia High with seconds to spare, her ears ablaze with the ticking of an imaginary bomb.

"Hurry!" Melinda shouted.

She had started reading Aubrey's diary, desperate for insight into the crucibles of her depressed child. Each day's entry read, simply, "FML." Her bright girl, once sociable in the playpens of daycare centers, was surly and distant and inscrutable. She spoke in grunts and snorts.

She was, as the lawyers used to say at Worthington Fairchild, a riddle wrapped in a mystery inside an enigma.

Melinda thought of the headlines on the CNN crawl: "Boy, 10, Saves Town Manager from Drowning," "More Americans Die from Spider Bites than Shark Attacks," "Boston Marathon Massacre Retrospective: Tonight at 8." She wondered how she could make Aubrey understand life was fleeting. You had thirty thousand days, if you were lucky, before you were strung up like an Angus steer on a hook. You didn't have forever.

So, get in the game, baby. Play to win.

What kind of person didn't care about winning? A spoiled person, a depressed person, a stupid person. Not a normal person.

Yet the world was full of losers, rationalizing their losing, learning to love their legacy of losing. *I did my best. I gave my all.* Jesus Christ, you moron, you lost. The flaming trash you called your best couldn't beat the scrub that choked in the next bracket. It couldn't free you. And you know why? Because losing is a *choice*. No one is born with everything they want. No one is born with *anything* they want.

Everything I have I had to take from someone else. I had to steal your father from his wife. I had to wrestle a job from the other law-school grads. I had to hang my own shingle, knowing it would knock somebody else's down. Do you understand that? Are you doing that math? Who do you think eats and who do you think goes hungry? God, girl, in the end they will turn on you like wolves. And you will need to go for their throats.

Sorry, kitten, but that is how the world turns. I didn't make the natural order, and neither did you. Do you want to be prey? I don't think so.

Calm down, she thought. She's just a kid. Why am I punishing my girl? Because I am a killer and I am killing her dreams.

Fuck.

Jim had said Melinda was cold. He had called her Queen Bitch. He had asked her one evening, after a romantic dinner at Marcel's, his puppy-dog eyes searching her insides, if she had been abused as a child.

People competed. They schemed. They fought. And the heat of competition brought out the best in them.

Oh, Aubs. When are you going to learn? The world will no sooner honor your whims than change its orbit. You have to earn your way. Our ancestors killed and were hunted. Do you think the world is different now? Human beings barely go a day without flesh in their teeth. I don't mean to burst your bubble, baby. But what kind of mom would I be if I said the world was a fairyland?

I would be a failure. And you would be a loser.

"With the god Shiva as my witness, I flip this egg and declare," Arjun said, his lungs swelling with fresh air. "It is a beautiful day!"

Candy smiled. "Yes!"

"We need only to appreciate it," he said, looking out the pass-through and into the lot. "And I need only to make you breakfast."

"I love mornings."

"I did not know that."

"Well, I do."

"You are a bud on the branch, a harbinger of things to come."

"A 'harbinger?'"

Arjun looked at Candy, at her bright eyes and loopy curls. When he was eight, he had fallen in love with a little girl called Asha. Her smile had filled his heart with butterflies. He had sat next to her in class and passed notes to her in the hallways. He had carried her books. But when she had pulled him under the Ashvattha tree, her lips puckering, he had broken free of her and run home to Amma. He wasn't ready then.

He was ready now.

He slid the eggs onto a plate. "Change is in the air," he said. "No more eggrolls. No more vestiges of Bollywood."

"'Vestiges?'"

"No more disembodied heads. They were not happy, beckoning to a world deaf to their charms. They did not take their nightly leave feeling satisfied. No, I sense their disillusionment. I am going to relieve them of their duties."

"They will thank you later."

"I think so."

"I have a friend," Candy said, "who paints cars for real estate agents. He could paint the truck."

"We have no money."

"He'll do it for burritos."

Arjun looked at the other trucks, at their bodies soiled by rust and grease and exhaust from the fryers. They were not appetizing. He thought of Seiko, framed by tubes and wires like an old tree wrapped in vines.

Antwaan pressed the microphone to his lips. "Beat 'em with a stick," he shouted, "beat 'em with a stick, Rick." The PA thumped, rumbling through the frame of the leather couch, rattling the coffee table. The new song was flowing like Cristal. "Let 'em take a lick, Rick, dump 'em in the crick. String 'em up the oak tree, crush 'em with a kick."

He pivoted on his heel, closed his eyes, and saw the crowd shouting through the smoke, waving their arms, swaying. He didn't need to explain. They understood every word. "String 'em up the oak tree, wrap 'em in the rope. Fling 'em out the tree branch, ditch 'em on the slope." He saw the fists, the lighters, the lines at the bar. He saw the high heels and the short skirts. He stuffed a bite of orange roughy into his mouth. All that separated him from Fiddy and Diddy was popularity. He had the rhymes and the beats. He had the bling and the colors and the passion for the prize. The words rushed from his lips: "Beat 'em with a stick, Rick, cut 'em with a nick. Tie 'em to the trunk lid, pound 'em with a pick." *Roil like boiling oil*, he scatted in his mind, *from a place too deep to trace*. He spat a fishbone onto the plate.

You might not ever be president, he thought, but you can be Snoop. You might not cure cancer, but you can jack a whip. You can do anything you set your mind to. Somebody on TV said Jesus didn't hate money, he just hated the moneychangers. He doesn't want us on food stamps. He taught the apostles to fish. Showed them how to be slick with the pick, Rick. He duped the loaves. He walked on water. He doesn't want us knocking over a liquor store. He doesn't want us in a cell. He wants us to use the tools. Throw the net in the water, and the fish will appear.

He picked up the flyer for the Gourmet Battle of the Vans™. Who are these fish? Is this a king salmon or some weak, farm-ass tilapia? God made all the fish, but some gillies were just flakes. He was the best MC they would ever see. He issued a call to arms. *Throw the net into the water*. He would dress it up like a revival. The ladies would faint in the aisles. Their husbands would plead to the pulpit. *Save us, Jesus*. The power would speak through him like sun bursting through an old oak. And his dreams would manifest like the Savior on the third day. *Can't touch this*. He would bless them all.

I ain't the rabble, I am the One. He would swing the rope in the air. *See? Who hangin' out now?*

He picked up his phone and called the number on the flyer. "Yo, Melinda McCoy," he said to the voicemail. "I hope you da *real* McCoy. 'Cause this is the Assassin. Know what I'm sayin'? I's callin' to *make* your show. Now, I know the way it is. You probably got a sorry folk singer and a beatbox. You probably got a juggler. But listen. I will bring the passion and the *people.* I will line 'em up like bowling pins at the window of yo' truck. You like the sound of that? Think of the chips, aight? I roll in, do my thing, and leave you rollin' in cheddar like a cheese doodle. Leave you dusty. Go on, ask around. Aight. Call me back."

He moonwalked across the floor. *Go on, baby, ask around. They'll tell you.* He would bring the noise. He would be the best ambassador that lady ever had. During junior year, he had sold more Tootsie Pops than anybody in the history of Great Falls Kiwanis. You don't just give them what they need, he thought. You *make* them need it. Because they don't *know* what they need until you *tell* them. You think you don't like hard candy, baby doll? Think again. This shit is delicious. You got a little brother or sister? Do something nice. Make their day. Worried about cavities? Sugar-free. I got you covered.

Throw the net. He thought of 'Pac and Biggie, rolling up to clubs on both coasts. He thought of the forces that brought them down, the jealousy and the pride. He rustled through his lyrics, each struggling like a salmon in a relentless current. He opened the door of the microwave, and the fish appeared.

Candy sat at the light, her foot pumping the brake, her thumbs tapping the wheel. *Let's go, now.* People lost hours of their lives to traffic lights. They lost years to standing in lines and waiting to be seated and talking into the night with strangers they would never see again. Thirty thousand days, give or take. No buttons for rewind or fast-forward. Only play and stop.

People mostly kept their fingers off the buttons. They watched the tape spool like silk on a wheel, wondering what would happen next. Most had no idea. They were headed out to buy a hamburger. Or they were driving to work. Or they were going to a baby shower for a coworker they didn't even like. Prisoners. They locked themselves up every night and hung the key on a hook.

The light turned green. Something was under her skin. She wanted it all now. Arjun and the children and the cute house on the quiet cul-de-sac. She wanted the minivan and the swing set and the picnics on the Fourth of July. She wanted security.

She pulled into the Walgreen's lot. She felt a lump in her throat. She imagined a train sounding its horn as it roared into the station. Passengers entered and exited. They had places to go and people to see, chores to do and dreams to pursue.

She walked down the aisle, past the greeting cards and the gift bags and the flip-flops. She stopped at a revolving display, tried on some splashy sunglasses, and checked her reflection in the tiny mirror. As glamorous as Jackie O. Who had Arjun talked about? Deepika Padukone? Maybe Candy would become a brunette. Arjun would arrive at the truck to find a sultry raven in a low-cut blouse scrubbing the fryer. He would wrap his arms around her and kiss her neck and take her ear in his teeth and—

"Can I help you?"

She looked up. It was Billy.

"Hey there," he said.

"Hey."

"Do you need any help?"

"No, I'm okay."

"Okay."

"Been busy?" she asked.

"Not really… just partying."

"Sounds good."

"Yep."

"Oh, well. Have a good one."

"Yep."

Candy vanished down the tampon aisle. The kid looked miserable. He looked like an emasculated five-year-old banished to the corner of the classroom. And she was his teacher, demonstrating the nature of carnality.

Her phone vibrated. It was Bobby. *Y u not @ curly?* She bit her lip. What part of total silence did he not understand? *Been busy*, she answered. Busy avoiding you. Busy cutting you loose. Busy forgetting the trainwreck of making your acquaintance. In the name of all things good and holy, please fuck off.

Miss u, he said.

She jammed the phone in her purse. No, he missed *it*.

She floated down the aisle, her eyes rolling over the pads with flexi-wings and the super unscented maxi-pads and the contour-shaped bladder-protection pads. Douche bags. Douche bottles. She appraised a full aisle, including packed end caps, dedicated to products of which men pleaded ignorance. She looked at the packaging, emblazoned with graphics of joyful women and butterflies. She figured for every moment a man spent watching porn on his phone, he should have to devote a minute to studying panty liners at Walgreen's. He should have to inhale dioxins and petrochemical additives. And every time Bobby took her without a condom, he should have to eat a contraceptive sponge.

Randy had always been so gentle. He had sensed and mapped her vulnerability through his own. He had stroked her hair on his parents' sofa for hours, kissing her temples, and making up whimsical stories about the tumbleweed in west Texas. One group of weeds, he said, was always plotting to overthrow another, tooling over the dustbowl under cover of night, marking their territory with scratches in the dirt. *And this one tumbleweed is named Davy Crockett. You may all go to hell, Davy says, and I will go to Texas.* The weeds roamed from town to town, fathering children, renewing oil leases, restoring order to unlawful outposts. The thistle that littered the landscape today was all descended from Davy. And now, whenever you saw tumbleweed bouncing across a state highway, you had to pull over to the shoulder and salute it. You had to remember the Alamo.

Candy thought of how she loved Randy's playful stories of yesterday but preferred Arjun's sunny vision of tomorrow. Life with Arjun would be full of possibilities. It would be all fun ideas and new friends and strange culture. She imagined a loft in a converted warehouse, ladders and bridges connecting the ledges, an open elevator descending to the lobby. She dreamed of their children playing in the park, their eyes shining. She saw their food trucks parked along the Mall, wedged into spots on K Street, and camped out at Gallery Place.

She would create colorful murals and dream up sensational menu items while Arjun managed the business. They would change the game through hard work and imagination. They would pass the secrets along to their children.

They would build a future.

Bobby hadn't used a condom. Arjun had. She stared at the cartons, stacked neatly and wrapped in cellophane as if they didn't contain the worst kind of chaos. She grabbed a pink box and took it to the counter. *Jesus*, she thought, *how close do I get to this beautiful mirage before it's taken from me? I want to believe there is a better tomorrow.*

I need to believe.

19 | Clowns and Jugglers

Arjun bit into the burrito. Crunchy, flavorful. Spicy. It tasted good to him, but he had no idea what a Texan might think of it. Maybe only a Delhi boy who had cut his teeth on dal makhani would cotton to a burrito like that.

Candy would know.

He sat down on the courthouse steps. He could almost hear the sounds of cricket in the streets of Lajpat Nagar, the shouts in the breeze and sneakers on the asphalt as the sun disappeared over the block. He looked at the statue of George Wythe, revolutionary, mentor of Thomas Jefferson, delegate to the Continental Congress, abolitionist, keeper and rapist of slaves. Founding Father.

He mused that Jefferson might never have written the Declaration if not for the example of his teacher. He might never have become president. He might never have impregnated Sally Hemings six times while she subsisted in bondage at Monticello. *Unalienable rights.* He might never have become an icon to a nation of immigrants seeking a brighter tomorrow.

Arjun thought of the judges and the lawyers and the court reporters, bustling through the hallways. He pictured the bailiffs, guns gleaming in their holsters. He thought of the sketch artists, grateful for the chance to make art for a living. He wondered how a judge could hold a man's life in his hands without bursting into guffaws or bottomless sobs.

He imagined the staff of EverSafe Solutions, walking on eggshells as their CEO barked orders from behind a desk of the finest African mahogany. There was room for only one person at the top of the pyramid. You either built your own pyramid or you died in theirs.

It took all kinds, he thought. Leaders, sycophants, cogs. Every dirty job was someone else's dream.

Where was Candy? Late on her first day, he mused. He imagined her eyes dancing in the morning sun. Life was a pendulum that swung between pleasure and paralysis. Feeling sad? Have an eggroll. Have a burrito. Have a drink. Dance naked in a fountain. Pour out your pain and love and longing until they join the stream that rushes down the mountainside to the sea.

Fill the void.

"Hey!" Eddie called out, waving a flyer. "Bitch can't do this!"

"Can't do what?" Arjun said.

"Carnival bullshit!"

"Oh, I think it is mostly clowns and jugglers, Eddie. Minstrels and tap dancers and clairvoyants."

"Shit."

"You will be selling hot dogs?"

"Bitch says I can't! Says I gotta have a truck! Says I need a license that shows I'm a *human being!*"

"She is an enigma."

"She is a bitch!"

"I think she is a little sad, maybe."

"She can rot in hell!"

"I am sorry she was unkind, Eddie. She is going through a difficult time."

"Yeah? Who *isn't?* I drag my ass outta bed every day and face this shit. And a bitch makes it *worse.* Sorry, Gandhi. I support the doctrine of the Church of Just Deserts, you know what I mean?"

"Um..."

"We give 'em what they got comin'. What do you idol worshippers call it? Karma? What goes around. They feed us a supper of *bird shit* and we serve them a dessert of *cow shit.* See how that works? Gook lopped off my friend's ear with a machete. So, I put a knife in his kidney."

"Melinda is not like that."

"The fuck she isn't."

"It is more like… she is a rabid dog. She cannot help herself. She bites, she chews. She does not want to be unpleasant. She just is."

"Well, ain't that nice. Get her to a vet."

"Maybe *we* are the vet."

"What?"

"Maybe we can help her."

"You can't tame a rabid dog. You gotta throw her in a cage or shoot her in the head."

"She is a person."

"Shit."

"Okay, Eddie. Calm down. Think of a sandy beach on a tropical island. Think of your favorite food. A tall drink. Pretty girls."

"What the—"

"Relax. You do not want to collapse in a heap."

"I know—I *know*—I am going to die on the battlefield. It's just taken longer than it was supposed to."

"No, no. We are going to get through this, friend. You are going to sell hot dogs from a truck. This truck. *My* truck."

Arjun imagined the far corners of Eddie's mind, canyons and echoes of artillery fire. A memory took the form of a ghost. The ghost became a fear. The fear stalked the former PFC like a tiger, silent and stealthy, until he was out of breath and scratching like a mole in the dirt. He felt the ghost on his back, tracking him, but couldn't fight what he couldn't see. He could only wake in the ˙ ‑f the night and sweat it out like a sniper in the throes of ‑s no relief from the flames engulfing the ᴛe from the women and children screaming. ʰent of the wronged, preying on his soul. ddie. It is a beautiful day. See?"

Tracking, check. Menus, check. Gallery of food trucks in the vicinity, check. Jared piloted the prototype like a driver on the circuit, pushing the engine, testing the turns. He stuffed the pork in his mouth. *I will pay you back tenfold.* He noticed the image of the Pig Rig was pixelated and formatted a replacement. He tweaked the background to match the Day-Glo orange of the Three Bucketeers truck. He pinged the nearest cell tower and got seven results: the six food trucks in the courthouse lot and an old funnel-cake van stowed at a tow facility on Columbia Pike. He still had some bugs to squash.

His phone buzzed. *Get OFF my network.*

Info is FREE, he replied.

Will show cops vid of you stealing food from Rig.

Will leak yr files.

Warning u.

Jared smirked. Melinda didn't encrypt anything. She just left it hanging on the branch, ripe and delicious, for anybody to pick and eat. She probably had an expensive alarm system in her house and left her jewelry hanging on a potted plant in the back yard.

Srsly. Vid of u. Taking trays.

Will Snowden u.

He popped a Paxil and closed his eyes. Life was a riddle wrapped in a mystery inside an enigma, baked in a sugary shell of thrill and dread. He loaded the home-screen notification scheduled for the morning of the carnival:

Hungry? You are only [user-generated distance calculation] *feet from the First Annual Gourmet Battle of the Vans™ at the Broadnax County Courthouse!*

Chicken, BBQ, Eggrolls, Doughnuts, Ice Cream, Burgers!

Come on down!

"In a world of culinary bondage, the courthouse offers freedom from the chains." —Tim Samsara, The Washington Post

Tap to MAP YOUR ROUTE!

He texted Melinda. *4 ur banner—"Freedom from the Chains." That one's free. Ur welcome.*

Get OFF or meet cops.

B nice or SNOWDEN.

He tore another scrap of pork off the pile and let its savory juices settle on his tongue. Once the app reached critical mass, with millions of users in hundreds of cities, he would monetize it by selling preferred placements. Proprietors would pay for access to the most powerful customer funnel ever devised.

He would build a mansion in the foothills. He would invest in silicon alternatives and wearable tech. He would bankroll a blockbuster and appear in a black turtleneck on the cover of *Wired.*

The silhouette of Lincoln stared up at the windshield. The change tray was full of dirt and paper sleeves from fast-food straws. A grimy Sacajawea dollar had blocked his vista for days. Finally, Jared had spent her on a McChicken sandwich. Lincoln looked at the birds on the telephone wires and a big, billowy cloud shaped, he thought, like the head of Stephen Douglas.

He saw a bluebird zip by the glass. The answers lived in the skies, yet people kept their eyes on the ground. They studied the ants, organizing armies, rebuilding after each rainstorm, and planned their own monuments. Soil and sawdust. Time and space floated above, beckoning, yet people scratched and dug and bloodied their rivals like animals. Surely God rued the failure of the frontal lobe.

The human race would either kill itself in a war of attrition, Lincoln thought, or destroy the world.

Antwaan coasted down Broadnax Street, riding the brake. He sailed around a corner, nearly toppling a couple French kissing against a telephone pole. He had been summoned to court to answer a charge of urinating in the courthouse fountain. He was guilty. His only concern was the mental state of the judge who would be sentencing him. That judge had seen him before. When he had peed in the fountain. Before.

He burst into the lot, popped a wheelie, and skidded to a halt in front of the Burger Bombs truck. "Yo! Melinda McCoy! It's your boy Antwaan come to firm up arrangements."

Melinda stuck her head out the window. "Who?"

"The Assassin!"

"Oh, right. Let me get my book." She slipped out the door and came down the steps. "You're a rapper?"

"The one and only!"

"Okay… Do you have a tape?"

"A tape?" he howled. "That's some twentieth-century shit! No, I don't have a *tape*. I'm standing right here! Check it." He lifted a fist to his lips. "I had a forty I had been bequeathed, but a brother can't get no relief. So, I explained it in a voice loquacious, and the popo got up all pugnacious. Chained me to a chair in court, with the lawyers and their writs and torts. In the fever of evacuation, the fifty shouted 'public urination!'"

"Well, I see."

"Do you?"

"Is that a true story?"

"Hell, yes!"

"How many people can you draw to the carnival? Any?"

"Shit. I got minions by the millions. And they all hungry."

"Okay, I am going to give you a set. Maybe let you headline. But if you screw this up in any way, if your people screw this up, I will take your mic and hand you a mop."

"Aight!"

Melinda handed Antwaan a stack of paper. "First, a few ground rules. This is a family-friendly event. No profanity. No crotch-grabbing. No pantomiming bong hits. Okay? Cross me and I will sue your ass. Damage this event and I will bankrupt you."

Antwaan laughed. "Can't get blood from a turnip," he said.

"Your daddy isn't a turnip. You think I'm stupid? Listen to every word I say. Follow my lead. Get your people on the lot. Talk

about the delicious food. Make everybody hungry. Line 'em up for
Bombs with the works. This is your chance to be a leader,
Antwaan. It's your chance to show the world you have talent, that
you can motivate people. That's what your heroes do, right? Jay?
Diddy? They've got portfolios of sweatshirts and headphones and
crystal candy dispensers. They use the *songs* to sell the *stuff.* See?"

"No shit. I know that."

"Do you know what a carnival barker is?"

"Um, yeah."

"That's you."

Billy leaned against the brick wall of the Walgreen's and took a drag
on a Marlboro. He was tired. If it wasn't for the nicotine, he
thought, he would be passed out on the floor with a box of Kotex
as a pillow. He would be dreaming of Candy cavorting on his twin
bed in a sheer black negligée. Instead, he had been up for three
days straight, working extra shifts so the night manager could take
the underage pharmacy assistant to Disney World. He had been
mainlining Mountain Dews.

He pulled out his phone and called Melinda McCoy. "Hi, um,
this is Billy, the guy from Quantum Leap. Did you get the press
kit?"

"Who?"

"Billy Shavers. I sent a package."

"Oh, okay. Yeah. Cover band, right?"

"Uh-huh. Creed and Staind and, like, Hoobastank. And Puddle
of Mudd. And Nickelback."

"Who listens to that?"

"You know, kids."

"Little kids?"

"No, I mean, like, bigger kids. More mature kids."

"Teenagers?"

"Yeah, I guess. We have a new original too, called 'Girl in a
Car.'"

"Um. Will these kids eat?"

"I guess so. I mean, yeah. Kids get hungry."

"All right. Tell 'em to bring their appetites. I'll have posters of burgers and fried zucchini we can hang over the stage. You can open for the rap kid."

"Oh, cool. Thanks a lot."

"Eight thirty sharp for setup and sound check. Don't be late."

"Okay." Billy hung up and took another drag on the cigarette. It was time to start living more dangerously. *Die young, stay pretty.* Break the shackles. For years he had been taking out the trash and doing busywork in study hall and trying to flirt with stacked little prudes who looked past him as if he smelled like Limburger cheese. Well, that was history. It was time to crank his Peavey amp to ten and rattle the rafters. He and Justin were playing a festival. This was the big time.

He checked his reflection in the driver's-side window of a Honda Accord, his long hair flowing. No more bowl cut, like in third grade. No more dorky side part, like in sixth. This was a fresh Billy, new and improved, like Jesus or Jared Leto. And this Billy could taste the Cuervo, as fragrant and alluring as the woman who had changed him.

The car window opened. A man in a suit sat inside, tapping his fingers on the steering wheel. "What are you doing?" he asked. "Were you trying to steal my iPad?"

"What? No."

"Don't lie. I'll tell your boss. I'll get you fired."

"Really, I was just... looking at myself."

"*Looking at yourself?*" the man chuckled.

The Accord sped away. Billy crushed the butt beneath his sneaker. He was a work in progress, sanding off the rough edges. Even Scott Stapp had been young and stupid once. But things changed. They got better. You learned stuff and you went to Harvard and you stopped smoking reefer. And you became a Black president. Or you stocked groceries and you lived in your parents' basement and became the quarterback of the St. Louis Rams. Or you grew up in a double-wide and fenced propane behind the 7-Eleven and came in fifth place on *American Idol.*

It happened all the time.

Candy dropped her purse and ran to the bathroom. She was about to dodge a bullet or take one. She tore open the box, sat on the toilet, and peed into the little plastic cup. *Jesus, don't tell me I fucked it up before I figured it out.* She stared at the liquid, rich in or devoid of human chorionic gonadotropin, and considered the possibilities: it was Bobby's, it was Arjun's, or it was nothing. Her future, she thought, was about to appear or vanish like some childhood dream. She dropped to her knees. She felt sick. She hung her head in the bowl, pulled her hair back, and vomited on the porcelain. Maybe she had the flu.

Maybe not.

She remembered another time she was late, after prom, when she and Randy had parked at the quarry and the condom had split open like a little water balloon. She had hidden in her bedroom all weekend, feigning a migraine, until she got her period and felt as if the sun had broken through the clouds. She held that feeling as the acid swirled in the bowl like a pinwheel. She heaved again. Maybe it was just nerves.

Maybe not.

She applied a drop of urine to the test stick. Five minutes was a long time. She walked into the living room, to the sliding doors, and over to the kitchen. She took a deep breath. Her heart thumped. She dropped to the sofa and pulled her thighs up to her chest. If she never went back to the bathroom, everything could stay as it was. She could have a normal day. She could see Arjun and work on the new menu and laugh at the choreography of the Three Bucketeers. She thought of her mother, drunk on a Saturday night, crushing butts in Bud cans and ranting about the liberal media. *The less you know about how the world works,* her mother sneered, *the better off you'll be.*

Candy got it. You had to embrace the good. Landmines killed children in Iraq, but not in Virginia. Despots committed genocide in Sudan, but not on her street. Life was love and longing, pleasure and pain. It was a reason to be until it stood up and killed you.

She glanced at the clock. Two more minutes. She had seen a boy shoplift a Hershey bar from the Walgreen's. She had watched a man pilfer a tip from the Curly's bar. She had stood by while a woman from the EverSafe data pool keyed the car of a coworker. She had minded her own business. And now some new business, fragrant and in full bloom, had arrived at her doorstep. She walked to the bathroom. She steadied herself against the doorframe and closed her eyes. *God, please. I know. I'm stupid. I'm selfish. I am trying, but I'm failing. I've been failing a long time. Daddy forgot my birthday. Daddy touched Callie at the lake. He made Mommy an alcoholic. Mommy is so angry. I don't care. I'm a bad person. I deserve whatever you're going to do. But I will get better. I'll turn over a new leaf, okay? Please, just this once. Set it aside. All the dumb crap I did. Forget it for a sec. I'll make it right. Give me a chance. You're listening? Okay.*

She peered into the bathroom. The light flickered over the vanity. She squinted at the test stick. Was that a plus sign or a minus sign? She couldn't tell. She walked to the counter. The bulb fizzled. She glimpsed her face in the mirror, wan and perspiring. *Jesus, it's hot in here.* She lifted the stick up to her eye. The light crackled and flashed and blew out with a hiss. The room was dark.

What the hell is that supposed to mean? She whisked the stick out of the bathroom and to the sliding glass doors. She slipped out to the tiny balcony. She grabbed the railing. Those guys never cared about her. They just wanted to get in her pants. Daddy never cared about her. He just wanted to diddle her friends. The bitches in school were just jealous. But the pretty girl?

She is the saddest girl.

She held the stick up to the sky. The little symbol appeared in the glare, a flat line, an expressionless mouth, neither smile nor frown.

20 | What Do We Learn by Thinking?

Aubrey stroked the tip of the blade. She imagined a carousel spinning through a summer night, its poles wrapped with ponies. Children cackled and held the horses' necks. *Mommy, I want to ride again! Hi, Mommy!* The mothers waved and snapped pictures. The merry-go-round was safe as long as it didn't twirl too quickly.

She retraced the little circle in her forearm. The blade deepened with each revolution, wearing a path. Maybe she would turn the knife until she could remove a little chunk of herself. Nobody would miss it. She could plant a little flag in the hole to signal her allegiance to nothing in particular.

She soaked a wad of toilet paper and pressed it against her arm. *Mommy, I want to bleed out! I want to cut myself again! Hi, Mommy!* Relief coursed through her body, reminding her she was in control. She could hop off the carousel whenever she wanted to. It was her ride.

She thought of the anorexics in the cafeteria, huddled together at a corner table, and the bulimics wolfing down pizzas. She saw the cutters, making wounds to dwarf those inflicted by others. She thought of the girls on the field hockey team, expelling it all in wholesome bursts of sweat.

She thought of the happy idiots with their scientific calculators and book bags.

She dropped the tissue in the toilet. Mom wanted her to work the dumb carnival. Greet people and make small talk. It sucked. Aubrey just wanted to fake a migraine and hide in her room with the shades drawn. She wanted to curl up in a ball and eat macaroni and cheese and watch reruns of *Buffy the Vampire Slayer*.

She thought of how she had caught Jared staring at her again, his eyes steely behind the car window. Mom hated that kid. Never mind that he was living in his car. *That kid is a pox.* Was she a pox too? Was anybody who didn't buy a Bomb a pox? Was anybody who didn't get a lot of toppings on his Bomb a pox?

Jared wasn't following orders.

She opened the bathroom window. She pulled a joint out of her purse, sat on the floor against the wall, and lit it up. She imagined her mother in a drill sergeant's olive drab, saluting herself in a full-length carnival mirror, barking at her own reflection. *Fall in! Forward, MARCH! Double time!* She watched Mom's face redden. *Do you HEAR ME? Mark time, MARCH! About, FACE!*

Aubrey walked up behind her daydream mother. "Hi, Mom."

"Oh, hi, sweetie."

"Are you in the army, Mom?"

"Yes. We all are."

"Did I sign up for that?"

"I signed you up."

"Why?"

"Because I love you."

Aubrey took another drag on her blunt. She didn't want to be in the army. She didn't want to drop Bombs for Mom. She just wanted to take a nap and dream she was Sarah Michelle Gellar, chilling in her trailer and waiting to shoot the next scene, making out with David Boreanaz. She just wanted to be held and caressed and touched and—

There was a knock at the door.

"Aubs? Are you okay?"

Melinda pumped the accelerator and merged on to I-66. Purity Farms was past The Plains, in the foothills of the Blue Ridge. It was nine-hundred-forty-one acres of free-range chickens and organic corn and grass-fed Angus cattle. It was pricier than shrink-wrapped vegetables and meat raised in stalls, but it was more flavorful too. Melinda gave credit where it was due—to fresh ingredients without preservatives, pesticides, or genetic modifications. No one had faked any of that successfully yet, and until someone did, she would drive to the foothills for what she called "the real."

To her surprise and disappointment, she had discovered from a discarded supply manifest that Purity Farms used paraquat dichloride to protect their tomato crops. She had struck a deal with them to help her meet budget while allowing Purity to stay pure.

Competition was about leverage.

She sailed down the highway, the horizon bleeding into the afternoon sky. She thought of her poor, tortured girl, wallowing in adolescent angst. At least Jim was out of the house. At least Melinda didn't have to smell lap dances on his clothes anymore or hear him stumble into the foyer like a blind cow at three in the morning. Now it was just the two of them making their way. Melinda still needed to teach her doe-eyed child the truth about men and their shallow wants and deceits. She still needed to teach her baby about the one thing for which men were useful. But there would be time for that later.

She ticked off the checkboxes in her mind: security, booths, carousel, sound, clowns, schedule, toilets, cleanup. She would have Jared's car towed around dawn. She would help set up the stage, introduce the opening band, and retreat to her truck.

She tuned in the classic rock station. *Ain't talkin' 'bout love. My love is rotten to the core.* She bopped in her seat. She thought of when she was a little girl, sneaking into her big sister's parties, lurking in the shadows and spying on the teenagers with their cigarettes and Stroh's. She had watched them laughing and locking lips while the stereo played the first Boston album. She had seen things her parents wouldn't have wanted her to see.

Would the bands attract the wrong element? Would the rides be safe? Had she ordered enough porta-johns? Her mind raced. She would be in the truck while a mob milled around the lot, drunk or stoned. It had all the makings of a disaster. What if she had to call the police? It would be a big, black eye on Burger Bombs, a setback for the plucky lawyer turned gourmet chef. It would send her and Aubrey into a financial tailspin from which they might never recover. And, and—

She was afraid—of failure, of bankruptcy, of leaving Aubrey alone in a house full of kitchen knives. Her imagination served up nightmares. Maybe she would crash the minivan into a vegan restaurant. Maybe she would perish in a house fire caused by an overcooked Hot Pocket.

She pulled into the parking lot of Purity Farms, wheels spinning on the gravel. She recalled the list: grass-fed Angus, Virginia ham (sliced), lettuce, sweet onions, portabellas, orange peppers, goat cheese, cabbage, radishes, red potatoes.

"Hello!" she called into the open-air shelter. "Anybody home?"

A gray-haired woman appeared. "Afternoon!"

"We all set?"

"Almost. Still pulling it together. Have a seat. Try the jam. Best apples I've tasted on the mountain. Won a blue ribbon at the Blue Ridge last week. Try the hummus. Getting the knack of chickpeas."

Melinda inhaled the brisk mountain air. Someday she would buy a farmhouse in Sperryville with a creek running through the back yard and an old barn tucked in the woods. She would keep cows and chickens and pigs and grow vegetables in a plot off the road. Aubrey would bring the grandkids to stay in the summer to camp out under the stars.

She thought of the food trucks and the crowd and the music echoing like a rallying cry down Broadnax Street. After Saturday, she would be in charge. She would tell the rest of them how it was going to be.

"Well, hello!" Arjun said, smiling.

"Hey," Candy said. "Sorry I'm late."

"Setting ground rules on your first day?"

She batted her eyelashes. "I don't want you to expect too much of me."

"Oh, I already do."

She draped her arms around his neck. "Life is funny, huh? Everything is."

"But not a whoopee-cushion kind of funny."

"No. More like a movie theater full of people who don't laugh at the joke… and their silence makes you laugh kind of funny."

"Yes."

She kissed him.

"What is wrong?" he said.

"Do you want babies?"

"What?"

"Do you?"

"Whose babies do you think I am wanting?"

She laughed. "Ours?"

"Oh, yes. I would like a baby with you. I feed the baby, you diaper the baby. And you dispose of the baby nappy. The baby is like a little factory, consuming precious resources and dumping waste into the Potomac River."

"Sounds wonderful, doesn't it?"

"It does."

She checked the time on her phone. "We have to leave for the paint shop. Appointment at noon."

"No more disembodied heads," he smiled. He remembered buying the step van from the guy at the bread shop, talking him down to the bills he had in his pocket. *Just get the truck*, Seiko had told him, *and then you can do anything.* Overnight he had gone from scrubbing woks to designing menus. *You were always a chef*, Seiko had said. *See?* It had taken four men to lift the fryer into the truck. He had shivered with excitement the first time he saw the bubbles in the oil. The carnivals of Lajpat Nagar, bazaars in the back alleys of the Central Market, had taught him that any savory snack—bread, potato, onion—was more delicious when deep-fried.

"Red is passionate," Candy said. "It makes a statement."

Arjun imagined a fire-engine-red race car burning through the turns at Buddh International. He thought of Candy in a tight red dress, her hips round like racing slicks. If all he ever did in life was delight the world, rolling out arresting snack after alluring treat, it would be enough. He would take the checkered flag.

"Champagne and roses," he said.

"Red roses."

"Victory laps."

"Fireworks."

He kissed her. "Bombs bursting in air."

"Pleased with yourself?"

"I am just pleased. With everything." He pulled her close. "When I was a little boy," he said, "my mother told me I was the fastest boy in the school. And I was nifty. Like quicksilver. Every day she asked me my time in the fifty meters. Was I faster than before? Was I faster than the other boys? I thought I would carry the flag for India at the Olympics. I thought I would win a gold medal and bring it back to Lajpat Nagar."

"What happened?"

"Well, when I was fourteen, I woke up one day and thought, *All right now, what is all this? Everyone gives everything they have to it, and nothing changes.* They just wanted the bragging rights. You know—*I* win and *you* lose. I cannot win *unless* you lose. I must take delight in your defeat because it brings me to my goal."

"You didn't want to watch them lose."

"I did not see why they *had* to lose. People are not rats in a race. We are on the same team! I had a dream one night after I ran in the relays. A voice spoke to me through the radio of my father's car. *We don't know why we were born,* it said, *and we don't know when we will die.* I woke up the next day and thought, *Hey Bhagwan, I need to figure out what I am doing here. I need to get to work!*"

"So you stopped running?"

"I stopped beating people."

"How?"

"It did not enter my calculation, cactus flower. They were cooking, and I was cooking, and we were all feeding people. One chef cannot feed the planet on his own. It takes many chefs, each making something. The world is full of people who need the same things, but each in his own way."

"So the eggroll people, they came to you... and the burger people and the chicken people... they went to those places."

"Yes."

"And I... was an eggroll person?"

"Yes."

"You went fishing for eggroll people and you caught me?"

"*You* caught *me*, did you not?"

"Ha! I'll have to think about that."

"You do not have to think about it. What do we learn by thinking? Why we were born? When we will die? *No.* We do not learn those things. We do not learn anything by thinking except the name of the street we need to take to this parking lot or the number of the station that broadcasts our favorite songs. If we wish to learn something, we must *absorb* what we see and allow it to grow inside us. We must monitor its progress. Only then can we know something others do not plainly see."

Candy looked at him quizzically. "You're a trip."

"Am I? Do you have trip insurance?"

"No."

"Then I will be your insurance carrier. I will cover you against damages."

"That's comforting," she laughed.

"I will issue you a policy. And my policy says this: you cover my back and I will cover yours."

"What, I have to insure *you* too?"

"That is how it works."

"Uh-huh."

"Okay, I hereby pronounce us both insured. I will drive to the paint shop and you will tell me what roads to take."

She kissed him.

The waiting room was painted a soft yellow, muted by the dirty business of slathering barium sulfate and resin onto steel. A small TV was bolted to a frame in the corner. Arjun watched a squad of police officers launch tear-gas canisters into a crowd. Candy thumbed through a worn copy of *Popular Mechanics*. The longer Arjun sat in the plastic chair, listening to the hand of the clock snap, the more he wondered if something was awry in the bowels of the shop. He remembered a joke he had heard in school: *We paint your car for only a hundred dollars! Windows included!*

"What will it say on the side?" he asked.

"You'll see."

"I am paralyzed by apprehension."

"Chill, baby. I designed the props for *Annie*. I built the street set for *West Side Story*. Color, composition… I get it. You want to stand apart from the crowd. You want to show the world how beautiful you are."

Arjun chafed. "I just want to show them beautiful food."

"Well," she said, sidling up to him. "You are what you eat, right? You are also what you make."

"An eggroll is foreign," he said.

"Yes."

"A burrito is American."

"Yes."

Arjun stared at the dirty floor. *Give me your tired, your poor, your huddled masses.* He was a stranger in a strange land. He stood out as much from the people around him as a black sheep from its flock. Yet something in him resonated with his surroundings. Something in him was American.

He thought of the millions of immigrants who had come through Ellis Island. They had fled their homelands to heed the call of a future stronger than sentiment or fear. They had risked it all for a dream.

A wiry man in an orange jumpsuit burst into the room. He pulled off his goggles and set them on the counter. "Had a little chippin' by the taillights. I took care of that. Had some rust under the fenders. Took care of that too. People think they need new cars when all they need is new paint."

"Were you able to match the red?" Candy asked.

"Sure. I can match anything. A woman came in with a VW Beetle, wanted me to match her polka-dot dress. So I did." He reached into his pocket and pulled out a bright-red bird's-eye chili pepper. "Here you go. Still good."

"What's that?" Arjun asked.

"It's a Thai chili," Candy said.

"Thai?"

"I thought you might like it."

Arjun thought of Seiko, of her fusion of cuisines and people. He thought of how she had changed him just by passing along ideas. He had absorbed something from her. And now he was more himself.

"Let's take a look," the painter said.

They walked through the door, down the hallway, and into the shop. The truck gleamed under the fluorescent lights. Candy had changed everything—the colors, the pictures, even the name. Arjun looked at the side panel, emblazoned with children skipping rope in a crowded barrio, teenage boys and girls flirting on the street corner, and old men playing cards on a stoop. Each was munching a red, yellow, orange, or green pepper. He read the words:

TEXI-DELHI
Curry Burritos
*Juarez * Pocho*
*Carne Asada * Carnitas * Shrimp * Chicken*

He scanned the painted horizon, a sunrise bursting through the clouds, a backdrop he knew well. Eagles and hawks dotted the sky. Pigeons waddled over the grounds. Colorful food trucks snaked around the back doors, calling out to long lines of brown- and yellow- and white-skinned people winding over the landscape.

"Do you like it?" Candy said.

"Yes."

He walked around the truck. He saw the steps to the courthouse and the benches by the dogwoods and the rows of shining office buildings. He saw a man in an American-flag ball cap pushing a silver cart. He saw kids on skateboards and roller blades. Finally, on the hood, he found a picture of a food truck with a smiling woman at the window and a man in a cowboy hat standing by a fryer.

It was a golden, deep-fried dream.

21 | Gourmet Battle of the Vans™

Jared awoke to the clanging of metal. A truck was parked behind him, belching smoke. A chain on a spool was pulling his car off the asphalt and up a ramp. He braced his feet against the floor and watched the pavement recede.

He rolled down his window.

"Get out!" Melinda said, standing by the front fender.

"What the—"

"No permit, no parking," she said, grabbing a flyer from under the windshield wipers. "You should read your mail."

"What the—"

"We have an event today. Maybe you've heard of it? Get out of the car unless you want to spend the day basting in a lot in Franconia."

Jared grabbed his laptop. "You're towing me?"

"Get off the truck."

Jared fell out the door. "You want me to sit on a curb all day? I am about to *launch the app.*"

"You're in the way of the jugglers."

"Jugglers?"

"And fortune-tellers."

He inched down the ramp. "What, you don't need help with this? You're already killin' it? You're already Guy Fieri?"

"We have to move the car."

"You don't like me."

"You are *not likable.*"

"I have been working. For you!"

"Not for me!"

"You owe me!"

"I don't owe you!"

"Well, you *will.*"

"Whatever. I need to supervise the setup. You can hang around, I don't care. You can sit backstage. In one of the folding chairs."

Jared gave Melinda the stink eye.

"Don't get in the way."

He watched the truck disappear around the side of the courthouse. He looked at the statue of George Wythe. Nobody gave a man forty acres and a mule anymore. Nobody cared.

He sat down on the curb. A crew of men unloaded the sound equipment from a truck, grunting and calling to one another as they rolled huge speakers down a ramp. They stacked the cabinets across the stage and ran lights up the rigging.

"Faster!" Melinda shouted.

Antwaan sped down Broadnax Street, popping wheelies, showing off for the patio crowds with their tablets and newspapers. He hopped a curb and skittered down the sidewalk, nearly sideswiping a feisty Scottie. He flew into the crosswalk with barely a glance. The sun blinded him as he dodged a man in a wheelchair. *Darkness cannot drive out darkness*, he thought. *Only light can do that.*

He coasted down to the stage, skidded to a halt, and tossed his bike to the ground. "Yo, Melinda McCoy! Sound the trumpets! The Assassin is here to lead your people to the Promised Land!"

"Have a seat," Melinda said, her eyes on the light rig.

"A change is gonna come!" Antwaan shouted. "Ain't nobody turning Sam Cooke away from no motel in Shreveport today! Look out, Memphis! Back up, Birmingham! Time to testify!"

"Calm down."

"I never *been* more calm, lady!"

"Calm down."

"You can't calm down a revival! Can't muzzle the Assassin!"

Antwaan jammed his hands in his pockets. The days practicing in the basement with only orange roughy to sustain him, the nights preaching to an empty room at the Annex, had all been worth it. He was headlining. And this was no blow in the park, no kiddie birthday party. It was a festival with a stage the size of a middle-school gym. Hundreds of people would be transported by the call of the Assassin.

An old Buick rolled up to the stage. Billy and Justin spilled out and started pulling drums out of the back seat.

"Drum stool on the duct-tape X!" Melinda shouted, pointing to the back of the stage. "They'll mic you up."

Melinda tapped Antwaan on the shoulder. "Hey, see that rope?" she said, pointing to the rafters. "It's hooked to those scrolls. When you start to perform, you pull the rope and the scrolls fall. See?"

"Yeah," he said. "I've seen those before."

"They've got pictures of a hamburger and fried zucchini. You shout 'get your Bomb on!' or 'Bombs away!' and point everybody to the trucks. Then you talk about how you're going to get something to eat as soon as you're done up there."

"Uh-huh."

Melinda marched to her truck and disappeared through the door. Antwaan walked to the back of the stage, to the statue of George Wythe, and lifted a pair of cylinders from the tall grass. He mounted the ladder and hauled them to the top of the scaffolding, snapped Melinda's scrolls out of the rollers, and replaced them with his own.

Aubrey wandered through the carnival alley, her eyes bouncing over booths of cotton candy and stuffed animals and ducks on the wall. She watched a carny slapping together a stand where a seer might tell a fortune. She saw a clown applying makeup. She watched men tightening bolts on the carousel, their wrenches black with oil. It reminded her of the Broadnax Fair, when Daddy was around, when he carried her on his shoulders and ran through the crowd. He tossed beanbags at Sylvester and Tweety Bird while she covered his eyes with her little hands. She remembered the soft-serve ice cream dripping onto his collar and buttons.

The carousel spun through its test run, blinking and dinging a Katy Perry song about a teenage dream. The horses passed, faces unchanging, front legs raised in a jaunty trot. Aubrey thought of the school bus running from Columbia Pike to Glebe Road to the condo canyons, the same sights whirling by each day while she stroked the tip of the Exacto knife in the pocket of her windbreaker.

She stood before the funhouse mirror and saw a distorted girl staring back. A tilt of the head transformed her into a cartoon character. She laughed. *This is how God sees me,* she thought. *Sad and silly.* She danced before the glass, her chest and hips thrusting in mock flirtation, her shoes jutting out like clown footwear. She pressed her nose to the mirror and made a duck face.

Jared watched her from his folding chair.

She turned and caught him staring.

The pepper-red food truck careened onto the lot, rolling on the edges of its tires. Arjun shivered with excitement. Candy fidgeted in the passenger seat, smiling in anticipation, her feet on the dash. She turned the recipes over in her mind. *Classic burrito, curry burrito, variations on classic and curry burritos.* She looked at her notes. *Add red pepper, cayenne, and brown sugar. Replace sprouts with romaine lettuce and carrots with yellow peppers. Add cinnamon whiskey.* She thought of the fryer and the oil and the faces at the window, a gauzy fantasy primed for real life. She surveyed the lot, teeming like some tent city.

"We should shred the cheese, not slice it," she said.

"Okay."

"And we should shred the cabbage too."

"Yes, okay."

"Look!" she said. "Up by George Wythe."

"Eddie!" Arjun shouted, leaning out his window. "The *dost* with the most! Come on down!"

Eddie wheeled his cart down the carnival alley, around a target-practice game called Big Bertha, past a scowling clown who resembled the famous Emmett Kelly Sr. He waved at Arjun and Candy in uncharacteristic amity, his 23rd Infantry Division ball cap shining in the sun.

"I want to be in the truck!" he shouted.

"You will *be in the truck*!" Arjun said.

"I want to feed the people!"

"You will *feed the people*!"

"Awright!" Eddie said, huffing and puffing as he rolled up to the Texi-Delhi step van. "Let's go."

Melinda hadn't seen her daughter in over an hour. She realized an absent Aubrey was an endangered Aubrey, a girl with the imagination of a kindergartner and the life experience of a coddled family pet. She scanned the booths—the twister of balloons, the guesser of weights, the arbiter of air rifles—and found only leers and strange odors. She envisioned Aubrey hiding in a ladies' room at the courthouse, or locking herself into a porta-john, carving a ravine in her forearm with a paring knife from Burger Bombs. Her eyelids twitched as she imagined sirens ringing from the food-truck court to the courthouse to the offices of EverSafe Solutions.

She broke into a trot, flogging herself for letting Aubrey out of her sight, biting back on a rush of acid reflux. *If you love her, set her free.* But Aubrey wasn't ready to be free. She wasn't prepared for a world that would nibble at her appendages until it swallowed her whole like a goldfish. No, Aubrey wasn't ready for real life or the real world or anything that might, in any light, appear real. Melinda remembered her laughing little girl barreling around the house in bunny pajamas, underfoot while Jim tacked up a family photo in the entrance hall. She could still see Aubrey tumbling down the stairs after knotting her ankles in the tangles of her blanky, landing with a thud and cackling with laughter. It was just another gambit in the life of a playful toddler. Nothing could hurt her because nothing was real.

But it was all real now. When had reality set in? On the first day of kindergarten? Of middle school? No, it had been incremental, a gradual loss of security as it invaded the psyche of her little girl. One day Aubrey had awakened to find reality living inside her like a tapeworm.

"Aubs? *Aubrey!*"

Melinda sprinted down the alley, around the corner, and to the handicapped parking spaces in front of the courthouse. She squinted past the benches, to the edge of the corporate campus. There she saw her darling daughter, squatting on the curb under a Kousa dogwood, laughing and relaxed, feeding the pigeons.

She exhaled.

Jared sat in his folding chair behind the stage. The screen on his phone animated a word like a rainbow: FOODSTR. The app executed its routine, from the montage to the menu to the buttons popping up like heads in a game of whack-a-mole. He looked around the lot. Fifteen minutes to opening, and no one was waiting. He logged in. *Compose, Edit, Target, Schedule, Send.* The notification was locked and loaded, waiting to be sprayed like buckshot over the hacked phones of Broadnax County. He imagined a field of land mines detonating.

He hit "send."

Melinda's phone vibrated. She checked her screen. *HUNGRY?* She tapped the badge with her thumb and saw Bollywood Eggrolls, Saturday Sundaes, Three Bucketeers, The Pig Rig, Doughnut Hounds. She shivered with excitement. Who was doing this? Where was it coming from?

"Look, everyone!" she shouted.

A map of the surrounding area appeared. *FOLLOW ME TO THE BEST FOOD IN BROADNAX.* A dotted red line skipped from the lot entrance to the food-truck court. It paused in the corner and circled icons of the five trucks.

But wait. Where was Burger Bombs?

Arjun, Candy, and Eddie followed the action on their phones, a scroll of culinary delights. Sharon and Sully cheered. Ron, Debbie, and the Finn Brothers paced around their trucks, watching a miracle unfold.

"*Where is Burger Bombs?*" Melinda wailed.

Eddie pointed toward the courthouse. "Incoming!"

People of all sizes and descriptions—kids, parents, young singles, middle-aged couples, Blacks, Whites, and Latinos—were pouring into the lot, their heads down, following the directions on their phones.

"Security!" Melinda shouted. "Stamp their hands! Put them in line!"

A guard in an EverSafe Solutions uniform stumbled out of a porta-john. The crowd ignored him, forming its own shapes, surging toward the food trucks.

"*Check*," Billy grunted into the mic, slinging his guitar to one side and throwing his hair back. "*Check*, one, two, three."

"Wait!" Melinda barked, running up the steps to the stage. "Good morning!" she shouted into the mic. "Welcome to the First Annual Broadnax County Gourmet Battle of the Vans. We have worked so hard to create this special event for you. It's the best brunch in Broadnax! We have music and clowns and games and vendors and a carousel. So, grab a burger! Or, you know, whatever! Have fun!" She paused to collect her thoughts. "And now, please welcome, um, Billy... and, um..." She turned around and read the words on the tie-dyed sheet hanging from the rafters. "*Quantum Leap!*"

"What's up, Broadnax?" Billy shouted. "Are you ready to party?" He slashed the strings of his Squier Strat, gripping the neck in an open E chord. Justin fired a roll off the snare and splashed the cymbals. "When you take to the streets," Billy intoned, "and the day is long, and the sun is hot and high in the sky... you know you can do anything. Because you're *invincible*, right? You're freaking Superman! But then all of a sudden something weird happens… and you're, like, oh no, shit, what's this… and your arms get weak and your legs are like noodles, and your vision gets all blurry like you're about to faint. And you start losing control of your *mind*. You can barely remember your name! And you're, like, WTF? What is going on? Well, I'll tell you what, people. It's *her*! She's *Kryptonite*! And she is sapping your strength!" Billy locked into the chorused guitar figure he had played a thousand times before. Justin joined in on the kick drum and then the snare. "Will you still be my friend at the end?" Billy sang, his voice cracking. "Will you still call me Superman?"

"Yeah!" Justin shouted.

Billy glared at the crowd, his eyes sizzling in a flare of rage and yearning. Justin exploded into double-time, his snare echoing through the lot. Billy held his guitar over his head and stood before the little Peavey amp, coaxing a shriek of feedback from its speaker.

"Dude always comes back!" Billy shouted. "Dude always survives!" The duo summoned a thundering *thrump* and basked in a smattering of applause. *Festival crowd*. "We're Quantum Leap," Billy said, catching his breath. "That means, like, a really big jump. Like when you travel through time. Or when you go through a wormhole to some other galaxy." He squinted at the carousel spinning and dinging. He saw the little kids holding the hands of their parents, safe and secure. He saw the teenagers roaming in packs, cigarettes between their fingers, staking out the periphery. "Okay, listen up, 'cause we wrote a song," he said. "It's about a girl. Yeah… it's about a girl who is, like, in a car, and she is leaving home. She is going someplace totally new and far away. She is making a *quantum leap*." He scanned the crowd. "Candy? Candy, are you out there?"

He stroked the soft, minor-key progression, his fingertips alive with anticipation. "Okay," he whispered into the mic. "It goes like this." He shot a glance at Justin and started to sing. "Girl in a car, on the road, doesn't know how far she's gone. Girl on the run, far from home, doesn't see how much she's grown. Girl, girl, you're lost in the world. Can you trade your swine for pearls? Oh, oh, oh, oh, ohhhhhh." He strutted to the edge of the stage, his eyes radiating soulfulness. "Girl in a car, on the street, doesn't know who she will meet. Girl on her own, lost in love, doesn't know that love can bleed. Girl, girl, your life is a pearl. Can you share it with the world? Oh, oh, oh, oh, ohhhhhh." He repeated the sequence: A-minor, C, E-minor, G, two beats each, riding the backbeat in a distorted alternative earworm. "Oh, oh, girl. You're the light of love in the world. A beautiful song and a twinkling star. My girl in a car."

The crowd was silent.

"Yay, Billy!" Candy shouted from the Texi-Delhi window. "Yay, Justin!"

"Thank you!" Billy said, a smile of relief spreading over his face. "That one is for you, Candy! Because you gave it to me."

"*Hey!*" a voice exploded in front of the stage, next to the booth with the beanbag toss. "Who you talkin' about? Who you talkin' to?" It was Bobby, plum-faced and sweaty, swigging from a bottle and waving his fist. "Who the fuck?"

"I'm the fuck," Billy said into the mic. "And I could split your head open with this tuning peg." He reached down the neck and turned the peg half a rotation, sending the low E string dive-bombing to low B. "Hear that? Sounds like a plane crash. Sounds like you were on the plane."

"Dude…" Justin whispered.

"You man enough for a plane crash?" Billy shouted.

The crowd hooted and clapped. Billy pulled his guitar over his head and held the end of the neck in both hands, twirling it like a baseball bat.

"Security!" Melinda screamed from the Burger Bombs window.

Bobby bolted up the steps. In a flash, he tripped on a guitar cord, stumbled over a mic stand, and flew, face first, into the corner of the drum riser. Blood gushed from his nose.

Billy tossed the strap over his shoulder and grabbed the mic. "You're my beautiful song and my twinkling star," he sang, his voice reverberating. "My girl in a car."

Candy glowed. "Are we about ready?" she asked Arjun. "Because I think *they* are."

"We must allow the flavors to mingle," Arjun said, stacking his creations under the heat lamp. He jiggled the basket in the oil. "Let the burrito sweat until it crunches like a pakora baked in the Texas sun. I impart this to you, cactus flower—the rapprochement of art and life."

"They're leaving," Candy said.

"They will come back."

"I'm serious."

Arjun handed Candy a tray. "Feed our multitudes," he said. "The ones who left were never ours."

Candy greeted the first customer. "What can I do you for?" She looked into the lot and saw Tim Samsara, fighting a sloppy Burger Bomb, his shirt stained with Dijon mustard. She saw Brad Paxton, working the crowd, his hands tracing the backbones of matrons and teenage girls. She saw the perps from the courthouse, free on work release, families in tow, eyes scanning the lot for the American dream. She saw Charlene, chomping on a drumstick and scowling at a baby in a knit cap.

She spied Bobby, detained at the side of the stage by the security guard from EverSafe Solutions.

She felt the fertile space between her and Arjun, the soil from which her life would soon spring. It felt big and vague inside her, like the glow of bourbon in her belly on a Saturday night.

She heard the customers chattering as they ate their burritos. "Hints of Delhi," one said. "Notes of San An-tone."

Billy and Justin ground to a halt at the end of Hoobastank's "The Reason," their heads mops of sweat, their eyes glowing.

Melinda climbed the steps and took the mic. "Let's hear it for Quantum Leap! Reminds me of the good old days! Okay, everybody, fasten your seatbelts. Our headliner is a rough-and-tumble ghetto prince from Southeast. From his bio... 'Growing up at 4th and Morse, he could have been a pusher, could have been a pimp. Daddy wasn't around. Mama worked three jobs. Slept on the bottom bunk to dodge stray bullets coming through the window. Crawled to the bathroom on all fours. Then one day he heard Fiddy and Jay and Biggie and 'Pac, and everything changed. He found he had a *gift*. And he knew he had to find somebody to give it to.' This energetic young man has a way with words. He talks my ear off! And he loves burgers! Please join me, on the stage of the Gourmet Battle of the Vans, in welcoming... *The Assassin!*"

"Yo!" Antwaan shouted. "Whazzup? You my people, and I'm your boy! And I come to this sorry patch of asphalt to lead you *out of the desert*, to what some y'all call the Black Canaan. But yo, Moses was Black, so it's *just Canaan*. I come to take you to the Promised Land. Yeah, yeah, I'm just a rapper. And it ain't all that. But a few years back, I was just a kid on a bike with two flat tires, hangin' at the corner store boostin' magazines and chocolate bars while my brother hit on the shorties. I was wastin' my life. My best friend was dealin' crack! Those little rocks was like candy, somethin' sweet everybody wanted, somethin' that made my boy *somebody* when he was a nobody to everybody but me. But he couldn't keep the sweets, no, and now he's gone to live with Jesus. Props to the Father! I know my boy is sittin' at the right hand, sippin' Cristal. But today, y'all, you know what? We're all still here. We still have a job to do. And you're probably thinkin', yo, shit, how do we do it? Well, I'll tell you. We look back. We *check the past* so we can *know the future*. We say, 'how did we get here?' and, hell, it ain't hard to see. It's right there in front of us. It's like some pigeon waddlin' around this lot, like that little chump over there with its dumb, beady eyes, waitin' for us to *feed it*. And if that ain't plain as day, I don't know what is! This shit was happenin' on the *Mayflower*. It was happenin' in the Declaration and the Emancipation. It's in every water fountain torn out of the walls in the schools of Birmingham and Montgomery. And it's *right here*, too, in this lot. Some crazy motherfucker shot MLK in his head. How 'bout that? He was like Biggie and 'Pac, bigger dead than alive. Homey had a dream, yo, he did, but after he was dead it was a dream for *everybody*."

Antwaan hit the beatbox. "I wrote this song in my crib. It's called 'Founding Father.'" He walked to the side of the stage and yanked the rope. The scrolls fell, bouncing like flags. "You see those?" he said, pointing to the banners. "That's our boy, Thomas Jefferson. Monticello motherfucker. He was a Foundin' Father, spreadin' his seed. Dude was prolific. And Sally Hemings, you know, she called her little ones Hemings, not Jefferson, 'cause they was slaves. That was some shit! Be fruitful and multiply, all you Puritan bastards. Listen up now. Did you know, while you sitting there all happy and satisfied and full of yo' box lunch, that *we all slaves*?" He turned up the beatbox.

Life and liberty, yo
But I don't know
'Bout happiness
'Bout happiness
A land of the free
On a roiling sea
Ain't happiness
Ain't happiness
Life and liberty ain't a flag unfurled
Ain't a scroll of lies in a fallen world
Who's your daddy, boy?
Uh-huh, uh-huh
Who's your Founding Father?

"Yeah!" he shouted. "When I was in school, I said to my mama, 'Yo, why we got pictures of Thomas Jefferson all over the damn house?' And she said, 'Ask your daddy'! Well, I asked him, and he didn't say. But I figured it out!"

Life and liberty, y'all
At every port of call
Like the KKK
Like the KKK
At the end of a rope
In the hairs of a scope
Like the MLK
On the judgment day
Life and liberty lost in history
The future ain't no mystery
Who's your daddy, boy?
Uh-huh, uh-huh
Who's your Founding Father?

The crowd erupted in cheers. Antwaan spied the crew from the Annex—the bartender, the bouncer, the stage manager—eating Bombs, moving to the rhythm, bringing the party downtown. "Yo, I spent some time over there," he said, pointing to the courthouse. "I got a little expressive with my bladder, like a bird in a fountain. You and me, you know, we're just like animals. Free to roam!"

He launched into "Sweet Roundy," a paean to the geometric allure of the female backside. Women were a marvel of symmetry, he implored, from their minds to their hearts to their downy, waxed cheeks. They were seraphs. As part of their duties as celestial emissaries, they embarked on Dionysian adventures to get down with the boys and make the world a funkier place.

"Woo-hoo, Antwaan!" Aubrey shouted. She was starting to relax, to realize this was just another day of people and situations. She tried some tenuous breaking, locking, and popping, stumbling and hitting her marks, drawing hoots from the carnies and the hip-hop kids. She saw Jared sitting in his folding chair and bopped over to him.

"Hey," she said.

He looked up. "Hey."

"You always look hungry."

"What?"

"Like you need to eat something."

"I haven't had any breakfast," he said.

"Like I said."

"Yeah."

"Do you want to get something to eat?"

"Not right now."

"You should eat."

"I should do a lot of things."

"It's not good to skip meals."

"Really?" he smiled.

"Really."

"Okay."

"What are you doing back here?" she asked.

"Waiting for you."

"No, you're not."

"Yeah, I'm not. But I'm glad I did."

"You're weird."

"Aren't you weird?"

"I guess. I mean, I do some weird things, so…"

"Like cutting yourself."

"Yeah."

"And hanging out with your dopey mom?"

"Yeah."

"You're weird," he said.

"Yeah, well, so are you."

"Everybody is weird. If you're not weird, you're probably super-dumb."

"Yeah, I know."

"You do?" he asked.

"I said I did." She sensed him moving closer. "I should probably go."

"Are you gonna drop out of school?"

"What? No."

"I'm going to Cupertino."

"Um, sure."

"I see stuff other people don't, okay? I can, like, see around corners and feel people's energy. Sometimes I know what they're thinking. I'm gonna go to Cupertino and walk into that spaceship building and find Tim Cook. I'm gonna show him Foodstr. And then I'm gonna get a Tesla and live in Mountain View and sell my company to investors."

Aubrey stood still, pinned like a pretty photo to a bulletin board.

"You don't like school," he said. "You don't like anything, I can tell. It's like you're trapped. Like a caged animal. But I've got space in my car. You can come along. We can hit the open road. We'll see things we've never seen. We'll do whatever we want. How about that?"

"I don't know."

"Yes, you do," he said.

"Um…" she said, her eyes blurring. "I…"

She had kissed a boy once in the ball pen at Chuck E. Cheese, and it had been totally gross. He had tasted like peanut butter. She assumed that was the way it always was, with somebody's teeth smashing your lips, but this was different. Jared was licking her ears and caressing her neck, whispering fascinating observations about her eyes and the aroma of her perfume. He was telling her she was beautiful.

She kissed him back. "I don't feel beautiful."

"You are gorgeous," he said.

"I hate looking in the mirror."

"Maybe you need a new mirror."

"Like a funhouse mirror?"

"Fun is good."

Aubrey laughed. Every boy she knew was a dumb jock or an awkward nerd or a straight-laced mama's boy with no boyfriend potential. Jared was like a wild animal. He lived outside. He was detached from polite society. He didn't seek approval from his parents or his teachers or even his peers. He followed a vision only he could see.

It was a lot better than algebra.

She felt his hands on her ribs, on her waist, on the small of her back. He fell to his knees and kissed her belly. He pulled her under the platform, into the shadows, onto the cool grass. She heard his shoes clanging against the light rig. She thought she saw the frame sway against the clear, blue sky, imagined she saw the lights teetering in the sun. He unbuttoned her jeans. She felt dizzy. His feet bucked against the supports.

His eyes shot open.

A crash enveloped them, shaking the stage, splitting the air like a bomb, and collapsing the supports. Echoes pounded the walls of the courthouse and EverSafe Solutions. Screams filled the lot. The pair struggled to move but found their bodies pressed together like slices of processed cheese.

The speakers shrieked, stuck in a deafening feedback loop. Aubrey saw feet sprinting past on the asphalt. She plugged her ears. Was this the way it ended? *I'm sorry, Mom. I was just so sad.* She tried to wriggle free, but Jared's torso held her in place like a bun on a Bomb.

"I'm trapped!" she squealed.

The sound dive-bombed from the shimmer of the cymbals to the bleats of the vocals to the rumble of the bass, shaking the stage, roaring like a propane tank exploding in the step van of the Three Bucketeers. The feedback hit a blistering crescendo. The light rig fell onto the statue of George Wythe, the scrolls of Thomas Jefferson tumbled into the cotton candy stand, and the scaffolding crashed to the booths of carnival alley. Antwaan jumped off the stage and sprinted toward the courthouse.

"Incoming!" Eddie shouted. He ran out the door of Texi-Delhi, stumbled over the staircase, and dashed toward the stage. He saw a little boy and a little girl, pinwheels spinning in their hands, and scooped one up in each arm. He rumbled across the lot and sat them under the dogwoods. "Heads down! Don't make a sound!" He scanned the alley for fallen comrades. "Edward John O'Day!" he announced, grabbing the dog tags jangling around his neck. "Reporting for duty!" He wrapped an arm around a mother and her baby and guided them across the lot. He looked at the fallen stage, at the mangled light rig on the courthouse lawn, at the massive scaffolding that had obliterated Justin's drum kit on impact. The speakers wailed, slicing the air, sending birds fleeing into the skies. "Incoming!" he shouted again. He scooped up an old woman and held her against his chest. "Hold on, baby, we're going home!" He deposited her frame under the trees, his heart pounding, his lungs heaving. Seeing the lot empty, he dropped to his knees. "Oh, God. Jesus fucking Christ. Keep them safe this time, will you? I was a dumb kid failing history and I did what those fuckers told me to! I tried, you *know* I tried, you know I would gladly have been blown to bits or burned alive never to lay eyes on their beautiful goddamn faces! Fuck you, asshole! A fucking *lifetime* of this! Oh God, oh God, *oh God.*" He sobbed and buried his face in his hands.

"Sir?" a voice said.

Eddie looked up. He thought he glimpsed a halo.

"Are you all right, sir?" It was a police officer.

"I'm okay…" Eddie glanced up at the rays of the sun falling through the clouds. He squinted at the sky, vast and sprawling and bluer than he remembered ever seeing it. "Thank you," he said.

Pidgey's heart fluttered. Cher Ami would know what to do when lives were at stake, when fear had the upper wing, when the split-second decision of a lone bird would shape lives for generations to come. He thought of Melinda, of the way she had bent his leg to affix the sticky note, of the way she had called him filthy and said, "do your thing, rat with wings." She knew nothing about him, or his parents, or his siblings lost in the DC derecho, or about his commitment to service. She was just a dumb human, no different from those who enslaved their own to enrich themselves, who fed on pain, who competed while feigning cooperation, who kept a scorecard of the times they got the best of their own flesh and blood in every trivial endeavor.

He stood up. A rat would eat anything. A discerning pigeon, however, sought fresh mushrooms, sautéed lightly with a little extra virgin olive oil and salt, with the edges slightly browned. He cooed to his comrades, who gathered around him in a semicircle. *The arc of the moral universe is long, but it bends toward justice.*

He set out across the pavement. He waddled toward the Burger Bombs truck, his compatriots following with military precision. He flapped through the window and onto the countertop, its surface slick with beef fat. The pigeons sank their beaks into the shiitakes, kicking utensils off the counters, knocking spice shakers off the shelves with their wings.

The birds took perches around the kitchen, from the grill to the fryer to the stainless steel sink, and opened their bowels in a blast of collective relief. The walls assumed the optics of a Jackson Pollock painting, spattered with colors and big, dripping blobs, rendered in creative freedom.

Pidgey nodded.

Sirens rang across the lot. Uniformed personnel leaped from vehicles. A fireman walked to the side of the stage, twiddled a knob on the sound board, and yanked an electrical cord out of its socket.

Silence.

22 | The Secret Additive

It wasn't a disaster. Although the stage had collapsed, causing a light rig to fall to the platform and obliterate a drum set, thrusting the sound system into a cacophonous feedback loop and driving the crowd into a stampede, wiping smiles off the faces of the clowns, sobering the carnies, and leaving the food trucks with more food than they could possibly use, Arjun felt the Broadnax County Gourmet Battle of the Vans™ had been a glowing success. Yesterday the lot was a village of plucky startups, refining their recipes, dreaming of the day Bobby Flay would call with an offer to compete in a shopping cart race. Today it was a spot on the map, a destination. Videos were circulating on phones.

"That," Candy said, laughing, "was a total disaster."

"No, no," Arjun said. "It was a breakthrough. For all of us."

Candy giggled and dropped into a folding chair outside.

Arjun looked around the lot, at the police interviewing witnesses, at the artisans packing up their booths, at the children climbing trees. He looked at the sky, at the vapor trails over Reagan National, at the clouds in their inscrutable float. Maybe it was just the caffeine. Maybe it was love. Or maybe it was something in his gut that had been sleeping, a creature now awake and hungry.

He scrubbed away the spilled curry and horseradish sauce and juice of the jalapeño peppers. He swept crumbs into his palm and dropped them in the trash. He swiped chunks of golden batter from the fryer and set them aside on a paper towel for the pigeons.

As if on cue, Pidgey appeared in the pass-through, his little head bobbing, and coasted over to the counter.

"Hello, friend!" Arjun said. "Are you enjoying your day? Have you foraged? Have you sought suitable mating options?"

Pidgey shifted his weight from foot to foot.

"Texi-Delhi filled more orders this morning than the disembodied heads filled all of last month. It is a big success, like winning the Super Bowl. Perhaps we will go to Disney World. Do you enjoy Wheaties, my avian friend? They are whole-grain healthy. Perhaps we will put our heads together and create a Wheaties burrito in your honor."

Pidgey's stomach growled, rocking him backward onto his tail feathers.

"It will be our crunchiest entry. A breakfast burrito. But not like Taco Bell. We will imbue it with the finest ingredients. We will infuse it with the secret additive. Do you know what that is, friend?"

Pidgey dragged his wings through the batter.

"It is caring."

Arjun looked at the community-service workers with their trash picks, skewering food wrappers and drink cups and dropping them in bags. He saw Melinda by a police cruiser, protesting some citation. He glimpsed Aubrey and Jared against the Burger Bombs truck, arms akimbo, lips entwined. He saw Sharon and Sully and Ron and Debbie, chatting and swaying to a famous old ballad by Dion. He saw Eddie standing in the midday sun, beaming to the sky. He thought of Candy's laughter as she lay on the pillow. It was a beautiful day. Despite everything.

"I have been wondering something, friend," Arjun said, throwing his voice over his shoulder. "If you have wings... then why don't you fly?"

Plunk. Hsssss.

Arjun turned. He gasped. He stumbled past the sink. *No.* He bolted to the fryer. *No.* Pidgey was floating in the oil like a little tugboat without a job to do. Arjun winced. He scooped the squab into the net and laid it on the countertop. It looked like his grandfather at the funeral home, pale and lifeless and all dressed up with no place to go. Arjun reached down and touched the bird's breast. It was still and firm and crunchy, a glistening, golden brown.

It was deep-fried.

He stumbled out the door.

Antwaan unlocked his bike from the rack. He rolled off the hillside and down to the sidewalk, yanked on the handlebars, and popped a wheelie. His performance had been a tour de force. Word would travel fast. No doubt his phone would ring in his pocket as he hung the next corner, or when he hit the lot.

He tore down the sidewalk, narrowly missing a telephone pole, dodging young women and their wide-eyed toddlers, dreaming of a day when his parents would understand what he had been doing all these years. He wasn't drifting. He wasn't lost. He was *MLK on the judgment day, murdering words in a world gone cray*. He flew into the lot, gliding across the gravel as he approached the food trucks. He slammed on the brakes, planted his sneaker on the asphalt, and turned out the back end of the bike in a fat fishtail.

"That's right, y'all!" he shouted. "Give it up for the Assassin! Tappin' your feet to the homeboy beat!" He darted around the corner, past Saturday Sundaes and Doughnut Hounds, toward the Texi-Delhi van. "Yo!" he shouted with glee. "*Ar-joon!*"

He saw Candy sitting in her chair, sunglasses shielding her fair skin, a smile spreading across her lips. He whooped and stood up on the pedals. In a flash, he saw a familiar figure stumble out the truck door. He swerved. He gripped the handlebars and spun them, but it was too late.

He staggered the man, sending him reeling backward.

Arjun rolled on the balls of his feet and tumbled into the step van. He threw out his arms to regain his balance, but spun into the fender, collapsing and striking his temple on the corner of the front bumper. He lay still.

"Mother of Exiles!" Antwaan wailed.

"Baby!" Candy howled, springing to his side. She forced air into his lungs, shaking him, gripping his wrist between her thumb and forefinger. "*No! No! Someone!*"

A paramedic, tending to the mild heatstroke of a matron across the lot, grabbed his kit and sprinted across the asphalt. He wedged himself between Candy and Arjun. He took the young man's vitals, spread gel over his chest, and pressed a pair of metal paddles into his flesh, sending bolts of voltage through his torso. *Ka-plunk!*

Ripples in the oil.

Arjun sailed over the farms and gravel roads, over the treetops and rock formations that jutted like sculptures from the foothills of the Blue Ridge. He soared over the strip malls and historic markers and municipal monuments, marking his trail, following a map seared in his mind. He glided onto the hospital roof, by the dynamos and the dirty skylights, past the cafeteria and the indoor pool, to a steel door secured with a deadbolt. He passed through the portal and floated down a hallway that led to the offices of the doctors and the administrators. He heard them complaining about parsimonious insurance companies and subpar medical equipment. He saw them admiring each other's golf clubs. He opened the cabinet and read the confidential medical histories dotted with terse, handwritten notations like "won't be long" and "gone soon." Inside a folder marked with the name Seiko Okuhara, he read a message scratched on a yellow sticky note: "Why is she here?"

He stood at Seiko's bedside, clad in a dark, tailored suit, a strange hat in his hand, a handkerchief folded in his breast pocket. He took her hand and rubbed the flesh of her palm with his thumbs. "Where are you?" he asked. "And where am I?" He thought of Jiyū, cool and glowing, a nourishing oasis in a desert of need.

"I am not coming back," she said.

"Why?"

"There is no why."

"There is," he said.

Seiko opened her eyes and looked at him. Her pupils were dilated, deep and dark like floodwaters. He was being carried away in her current. He saw the detritus, the sofas and the subcompact cars, the torn-out trees and children's toys, the roofs and rugs and patio chairs. He watched the ants rush by without their colonies, lost and alone. He saw the netting and the bubbles and the crunchy little beads of batter, bobbing up and down.

He watched her vanish in the oil.

Pidgey winced. He was stiff and creaky, encased in a crisp, golden glaze. *If you have wings, then why don't you fly?* He willed the muscles of his feet to move, stretching his legs on the cutting board, rustling his wings. Every part of his body was tender, as if he had flown into the back of a truck. He rolled off the cutting board, onto the countertop, and into the sink.

Plunk.

His feathers soaked in the suds, dissolving the crunchy bits, freeing him, crumb by crumb, from the bonds of batter. He flapped his wings and grunted, splashing water across the counter and into the fryer.

Hsssss.

He climbed to the edge of the sink. He remembered the Lost Battalion, demoralized by friendly fire. He thought of the only pigeon still alive, carrying a plea for help through a hail of bullets. He wobbled to the sill.

He took a breath, spread his wings, and soared into the sky.

Pidgey saw his brothers and sisters in the derecho, torn by gusts from their perches. He heard their cries and watched them vanish into the black. He rose into the clouds and felt the sun on his wings. It was preparation, all of it, from the days in the egg to the weeks in the nest to the months on the cool, green grass.

He had a message to deliver.

He dove earthward. He saw the ants in their toils, erecting boxes of dirt and stone to protect themselves from unseen dangers. He saw them killing each other.

He was Cher Ami.

He spread his wings to steady his dive but caught a blast of wind and tumbled through the air. He saw the sun, the trees, the courthouse, and the buildings and the benches, the trucks and the cracks like capillaries in the pavement. He saw his reflection in the windshield of the Texi-Delhi truck. He shrieked and flapped and crashed into the skull of Arjun Chatterjee.

His beak snapped. His lungs collapsed. He was still.

Candy cried out. Arjun and Pidgey lay side by side like a pair of bowling pins after a spare.

Arjun stirred.

"Baby!" she said.

He opened his eyes.

"Oh, my God!" She looked at the pigeon on the pavement, motionless. "Pidgey—"

Arjun groaned.

Candy saw the yellow sticky note wrapped around the bird's leg. She peeled back the adhesive, slipped the note off the bird's foot, and opened it.

It was blank.

Arjun took her hand.

"What, baby?" she said, tears on her cheeks.

"It's—"

"What?"

"It's a beau—"

"No!"

His eyelids fluttered and he was still.

JUNE 2018

23 | Candy

Candy sipped an iced tea. She restocked the lazy Susan—sea salt, garam masala, hot sauce—and centered it on the round table. She wiped down the vinyl placemats and moved a little metal truck to a toy box by the fireplace. She folded the blanky and set it on the sofa.

She freed a sippy cup from behind the refrigerator.

She opened the *Post*, which a man delivered every morning despite cancellations, and read about a woman in a small Mississippi town who weighed six hundred pounds. A year earlier, she had weighed a hundred-and-thirty-five. When the pastor of her church was arrested, she had stopped teaching Sunday school. She had stopped attending services. She had retreated to a bed in her trailer.

Now she couldn't get out of it.

Candy figured the woman's dreams had been crushed. Maybe she had forgotten who she was.

She refilled her glass. The fleeting moments of the afternoon nap were precious. She scanned the national news. Ants had overrun a neighborhood outside Topeka. The colony had grown over a period of years and invaded the garages and basements and walls of the local homes.

A seventh-grade boy, protesting the repossession of a PlayStation, had shot up a table in the school cafeteria.

A venture capitalist was buying a national charity.

Employees of a big-box retailer were living in a tent city.

The nation's largest debtholder was underwriting a community garden in Camden, New Jersey.

The US Congress was debating legislation to retire the penny.

The news, Candy thought, was nothing new, but life got better every day. Once upon a time, she had climbed the jungle gym with her pigtails swaying. *Don't mess with Texas.* She had commanded the spotlight at the proms and the football games. She had landed a professional job. She had signed apartment leases and car loans.

She had gotten busy.

Now she washed no windshields. She made no spam calls. It wasn't just a state of mind, it was a state of being. And the war between those states, freedom and bondage, friends and adversaries, survival and the arduous flight of the soul, lingered like yellowed newsprint on the driveway.

She spun the lazy Susan.

She thumbed through the Metro section. Liberty Stage was holding auditions for its revival of *Annie*. She was too old to play the little girl now. But she could still play Grace, the assistant who loved Annie from the beginning.

Her phone vibrated. Arjun was closing up the trucks for the day.

She turned the newspaper over to the last page and read the weather forecast. It was beautiful out.

Tomorrow would be too.

Acknowledgments

I spent a decade writing *Deep Fried*. I meant to finish in two or three years, but the book had other plans.

That is my excuse.

I divulge that I think of my editor Neil Kelly as "the litmus test." I exalt him for his skill, wisdom, patience, and friendship. I salute developmental editor Marla Daniels for challenging my preconceived notions, cultural editors Anita Jain and Hannah Gómez for their guidance on diversity, and proofreader Joel Pierson for his eagle eye. I hail fellow writers Kevin Kerr, Jerry Januszewski, Jason Warburg, Richard Fulco, Peter McDade, Keith Donohue, and Matthew Broyles, who read my drafts with wit and kindness. I am indebted to my grown children Alison and Matthew, who gave me the characters of Pidgey and Antwaan, respectively, through colorful accounts of their own real-life experiences. I laud visual artist Robin Doyon for her beautiful cover design.

I am grateful for the friendship of Eamon Loftus, John Watts, Scott Holmes, Paul Golder, Steve Walker, and Doug Burmeister, as well as the love of my parents Muriel and Roger, my brothers Scott and Craig and their families, and the members of the Lewis family. I extol Scott Donaldson, Walter Wenska, David Jenkins, and Wendy Weiner, mentors all, and J. Thomas Hetrick, who rescued and published my short stories in 2001. Warm thanks, too, to the indelible creative people—musicians, coders, dreamers—I've met in my travels, many of whom inspired the composite characters in

Deep Fried. Safe sojourns to Evan Pollack and Alisa Mullins, artists and dear friends who flew too soon into the sun.

Most of all, I thank my partner in crime Kathleen, who giggled and sobbed and commiserated with me, and shared rare insight, always with a love and patience I can only hope to return.

Winchester, Virginia
June 2024

About the Author

Mark Doyon received a B.A. in English from the College of William & Mary and a master's in arts management from the Shenandoah Conservatory. He wrote the short-story collection *Bonneville Stories* and edited the literary magazine *Friction*. His work has been featured in *PopMatters*, *The Washington Post*, *The Daily Vault*, *Hybrid*, *Skope*, *The Absinthe Literary Review*, *3AM Magazine*, *Hypebot*, and *Riffraf*. *Deep Fried* is his first novel.

Praise for Mark Doyon's *Deep Fried*

"*Deep Fried* feels like *Our Town* reimagined by Kurt Vonnegut on a nitrous buzz, a vital, shaggy, distinctly American tale of dreamers and strivers colliding in a courthouse parking lot. 'Never let them change you. Never give up,' advises one character's mentor in this sprawling tale enlivened by Doyon's vivid prose; it's a message each of these characters takes to heart as they work to piece together the puzzles of their own lives. In the end *Deep Fried* strikes an affirming note: life is hard, full of capriciousness, bad luck, and bad actors, but inside its crunchy folds lies a sweetness powerful enough to sustain any who taste it." –Jason Warburg, author of *Believe in Me*, *Never Break the Chain*, and *Home Was a Dream*

"A quirky, thoughtful meditation on creativity, purpose, and the American dream... Doyon blends humor with moments of profound introspection. This savory slice of contemporary American life will edify readers who have ever dared to follow their dreams or wondered, 'Why am I here?' [Editor's Pick]" –*BookLife Reviews*

"Draped in humor and slice-of-life realism, Mark Doyon's ambitious debut novel takes the reader on an invigorating journey, extolling the individual's need to seek a better life and a better tomorrow. Arjun Chatterjee, a highly motivated and optimistic chef, is in search of the elusive American dream. 'Sometimes he's the eggroll, and sometimes he's the oil,' but what's really being dished up for him and his cohort of colorful characters is the ability to change and evolve while maintaining hope. *Deep Fried* raises vital questions about freedom, about how we define success, and the true cost of the pursuit of dreams." –Richard Fulco, author of *We Are All Together* and *There Is No End to This Slope*

"With twists both humorous and heartbreaking, *Deep Fried* is a touching story about pursuing freedom in a world that wants to knock you down... Doyon keeps things fresh by rendering characters exquisitely—detailed backstories, alarming conflict, charming and just-weird-enough dialogue... *Deep Fried* feels like modern-day folklore—lively, odd, and full of familiar, old-world proverbs." –Frankie Martinez, *Independent Book Review*

"*Deep Fried* beckons: *Give me your discouraged, your angry, your bitter, your gluttonous, your deluded, your blind and greedy. But most of all, give me your hopeful.* And this hopefulness lingers with Doyon's characters like a sweet aftertaste." –Jerry Januszewski, author of *An Apprenticeship in the School of Anxiety*

"Doyon crafts a narrative that is both a love letter to creative freedom and a brilliant exploration of the trials and triumphs of the American dream." –Heena R. Pardeshi, *The Reading Bud*

"*Deep Fried* has what I value most in fiction, but too rarely find: empathy, heart, and a deep understanding of the human condition. Doyon conveys the thoughts and emotions of a wide range of characters, from cooks to immigrants to musicians to troubled teens to pigeons. They are all brilliant and flawed and very much alive, and the reader finishes the book feeling grateful for the chance to get to know them." –Peter McDade, author of *Songs by Honeybird* and *The Weight of Sound*

"Doyon weaves deceptively ordinary lives and aspirations into a fine tapestry, with a wisdom that juxtaposes the simple and sublime in perfect proportion. *Deep Fried* is a modern American story, with all the attendant dissonance and humor that implies." –Matthew Broyles, author of *Rewired* and *Threnody*

"Witty and compelling... Doyon's brilliantly observed culinary world is wrought in intoxicating splendor." –*The BookLife Prize*

Made in the USA
Middletown, DE
13 September 2024

60402543R00139